Acclaim for the Author's Books

In Too Deep

"*In Too Deep*, by newcomer Ronica Black, is emotional, hot, gripping, raw, and a real turn-on from start to finish, with characters you will fall in love with, root for, and never forget. A truly five star novel, you will not want to miss *In Too Deep* and will look forward to Black's next novel, *Wild Abandon*, coming out in 2006." – *Midwest Book Review*

"Ronica Black's debut novel *In Too Deep* has everything from non-stop action and intriguing well-developed characters to steamy erotic love scenes. From the opening scenes where Black plunges the reader head first into the story to the explosive unexpected ending, *In Too Deep* has what it takes to rise to the top. Black has a winner with *In Too Deep*, one that will keep the reader turning the pages until the very last one." – *Independent Gay Writer*

"…an exciting page turning read, full of mystery, sex, and suspense." – *MegaScene*

"…a challenging murder mystery – sections of this mixed-genre novel are hot, hot, hot. Black juggles the assorted elements of her first book with assured pacing and estimable panache." – *Q Syndicate*

Wild Abandon

"…intriguing, original, and quite well-developed…a sexually-charged romance about two very different and guarded women. Black carries the reader along at such a rapid pace that the rise and fall of each climactic moment successfully creates that suspension of disbelief which the reader seeks. *Wild Abandon* is a novel that displays the author's creative imagination while at the same time boldly exhibits the author's maturation as an author." – *L-Word Literature*

"…Black is a master at teasing the reader with her use of domination and desire. Black's first novel, *In Too Deep*, was a finalist for a 2005 Lammy and is a finalist for two GCLS 'Goldie' awards. With *Wild Abandon*, the author continues her winning ways, writing like a seasoned pro. This is one romance I will not soon forget." – *Just About Write*

"If you enjoy complex characters and passionate sex scenes, you'll love *Wild Abandon*." – *MegaScene*

By the Author

In Too Deep

Wild Abandon

Visit us at www.boldstrokesbooks.com

HEARTS AFLAME

by

Ronica Black

2007

HEARTS AFLAME

ISBN: 10-digit 1-933110-82-1
       13-digit 978-1-933110-82-0

This Trade Paperback Original Is Published By
Bold Strokes Books, Inc.,
New York, USA

First Edition: July, 2007.

Credits
Editors: Jennifer Knight and Stacia Seaman
Production Design: Stacia Seaman
Cover Photo by Ronica Black
Cover Design By Sheri (GRAPHICARTIST2020@HOTMAIL.COM)

Acknowledgments

Bold Strokes Books, the entire team. Thank you. When I say you've changed my life, I mean it. I really, really mean it.

Thanks to Carrie and Jan Carr for your valued input and most importantly, your friendship.

Linda and "Prince," thanks so much for all your help! I hope you're enjoying Flagstaff. I'm still jealous.

Sheri, the cover is amazing. Thank you.

My family, Dad, Dom, and Beck, your continued support means the world. Most especially to my mother, who went with me on a quest to "smell a horse."

And to my sister Robin, the strongest woman I know, for taking another chance on love.

Caitie. Thanks for posing for me in the dead of winter for the cover photo. You're absolutely beautiful. Thanks for all you did to ensure that this book was the best it could possibly be. Thanks will never be enough.

Dedication

For Cait,
for everything

CHAPTER ONE

Music and laughter echoed throughout the crowded restaurant bar. Friday happy hour was in full swing. Krista Wyler sat alone, elbows on the worn wooden bar, wishing she had taken up smoking so at least she would have something to do with her hands. Across the room, she watched a man and woman smiling and talking. They kept their eyes trained only on each another, ignoring everyone else. They inched closer, his hand finding the small of her back. The woman tossed her head in laughter, exposing her pale neck, an unspoken offering. The man leaned in, whispering something intimate in her ear. She gripped the arm of his expensive suit as her eyelids grew heavy with desire. Her lips trembled for a brief instant before she mouthed the word *yes.*

And just like that, another two connected.

The sight depressed Krista even though she knew it could easily be *her* engaging with an attractive woman. She could have another meaningless tryst, but she wasn't in the mood. Sighing, she fiddled with a matchbook and tried to unwind from a hectic week spent trying to sell homes in the midst of a dark pit of a market. Even though current times were tough going, she loved her job. She set her own goals and punched her own time clock. Problem was, she rarely punched out. When she did, like right now and only at her best friend's insistence, she didn't know what to do with herself.

She dropped the matchbook and tapped the bar impatiently, resisting the urge to dwell sullenly on her life. She had only just started her beer so her mind was top notch, sharp as a tack, and brutal with its realities: The loneliness she worked long, hard hours to avoid facing. The happiness she fooled herself into believing she had, buying material things. The success she shared only with coworkers, people who, like her, were all about competition rather than compassion.

A heavy sigh shook her body at the discomforting thoughts. She sipped her beer and mindlessly began to peel at the wet label.

"Hello, Krista."

Krista glanced up from another tasteless sip.

"It's been a while." The voice was husky and familiar, the face flawless with detailed, high-priced beauty.

"Megan, hello." Krista kept her own voice low in indifference, but as Megan raised her eyebrows, it was obvious she mistook this for seduction.

She held that intrigued, predatory look for a long moment and then signaled the bartender for a drink. She flipped her hair as she waited, purposely allowing Krista ample time to take her in. When Krista didn't rise to the bait by voicing an interest, Megan took charge without missing a beat.

"You're looking well, as always." A knowing smile accompanied the self-assurance as her eyes slowly swept up and down Krista's fit and curvy body. She slid onto the neighboring bar stool and cupped a hand over Krista's. "I was hoping you would be here tonight."

Krista studied the well-manicured fingernails and wished she felt more than just the warmth of another human's touch. She sipped her drink and fought off disappointment. This had been her reality lately. Her lack of interest in available women, her nonexistent sex life. As much as she went over and over her situation, only one thing seemed certain. She wanted more. She wanted sparks. But she was beginning to wonder if such a thing even existed. Up until now she'd led her life based on what she did know. Sex and lust. She'd experienced those all too well. She knew for certain what they were all about.

Megan, obviously clueless as to her mood, leaned in closer, whispering in her ear. "Come on, let's get out of here."

Krista felt the gentle pressure of the breath against her skin. It caused a reaction, a quick ignition of her flesh. She closed her eyes and willed the rush of awakening nerves to remain for longer than a few seconds. But this was wishful thinking, a hopeless, romantic dream.

Insistent and unperturbed, Megan tightened her grip and brushed her lips across Krista's cheek. The contact sent flashes of their last encounter to Krista's mind.

A posh hotel room, dimly lit, with the scent of the fresh linen sheets and hungry, wet sex tingling her senses. Megan atop her, peeling off a black teddy and tossing it aside, her body covered in a thin sheen of sweat, her long brown hair clinging to her skin. Panting and moaning, she undulates, with Krista's fingers up deep inside her.

"I'm going to come," Megan whispers, biting her lower lip. "Make me come." Her body jerks and waves, slow then hard. Her eyes open with fierceness, full of flames, and the tendons in her neck strain. She reaches out, grasping Krista's free hand, linking their fingers, pinning Krista against the bed. She comes like lightning, bright and furious, charged and fast. A long cry finds birth from deep in her chest as she rides out her climax, clinging and grinding and taking and holding.

Krista watches in wonder, her fingers long ago sweetly pained and numbed. As the last of the orgasm escapes her body, Megan collapses. She breathes hard against Krista's chest, her body moist and pulsing. Krista turns her head and focuses on the hand that she can still feel. A sharp, stabbing pain registers as something presses into her finger. Megan squeezes their hands tightly together, intensifying the sensation. Krista squints. In the dim light she catches the source of the pain as their hands separate.

A marquise cut diamond, twinkling in the moonlight. Megan's wedding ring.

Krista blinked herself back into the present and trained her eyes on Megan's hand. The ring was still there, doing all it could to stake its claim. Krista wondered if Megan's husband had any idea of her philandering. She met her colleague's eyes and wondered why she suddenly cared.

"I can't. Not tonight." She turned on her stool to examine her numerous coworkers. A sea of people moved about, laughing, socializing, boasting about their latest month of sales.

Megan turned alongside her, not seeming the slightest bit fazed. "Got other plans?"

Krista considered the question as she continued to observe some of the other women around her. Real estate agents, mortgage specialists, and loan officers occupied the large party room of the popular Mexican restaurant. She knew most of them, having worked with them on a daily basis for the past six years. Some she considered friends, but most she considered mere acquaintances. And a small, select few she used to consider one-night stands.

"No, I'm just not in the mood." *Not in the mood? What the hell is going on with me?* She downed the rest of her beer, confused by her own behavior. She could feel Megan's eyes on the side of her face.

"You sure?" Megan's warm hand found its way to Krista's thigh as she tried one last time.

Krista felt its intent and registered its warmth and pressure, but the sensation didn't shoot up her leg like it should have. "Yeah." She offered a regretful smile. "Maybe some other time."

Megan touched her cheek, smiled in return, and then stood. "You have my number."

She left Krista at the bar along with the lingering scent of her expensive perfume. Krista watched as she mixed into the crowd, a hungry hawk focused on the hunt.

"What are you still doing here?" another familiar voice asked, and an elbow rested on Krista's shoulder. "I thought for sure you and Miss Thing would be long gone by now."

Krista smiled genuinely at Suzanne Key, her closest friend. "Not in the mood."

Suzanne studied her with concern. "You feeling okay?" She felt Krista's head in search of a fever.

Krista laughed. "Fuck off!" She swatted the hand away, only mildly offended.

"No, I'm serious! You look like shit."

"Thanks."

"You need some color. You're locked up inside that office of yours too much."

Krista rolled her eyes playfully, knowing Suzanne really did care. As the bartender slid Suzanne her cosmopolitan, the duo observed the crowd with mock interest. Suzanne sipped her drink and sighed.

"So, what's going on?" It wasn't really a question, but rather a bored series of words spoken aloud.

"Nothing," Krista responded.

"I can see that." Suzanne worked on the plastic swizzle stick, happily chewing it down. "When's the last time you got laid?"

This time Krista sighed. "I don't know. Sometime before Christ."

It really hadn't been that long ago, had it? She thought back, unable even to remember who she'd been with the last time. Maybe it was a good thing she was no longer interested. Casual sex had become way too, well, casual.

"Why's that?" Suzanne knew Krista had her flings and knew she could have them anytime she wanted. She was obviously just as confused as Krista was.

"I don't know."

But that wasn't quite true. Krista had her suspicions about the lack of interest she'd felt recently. Sex was the same old game, just played with different pawns from time to time. No fireworks, no heartfelt emotion. Just fucking. And Jesus, more than half the time she didn't even enjoy her encounters, leaving with her shirt wrinkled and untucked, her libido still starving with need.

"Maybe that's what's wrong. Maybe you need to get some." Suzanne fussed with Krista's hair as if she were readying her only daughter for a prom date.

"Maybe," Krista whispered, mostly to herself. Sex used to cheer her up, keep her level.

Megan came into view again and Krista studied her fit body and gloriously long legs. But desire didn't tighten her throat or turn in her gut. The sparks she longed for might as well be figments of some delusional fairy tale. They weren't happening, and she was starting to wonder if she would ever feel them again.

As if she sensed Krista's sudden somberness, Suzanne slung an affectionate arm around her. "I still love you if even you do have better hair than me."

Krista laughed. "Gee, thanks." She'd always hated her auburn hair but everyone else seemed to love it. So she left it shoulder length, and when its thickness got in her way she simply pulled it back into a ponytail.

Suzanne settled in next to her and changed the subject altogether, like only a true friend would. "Rich Hamilton is all over me tonight."

The two watched as the short, stocky mortgage banker worked his way through the crowd, flashing his best smile.

"Yeah?"

"Uh-huh. What do you think?"

"You could do worse." Rich wasn't a bad-looking guy and he made a good living. Important qualities to a single straight woman, according to Suzanne.

"What about you?" Suzanne asked. "You gonna be all right tonight?"

Bless you, Suzanne. Always there for me. I don't deserve you. Krista was about to tell her so when something caught her attention. Her cell phone was vibrating on the waistband of her slacks. She unclipped it to identify the caller, expecting a client, as usual. A realtor doesn't know the meaning of "time off."

The name Judith flashed on the screen. Quickly, her mind flew, registering both simple fact and thorny possibility. There was only one Judith she knew. Her *aunt* Judith.

Oh, fuck.

A dark, thick mist settled over her insides, churning her stomach. Krista rarely heard from family and when she did, the news was never good. Judith was her one and only local relative too.

Damn it. Suddenly, she wished she was hard at work, calling back clients, showing a house, or doing paperwork. Too busy to pay attention. Too busy to think about why the aunt she hadn't spoken to in over a year was suddenly calling. Krista pocketed the phone and paid her tab, nerves on edge.

"Something wrong?" Suzanne asked.

Krista averted her eyes, not wanting to alert Suzanne to her sudden change of mood. After all, at least one of them still had a shot at a good night.

"I'm not sure. But don't worry, I'll be fine." She gave her best friend a peck on the cheek and rose from the bar stool. "Go talk to Rich. I'll call you later." She waited for Suzanne to nod and wave before she wound her way out of the bar.

The fresh February air felt good against her skin as she strolled to her car. She climbed inside the BMW Z4, let the top down, and started the engine. The sun continued to fall behind her, watching as the cool wind played with her hair. A series of beeps called from her pocket as she braked for a stoplight. She retrieved the phone and stared at the voice message light, deep in contemplation.

"Shit."

The traffic light turned green. She floored the gas pedal and flew down the road, cell phone to her ear.

Chapter Two

The cool spring air blew a welcome greeting across Krista's face as she slowed the car and turned onto the dry dirt road. Lowering her sunglasses, she peered up at the hovering gate that marked the entrance. It was in dire need of a fresh coat of paint, the exposed steel rusted in various patches. A squeaking caught her attention where the Wyler Ranch sign swung halfheartedly in the wind, faded from years of sun exposure.

A noticeable ball formed in her throat, and she pushed her shades back into place and eased the car along the dirt path. Large mesquite trees, sagebrush, and salt cedars shaded the often harsh terrain of the high Sonoran desert. Saguaros as tall as fifteen feet loomed proudly in the near distance, many flaunting their old age with numerous arms growing out of their sides. Barrel cacti displayed their green-gold blooms while nestled safely amongst the thick orange blooms of wild brittle brush and globemallows. Two prairie dogs playing tag scurried across the road where they disappeared into a hill of brilliant gold Mexican poppies.

Krista smiled briefly, remembering long walks with her aunt Judith, learning the names of each and every plant. The scent of the desert in the springtime relaxed her a little, as did the memory. But as she drove on, the earthy smell of manure began to overpower the numerous desert blooms. The scent was familiar, though long ago forgotten.

Wyler Ranch was built and run by Judith and Clinton Wyler. They'd started the cattle ranch over thirty years ago, moving out from Oklahoma to do so. Starting when she was five, Krista had stayed out here every summer, helping with the cattle and caring for the horses.

She could still remember learning to ride and loving to work alongside her aunt, with her rough, overworked hands, long, braided hair, and twinkling blue eyes. Krista had wanted to be just like her.

Another smile overtook her and then vanished into the wind.

That was before the accident.

Absently, she reached up and touched her temple, fingering the scar. The ball in her throat began to burn like fire. Krista did her best to swallow against it and drove on.

The little Z kicked up dust as she took in the sights and smells, climbing a bit and then rounding a large turn. From there the road opened up into the vastness of the ranch property, and she couldn't help but smile at its simple beauty. Miles and miles of grasslands and fences were nestled in the center of the surrounding desert terrain. The Wylers owned two thousand acres, and they'd settled their house, and the stables and pens, right in the middle of the property.

To Krista's surprise, there were no cowboys on horses whistling at cattle, sorting them in the pens. She blinked. There were no cattle. She looked to the surrounding stables and bunkhouses. There were no cowhands moving about the ranch, doing their daily chores. There was nobody and nothing.

Jesus Christ, have I been away so long that everything has changed? Pangs of regret expanded within her chest. She used to love this land. Worship this land. *So why have I stayed away?* She could've come back anytime she wanted. The invitation was always there. Again she touched the scar and her foot ached. It had just been easier to stay away.

"And now, some fifteen years later, I'm back." She wiped angrily at a stray tear as she pulled up to the ranch house. "Fifteen years," she whispered.

The house didn't look anywhere near as big as she remembered. It looked just like an average ranch home, wide and single-storied with an ample stone front porch and wide windows. Only now, the 3,500-square-foot house looked every bit its age. The stucco needed painting near the bottom, there were tiles missing on the roof, the grass in the front was overgrown, and the hanging flower pots that were once her aunt's pride and joy now held dead, dried plants. Some of the sun screens were missing from the windows, giving the house a "toothless" appearance. The large rocking chairs on the porch were faded and worn. There was no food in the bird feeders, and chimes were missing on the homemade wooden wind chimes her uncle had made years ago. The wood on the remaining chimes was weathered and bleached out by the sun. She could remember the day her aunt hung the one in the center, grinning from ear to ear, loving when her husband made things for her.

That had been the last summer Krista had been here. June. She remembered because the chimes had been a birthday present for her aunt. She studied the house in silence, the sadness of it all weighing her down. Even though she'd been away from the ranch for many years, it pained her to see the current state of disrepair. It was as if the house mirrored what was happening within its walls. Just like a sick body— trouble on the inside would eventually show on the outside.

The ball of fire was now burning, a liquid lava of raw emotion in Krista's throat. Tears formed as she cursed herself for her long absence. She'd been selfish all these years, making excuses for failing to come during the holidays and any other time she'd been invited. It had taken her aunt's falling ill to bring her back. Facing that fact made her almost sick at herself.

The car crunched onto the gravel drive as she swallowed back more tears. She slammed into park and killed the engine, forcing herself to look into the rearview mirror. She plucked off her sunglasses and stared into the cool green eyes. They were large and liquid, framed by moist mascara marks. She hated herself at that moment. Hated the hurt from the past, hated the hurt here and now, and hated the hurt that was sure to come.

Angry, she straightened her hair and gritted her teeth. There was no sense in crying. Not now anyway. Her family needed her and she was determined to be there for them.

The squeaking of the screen door made her refocus her attention on the house. Squinting into the sun, she opened her door and stepped out to stand alongside the car, shading her brow with her hand.

A little red rooster came running at her from her left. He angled his wings like a fighter jet on the attack and then slowed to peck around her feet, sizing her up.

"*Mija*, is that you? Is that my Krista?" Uncle Clinton's voice came out of the dark doorway before he did.

Krista at once smiled, her heart swelling at hearing his voice.

"It's me, *tío*, it's me." She had always called him *tío*. Spanish for "uncle." Half Hispanic, Clinton often spoke his mother's, and Krista's grandmother's, native language.

Laughing, he stepped out onto the porch, placed his Stetson on his head, and said, "Well, git over here and give me a hug."

Krista hesitated, searching him for the signs of deteriorating health her aunt had told her about. She'd been a little worried about him after their conversation a couple of weeks ago, but he seemed fine. Relief rushed through her.

He held out his arms in welcome, and as she walked toward him she noticed he had hardly changed. Worn, scuffed boots led up denim Wranglers that hugged his long, lean legs and ended at one of his numerous rodeo belt buckles from his days riding wild broncos back in his youth. Clinton always reminded Krista of her father, who'd passed away when she was very young. Her memory of him was mostly based on old photos, so seeing Clinton always brought him to life somehow. Something she cherished.

Smiling, her face flushed with warm heat, she stepped up onto the creaking porch and fell into his arms. His denim shirt was ironed and creased down the arms and she could smell his Stetson cologne. Something he'd always worn because "It drives your aunt Judy wild." And he would always wink at her after saying this. She sighed in his arms and felt the hot tears flow down her cheeks where they dropped onto the denim of his shirt, leaving dark splotches. Despite his seventy-plus years, he felt strong and safe and soothing. It was like being enveloped by *home,* a place you may leave but never really go far from.

She held him tighter, the sound of the wind chimes and the curious rooster behind them. She could hear clawed feet clicking on the stone porch. It was strangely comforting.

"I'm sorry I've been away so long." The words floated out, followed closely by chest-ripping sobs. All the courage, all the success, all the bravado in the world seemed to crumble at the old cowboy's feet. She must've been crazy to think that she could put on a brave face.

"It's okay. It's okay. Shh." He patted the back of her head.

They pulled apart and she wiped at her tears, upset and a little embarrassed at having lost control. But Clinton merely smiled down at her, his brown eyes alive and vibrant and his hair a thick, stark white. He stroked her cheek, wiping at the wetness. "Come inside and see your aunt."

Krista straightened herself up and then followed, unsure as to whether she was ready to face what the house held, but knowing she had to. They stepped inside the front door and the first thing Krista noticed was the familiar smell. Warm spice, pipe tobacco, and freshly cut wood. She closed her eyes and imagined she was ten years old and just arriving for the summer. She felt warm all over, and as she opened her eyes, she noted the same varnished vaulted ceiling, the same dark wood floors, along with the familiar colors of the Navajo rugs. The worn leather furniture sat where it always had. Her favorite painting still hung above the large stone fireplace. The white buffalo. Sacred and immortal as the timeless setting it still inhabited.

So much had changed, yet so little. The last time she had stood here the fireplace had been roaring and crackling, and the smell of fresh cornbread had hovered in the air. Her fingers had ached from their intense grip on the cane at her side.

Blinking back from the past, she held up her hand and stretched out her fingers.

"Clinton? Clinton, is that you?" a weak voice beckoned.

Krista glanced behind her but her uncle had disappeared. She refocused on the living room, searching for the source of the soft voice. Around her she began to notice the same neglect that marked the outside of the house. A thick layer of dust covered the furniture, and the rugs needed vacuuming. Stacks and stacks of mail sat on every end table, most unopened. Krista fumbled with a lamp, hoping to brighten up the dim room, but the bulb was dead.

Blinking, she stared at the back of her aunt's favorite recliner. The chair appeared to be empty, but slowly, a figure rose and turned, piercing Krista with blue eyes.

"Aunt Judith." The words came out on a shocked breath. Krista tried to regain her composure but failed miserably. Her aunt stood with one hand resting on the back of the recliner, a soft, knowing smile on her face. Her once-strong body was painfully thin and hidden poorly under a baggy pair of sweats. "I'm sorry, I..." Krista tried to explain why she had not come sooner but her voice shook.

"I look like an anorexic old cow, don't I?" The smile was etched into her aunt's sunken cheeks, yet her eyes seemed to dance with her wit.

Krista laughed, shaky and emotional, unable to form words for an answer.

"I thought so," Judith spoke for her. "Someone needs to go on ahead and shoot me but your uncle won't hear of it." She waved Krista over hurriedly. "Come hug me before I up and croak."

Krista wrapped her arms carefully around the older woman, afraid of hurting her, but Judith responded by squeezing her tightly and kissing her roughly on the cheek.

"How are you, Krissy?" She stepped back to get a good look at her only niece. "You look well."

"I'm fine." Krista searched the bright eyes and felt the cool, soft skin of the hands on her arms. *She's skin and bones. My God, she's just skin and bones. My aunt Judith. What happened?* "I'm sorry." She began to choke up again.

"Nonsense." Judith waved her off. "No need wasting anyone's time with what's already happened. I'm sick and dying and you're here. That's all that matters." Judith maneuvered herself back into the recliner. "Forgive me, but I can't stand for very long." She rested her head and took several deep breaths. "Sonja's gonna let me have it any minute now anyway."

Puzzled, Krista asked, "Who's Sonja?"

As if on cue, a middle-aged woman with skin as dark and as smooth as morning coffee entered from the hallway. "Mrs. Wyler, where did you get to?"

Judith laughed. "That's Sonja." Turning in her direction, she said, "My niece is here. I had to come out to welcome her."

Sonja approached them and smiled worriedly. "I understand that, but you know you can't be off your IV."

"I'm dying, Sonja. Don't tell me what I can and can't do."

Sonja rolled her eyes and then offered her hand to Krista. The other held a fresh lightbulb. "I'm Sonja Jonas."

"Krista Wyler." Krista noted Sonja's colorful scrubs. "You're a nurse, then?"

"She's a goddamn drill sergeant is what she is!" Judith shouted, winning herself a light slap on her upper arm from the larger woman.

"That's right," Sonja responded, crossing the room to switch out the lightbulbs and turn on the lamp. "So you better get your butt back into that bedroom of yours. You can't be off that IV." She wiped her hands on her scrubs and went back to Judith. Carefully, she helped her stand. Krista immediately went to her aunt's other side, but Judith wouldn't have it.

"I can do it. I can do it." Krista stepped back but Sonja continued to hold on to her, walking with her toward the hallway. "I said I can do it."

"I know you can do it, but you're just going to have to do it with me."

"If I wasn't sick I'd kick your tail."

Sonja laughed. "I know you would, Mrs. Wyler. Believe me, I know you would."

As the two neared the hallway, Clinton entered, meeting them head-on. His hat was gone, showing off his distinguished white hair and tanned skin. He held his pipe in his hand, probably getting ready to stuff it with tobacco. Upon seeing Krista, his face lit up like a child's.

"Judy, Judy, did you see?"

Krista smiled, glad he was so happy to have her there.

"It's Becky! She's come to see us."

Again he looked to Krista and then back to his wife, completely serious.

Krista felt her stomach turn to cold steel. *What? He thinks I'm my mother.* She was the spitting image of her mother, who'd been gone for years. "*Tío*, it's me, it's Krista."

He blinked. "Krista?" Then he smiled. "When did you get here?"

Krista reached out for the recliner. Suddenly the conversation she'd had previously with her aunt sank in and nearly caused her to faint with dizziness. Her uncle might look fine, but he wasn't well.

"Krista's going to be staying with us for a while," Judith said, touching his arm.

"She is?"

"Yes," Sonja said. "Why don't you help her bring in her things?"

Clinton nodded and headed for the door, his pipe sticking out of his pocket. As he stepped out Judith said, "I'm glad you're here, Krissy. We need you."

Krista nodded and lowered her head as Sonja led her aunt down the hallway to the bedroom. She looked around and felt a chill sweep over her body. As warm and familiar as the ranch home felt, there was nothing warm and inviting about what lay ahead.

Chapter Three

Two days later, Krista was sitting slumped at her aunt Judith's antique rolltop desk up to her eyeballs in bills. The sound of the vacuum cleaner buzzed in her head, making it damn near impossible to concentrate. Dropping her pencil, she leaned back and massaged her temples as the cleaners she'd hired moved about the house. Her aunt had had a hissy fit at the idea of someone else cleaning her house, but Krista had little choice. Sonja had been doing what she could, but Krista wanted her to focus on caring for Judith, not worry about the house. And her uncle Clinton—a sigh escaped her at the thought of him. He would start to clean, but then something else would get his attention and off he would go to chop more wood. He lost his concentration incessantly. Lighting a fire every night, even though it was now too warm to do so, and then chopping and stacking more wood the next day. He did the same with the ironing. For hours he would stand in the spare bedroom ironing creases into every piece of clothing he could find. His state was much worse than she could've imagined.

His inability to think clearly and remember was very evident in the Wylers' finances. Krista glanced down at the stack of papers before her. It was going to take at least another couple of hours to get the majority of the paperwork straightened out and more than a few thousand from her own bank account to cover all the bills. She didn't mind, of course; she had plenty of money and was glad she could help. But just realizing how close her aunt and uncle were to going under frightened her.

Since Judith had fallen ill, the ranch had nearly ceased working. Clinton's memory problems had started the year before, and he did what he could just to take care of his wife. Things were a mess. Hell, they were a nightmare.

Needing to escape the noisy confines of the house, Krista rose and took a short stack of paid and stamped bills with her. She stepped outside into the afternoon sun and breathed in the scent of the ranch. Instead of walking the near half mile out to the mailbox, she headed over to the large stock pens, where she leaned on the barred fence and stared off toward the quiet stables. Like the gate at the entrance, the welded pipes of the pens were rusting and in need of paint. The stables and bunkhouses also needed tending to, the wood worn and weathered. She blinked toward the chicken coop as the red rooster she'd seen before came running out to her. He seemed to be the only one and he was very protective of the property. She let him inspect her feet as she stared back toward the stables. At the very least, the ranch and its current state of disarray left her little time to think about her own life and its shortcomings.

She listened to the distant sounds of the horses, enjoying the peace and comfort of the ranch when her cell phone rang. It was Suzanne. She sounded chipper as always.

"Hey you. How are things?"

"Not good."

"Is it as bad as you thought?"

"Worse," Krista said. Suzanne knew she'd had to drop everything and head off for the ranch. Something that before then would have been damn near impossible to get her to do. "I'm sorry to hear that. Is there anything I can do?"

Krista laughed. "Oh sure. Can you continue to run my business while I take care of things here?" It had only been two days and she was already way behind on her own work.

"You know I would if I could. How much longer do you think you'll be needed?"

"Another couple of weeks at least." An image of her aunt came to Krista's mind, followed by the screen door banging and her uncle attempting to carry in more firewood, dropping some in the process. "Maybe longer."

"Are you gonna be able to work from the ranch?"

Krista grimaced at the thought. She now had her workload plus the ranch to look after. Not to mention her aunt and uncle. "I'm going to have to."

"Well, let me know if there's anything I can do."

"I will."

"Promise." It was a demand, not a request. Suzanne knew her all too well.

"Promise."

They hung up and Krista felt worse than before.

"Krista Wyler. Is that you?"

Surprised, she turned and looked into the sun-weathered face of Dwight Tanner, the Wylers' oldest friend and employee. Krista had known him and his father Douglas since her very first visit to the ranch. Smiling, she stepped up to give the large man a hug. The strong scent of chewing tobacco tickled her nose and his gray stubble tickled her cheek. He blushed at the contact and kept his hands in his back pockets.

"Dwight, it's good to see you." Krista studied his dark eyes, which were nestled beneath thick webs of wrinkles. She noted a sadness there, a silent defeat to his aura.

"It's damn near great to see you," he said with the ball of chewing tobacco kept to the side of his cheek. "This ranch, it's dying." The words struck home, and an anxiety at hearing them aloud knotted her insides.

Dwight came to a stand next to her and they both leaned on the barred fence.

"I know," she admitted. "I've been going over all the bills." She showed him the envelopes. "This isn't even half of them."

"I kept telling them to call you. Kept telling them they needed to do something. Ever since that drought a few years back, things have just gone downhill." He spat, marking the dirt in the pen. "But you know how damn proud your aunt is. And Clinton." He paused. "Hell, he's been my friend since I was knee high to a grasshopper. My daddy's best friend. It's hard to see him like this."

"How is your father?"

Dwight cleared his throat and linked his fingers. "He passed away two years back. Lung cancer."

Krista felt a fool for not knowing. "I'm sorry, I didn't know."

"I don't suppose you would, you being away so long and such." After a pause, he glanced down at the cocky rooster pecking his boot and shook him off. "Pepe, git outta here." He whistled and a red-and-white border collie came flying from behind the house.

Krista smiled and bent to pet the wriggling dog, then watched with amusement as it faced off with the rooster in aggressive play. "That's not Pete, it can't be." But the dog looked just like the one she remembered from years ago.

"That's Repeat. His son."

The Collie knelt and barked at Pepe, then hopped at him before they gave chase.

"They're friends," Krista observed, smiling.

"Yeah, they keep each other entertained."

Krista straightened next to Dwight and they both leaned on the bars and stared off into the afternoon sun. "Where are all the cattle?" she finally asked.

Dwight knew the ranch inside out and she figured he would be the best one to get accurate information from, especially since Clinton had given her three different answers to the same question. "They're out to graze."

Krista looked out past the house to the some two thousand acres that made up Wyler Ranch. Way out in the distance she could see numerous dots that she assumed to be cattle. They were eating bottle brush, no doubt, needing the roughage to help their digestive systems. "How long've they been out?"

"Two days. The creek's half full again."

"Anyone ride out with them?"

"Nah."

"You no longer worry about coyotes?" They used to have at least two cowboys ride out with the herd to look out for such predators, especially if they had more than a few calves.

"Yeah, they're still a problem, but I can't be everywhere at once."

"You're the only one working?" She stared down at the dirt. It explained why she hadn't seen anyone wandering around doing chores.

"For the most part. We got a young cowhand by the name of Cody that comes in to help me round up the cattle. He's due in tomorrow to go out on the ATVs with me."

"ATVs?"

Dwight took his time responding. "There's only two of us. It's easier that way."

"What about the horses?" After all these years she was still uneasy just thinking about them. She hadn't gone anywhere near the stables since she'd arrived.

"There's seven. I had to sell our latest colt and two others several months back. We needed the money."

Krista knew the ranch needed several horses for the cowboys to ride when they came in for work. The last summer she'd been here they'd had fifteen horses. But keeping a horse was costly, which also explained the ATVs.

"How many cattle do we have?"

"Couple hundred head."

That was way lower than the herd size she remembered. No wonder the ranch was in such dire straits. They couldn't possibly make enough money with that few cattle being sold. The throbbing in her temples returned as she mulled it all over. The mountain of bills, her aunt's medical expenses, the disrepair and the struggle of the ranch... there was only one option, in her eyes, and it had kept her up the past two nights.

"Well, I got chores to do," Dwight announced, pushing away from the fence. "It's good to have you back." With a tip of his hat he left her alone to stare after him as he headed toward the stables.

❖

That evening Krista settled into a chair beside her aunt's hospital bed after handing her a mug of fresh coffee.

"Mmm. I can't seem to eat a damn thing, but this coffee sure smells good."

Krista smiled, glad to see her aunt alert and full of personality. Judith slept a lot during the day, something she never did when healthy. She sipped the coffee and made another audible sound of delight. Her eyes twinkled as they flicked toward the window across from the bed.

"Krissy, pull open those blinds for me, would you? I want to watch the sunset."

Krista rose and did as requested. Then she made sure Judith was comfortable by stuffing some pillows down behind her back so she could sit up easier. She tucked her favorite homemade quilt around her feet.

"Now, that's better," Judith said with a smile. "Coffee and a sunset."

Krista stared out the window, watching the sun disappear behind the mountains with brilliant oranges and pinks. It was a beautiful, peaceful sight, just as it always was. But in her heart there was no light. There wasn't even a nervousness in what she had to do. There was only a dark, calm sadness.

"What's on your mind, girl?" Judith asked, somehow knowing that Krista was troubled.

Krista sat down beside the bed once again, but this time she couldn't bring herself to meet her aunt's lively blue eyes. She played with her hands, not knowing what to do with them.

"My Lord. Spill it, child. You look like you're the one dying."

Krista sighed and looked up. She hated doing this. Especially when Judith was feeling a bit better. "It's about the ranch."

Judith lowered her mug, suddenly somber. "It's bad?"

Krista clenched her hands together. "Yes, I'm afraid so."

"It will all work out. Don't worry."

Krista felt her mouth fall open. Surely her aunt wasn't sick in that way. Her mind was sharp as a tack. She had to know how bad it truly was. And to say it would all work out? How could she even think that? "I've gone over everything, Aunt Judith." Krista spoke softly. "The ranch is faltering. It's not making money. In fact, it's costing more than it makes just to keep it up and running."

Judith said nothing.

"I've paid some of the bills, all the ones I could cover, anyway. Got everything caught up as best I could, but…" Krista paused, unsure as to how to say it. "The way I see it, there's only one way out. Only one way to keep your head above water." She paused again, watching her aunt's blank expression. "I think we should sell the ranch."

Judith whipped her head up, pinning Krista with her serious eyes. "Absolutely not."

"Aunt Judith…"

"No, I don't even want to hear you say it. I said no and that's final."

Krista felt the heat rise to her face. "It's the only way."

"I said no."

"You can't say no." Krista got to her feet, frustration taking over.

"I can and I will."

"Fine, you sit there and say that. In the meantime the ranch goes under. You called me for help. That's what I'm trying to do. If we sell the ranch now you can still come out ahead."

"We're not selling the ranch!" Judith trembled and nearly spilled her coffee.

Krista offered to take it from her, but Judith tugged it away like a spoiled child.

Krista was at a loss. All the frustration from spending hours on end staring at the numbers came out. "Then what the hell do you want me to do?"

"I told you not to worry about it!" Judith countered. "There's another way."

Krista took several breaths and closed her eyes, trying to control her emotions. "What way is that?"

Judith sipped her coffee, suddenly calm. "I have life insurance."

Krista blinked, surprised. From the state of the ranch and the bills, it was honestly the last thing she expected to hear. Her aunt and uncle had led simple lives living off the cattle and the land. To find out that they had something like life insurance truly surprised her.

"You do?"

"Yes." Another long sip of coffee. "I bought it years back. And only because Molly Singer's girl was selling it." Molly was their nearest neighbor, another rancher.

Krista again closed her eyes. Her aunt lived a life completely different from Krista's. In a way the older woman was very naïve about the real world and its ways.

"I should probably look at the policy," Krista said. There were most likely stipulations, and a part of her was afraid the thing wasn't even legit.

"It's in the nightstand drawer there. Your uncle doesn't even know about it."

Krista opened the top drawer and pulled out a large manila envelope. "Do you know how much it's for?"

Judith stared out the window. "A hundred and fifty thousand."

Krista lowered the envelope. It was a good amount, but not enough to keep Clinton or the ranch cushy. The medical bills alone were pushing fifty thousand. The Wylers didn't have health insurance and it was costing a lot to keep Judith at home with twenty-four-hour care. Not to mention the treatments, the hospital visits. Krista placed a hand on her aunt's frail shoulder, not wanting to upset her any more that evening. "I'll take a look at the numbers again."

She fought off tears at the older woman's secret savior of life insurance. Judith really thought it would save them all. That even in her death, she would somehow take care of things. Krista bent and kissed her on the forehead. Her aunt was a good woman. Krista owed it to her to try and find another way to save the ranch. Taking her coffee cup, she eased Judith back down into the bed and left her staring into the sunset.

CHAPTER FOUR

There's no way. There's just no way!"
Krista threw down the fountain pen and knotted her hair in her hands. She stared out the window at the morning sun and wished to God life could be as simple as Mother Nature made everything seem. She wished she could just step outside where the warmth from the sun would massage her shoulders, and all her troubles would disappear.

A beep on her laptop alerted her to a new e-mail. Working via the Internet had kept her clients at bay for only a short while. They were now demanding her presence. Fingers flying, she responded to yet another home buyer, recommending Suzanne for all their house-searching needs. She'd done her best, e-mailing and showing houses online, but people still wanted a physical person to show them through the homes they were seriously considering. And right now, she couldn't be that person.

"Shit!" She sent the e-mail and sank down into her arms on the table. The loss of control she was feeling made her head pound and her heart race. Her eyes closed with exhaustion just as a soft hand came to rest on her shoulder. A mug of coffee was placed in front of her.

"You need to eat something."

Krista offered Sonja a weary smile. "Please, sit."

Sonja pulled out a chair and sipped from her own cup. Her dark hair was tied back into a ponytail that held numerous long, thin braids.

Krista could smell her plumeria body lotion and thought she looked beautiful in her lavender-colored scrubs. "I don't seem to have much of an appetite."

Sonja nodded. "You need to keep up your strength if you're going to run things around here. You've got a long road ahead of you yet."

Krista allowed the heat of the coffee mug to mesh into the palms of her hands, almost stinging them. "We're going to have to sell the ranch." She stared out the window as she spoke the defeated words.

"I thought so." Sonja rose to pluck the bread from the toaster. She buttered it in silence and put the plate in front of Krista along with two jars of jam, one strawberry, one peach.

"Thank you." Krista picked at the toast as Sonja sat back down.

"Mrs. Wyler isn't going to be happy."

"I know." Krista chewed a bite and then decided on the peach preserves to flavor it up.

"She's been on the phone all morning. Cursing up a storm."

"Really?" Krista had yet to give the final bad news to her aunt. She'd gone over and over the numbers. Even with the life insurance, the ranch wouldn't make it for long. Something had to be done. The sooner the better.

She swallowed more coffee and thought briefly about spiking it with something stronger to help her get through giving Judith the bad news. The woman was dying. It was terrible to have to tell her all that she had worked for was dying too.

"God damn it. Curse this thing!" Both women turned at the shouts of Judith Wyler. She was nearing the entrance to the living room, walker in front of her and the tall IV pole next to her.

"Mrs. Wyler!" Sonja exclaimed as they both stood and flew to her side. "What in the world are you doing!"

"I'm walking into the living room, what does it look like I'm doing!" Angrily, she grabbed at the pole to tug it along. "But this damn thing doesn't want to move!"

Sonja reached for the portable lifeline and assisted the older woman while Krista stood helpless. "Krista, why don't you turn the recliner around for her?"

Nodding, Krista did as instructed and they both settled Judith into the chair.

Breathing heavily, Judith licked at her parched lips. "Sonja, be a doll and get me some ice chips?"

As Sonja headed into the kitchen, Krista covered her aunt with a light blanket. "What are you doing out here? You know you should ask for help if you want to move around." She tucked the blanket in firmly, making sure the chilly morning air couldn't penetrate.

"I've got company coming and I can manage just fine." Judith eagerly took the cup of ice from Sonja and sucked on a small chip. Next to her, the IV beeped and continued to work, dripping much-needed nutrients into her veins.

"Company?" Krista asked. "Who?"

"Mrs. Wyler, how about some toast this morning?" Sonja tried.

"I don't want any toast." Judith's eyes traveled over Krista. "Rae's coming by to visit with me this morning."

"Ray?" Krista had never heard a Ray mentioned before.

Behind them voices came muffled through the walls. The front door opened and Clinton walked in, followed closely by two men. Clinton pulled off his hat, as did the second man, and Krista smiled, recognizing Dwight.

"Morning, ma'am," he said, nodding at each of them.

Krista murmured a hello and waited as the third man closed the door and turned to face them. He wore Wranglers and a faded collared shirt along with a worn baseball cap.

"Rae." Judith smiled. "Come give me some sugar."

The capped stranger walked confidently into the room, removing the ball cap to bend and kiss Judith on the cheek. "How are you, Mrs. Wyler?" The voice was deep and smooth, but definitely not a man's.

Krista stared, startled and moved by the sight before her. Rae held her ball cap in hand, the tanned muscles in her forearms straining as she smiled down at Judith. Errant strands of short dark hair fell onto her forehead, framing a classically angled face. Krista felt her own cheeks burn as she noticed the small, round breasts and a hint of a flare in the hips.

She's a woman. Rae's a woman.

She cleared her throat, trying to get control of the strange excitement that suddenly coursed through her. Everyone else took her cough as a polite request to be introduced.

"Rae, this is my niece, Krista," Judith announced proudly.

Rae met Krista's eyes with her own deep hazel ones and stepped forward to shake her hand. "Hello."

"Hi." Krista returned the firm handshake and hoped the heat in her face wasn't visible. *My God. What is this I'm feeling? Sparks?* She shook the thought away. It had been a long time since a woman had caused any kind of a reaction in her. And never one who looked like this. One who obviously worked outdoors, judging by her worn boots and strong-looking body. She was gorgeous, in a very raw and wild sort of way.

"I've heard a lot about you," Rae said with a friendly smile that had no doubt melted millions of hearts.

"Really?" Krista was surprised. "I'm sorry, I don't think I've heard your name before." She struggled to keep her composure. A pang of jealousy also shot through her as Judith beamed. Who was this woman her aunt was so obviously happy to see?

Rae merely raised her eyebrows. "Your aunt's always going on about you." She glanced back down at Judith, who reached out to hold her hand. "About how she wished you would visit more often."

Krista forced a smile to hide the guilt the statement brought on.

"Krissy, this is Dr. Jarrett," Judith said, "the veterinarian we've used for years."

Krista thought for a moment. Yes, she had heard Clinton speaking of their vet with great fondness. He'd been mumbling about Dr. Jarrett on and off as he wandered around doing chores. Maybe she should've paid more attention.

"You're here to care for the horses, then?" Krista noticed the thick leather belt and the insignia on her polo style shirt. *Jarrett, Inc.* An emblem of a galloping horse was embroidered next to the words.

Rae met her eyes and then glanced away, squeezing Judith's hand before releasing it as she sat down. "Not exactly."

Not exactly? Krista began to grow nervous as the looks between her aunt and Rae continued.

"Why doesn't everyone have a seat?" Judith encouraged.

Krista sat slowly, watching as Dwight and Clinton did so across from her. Sonja gave her a concerned look and quickly disappeared into the kitchen, claiming there was more coffee that needed to be made. Krista felt strangely alone as she waited for her aunt to voice what was really going on. She didn't have to wait long.

"Krissy, I've been on the phone with Rae all morning. I asked her to come over to talk about the ranch."

Immediately, Krista felt resentment. Dwight wouldn't even look at her. And Clinton sat rubbing his hands together. She decided to go on the offensive. "Well, I think we do need to talk about the ranch.

As promised, I went over the numbers again." She took a breath and looked to her aunt. "I'm sorry, but I just can't see how to make it work. We need to sell the ranch."

There was rustling of sorts as everybody repositioned themselves and began clearing nervous throats.

"That's unacceptable," Judith let out. "And that's exactly why Rae's here."

Confused, Krista asked, "I'm sorry, am I missing something?"

Rae bent the bill of her ball cap in her hands. "Judith called me for some advice. She's hoping that I can help you figure out a better way, other than selling."

"I don't see how that's possible. Unless you're prepared to buy the ranch?" The resentment trailed out on her voice. How was this woman in any way qualified to handle this situation? And if Rae's help was so important, Krista wondered why had they asked *her* to drop her life and come out here in the first place.

"Actually, I am prepared to invest in Wyler Ranch. If that's what it's going to take."

"Excuse me?" Krista couldn't believe what she was hearing.

"I don't want the ranch sold, Krissy," Judith said.

Krista turned to her aunt quickly. "I got that. Loud and clear."

"You're upset."

"I'm not upset, Aunt Judith. Just confused. I guess I'm wondering why I was called here to begin with. It sounds like you and your friends," she glared at Rae, "have got it all figured out."

"Your aunt just thought you could use some help, since you aren't experienced, as far running a ranch goes," Rae explained.

"Is that so?" Krista rose, unable to sit still any longer. The vet's eyes were penetrating. Too penetrating.

"I still want you in charge," Judith added. "You're family. And a smart businesswoman. I know you'll take good care of things."

"Thanks for the vote of confidence."

"Don't sass me, young lady," Judith snapped.

"Do you think I like doing this?" Krista demanded. "You think I want to sell the ranch? You think I want to sell the one thing that means the world to you?"

The cowboys lowered their eyes.

"Well, I don't."

"Krissy, calm down," Judith said.

"I'm sure together we can come up with a solution." Rae looked sincere and determined.

Krista placed her hands on her hips and did her best to breathe as she looked to her aunt. "You know I love you."

"Yes I do. And I know you'll do as I wish."

Krista didn't respond. She merely nodded.

"Good, then I want you to work with Rae," Judith concluded. "Find a way to keep the ranch running. For me. For your uncle. It's my final wish."

With those words echoing in her mind, Krista quietly walked out the door.

CHAPTER FIVE

The cigarette tip burned between Krista's fingers. Its scent, along with numerous others, was too overwhelming for her to pay it any mind. She glanced around the smoky lesbian bar, unable to concentrate on anyone for longer than a second or two. Her mind was on the ranch and the words her aunt had spoken earlier that day. And Rae. Who the hell did she think she was? Krista would be damned if she was going to work this out with a perfect stranger. And she wouldn't even allow her mind to linger on the attraction she'd felt for her.

"Fuck," she said softly and stubbed out the cigarette. She hadn't ever smoked before. But she needed something to comfort her.

"With pleasure," a woman's voice whispered in her ear.

Krista turned and found a short-haired dyke staring her down, inches from her face.

"Really?" Krista resisted the urge to roll her eyes. The woman wasn't bad looking, just a little too cocky. A huge turn-off.

"Yeah." The stranger's hand rested on Krista's forearm.

"Not tonight, chief." Krista shook out another cigarette, needing an excuse to move her arm.

"Why not?"

"Because." But she didn't have a good reason, not one that made any sense. The self-assured woman saw her chance and took it quickly, grabbing the lighter and assisting Krista with firing up her smoke.

Krista inhaled sharply and fought the urge to cough. Suddenly feeling playfully curious, she studied her new companion. Her hair was dark with red streaks, cut short and spiked, her T-shirt tight fitting, and her watch oversized. She was shorter and smaller in stature than

Krista's five foot six but she made up for it with attitude. She was cute and very much interested.

"How old are you?" Krista asked, feeling a slow smile spread across her face.

"How old do you want me to be?"

"Legal would be nice." Maybe this was what she needed. A mindless fuck to help get her head straight. Yes. God, suddenly nothing sounded better.

"Well, you're in luck. I'm twenty-one." She reached out and stroked Krista's arm with her fingertips.

"Goody, goody," Krista replied, allowing a false sense of bravado to overtake her. She stood, stubbed out her cigarette, and dug in her pocket for her car keys. "You coming?" she asked, raising an amorous eyebrow as she headed for the door.

Forty-five minutes later, Krista was sitting on the back of the Z, the roof down, with her legs slung over the headrests, staring into the brilliant purple-blue sky as the younger woman licked up her thighs. They'd driven hurriedly from the club and left the main road far behind for a secluded spot in the nearby desert. Their clothes had soon come off after a heated session of aggressive kisses. And now the young woman had her knees in the seats, groaning as she knelt and leaned in closer.

Eyes closed, Krista clutched the spiked hair and tried to just *feel* rather than think. But a face flashed in her mind. Classic, tan and angled, with a friendly, heart-melting smile. Krista opened her eyes, frustrated. She focused on the head moving up between her legs, felt the agile tongue find her clit. Yes, this was what she needed. She just had to put everything else out of her mind.

A strong, warm hand shook hers. The smile was genuine, the gorgeous face partially hidden by a ball cap. Her aunt's words echoed in her mind.

"Damn it!" Krista tugged back on the spiked hair.

The woman looked up her with heavy-lidded eyes. Her mouth was open, her lips swollen and hungry with desire.

"What's wrong?" She grinned.

Krista stared hard, determined to take this pleasure. "What's your name?"

"Erica."

"Erica?" God, she was young. But that wasn't the problem.

"But I can be whoever you want me to be."

Can you be a thirtysomething vet with a face I won't soon forget? Krista winced.

"I'll do whatever you want," Erica continued. "You're so hot, you could charge people to do you." Her grin widened as she inched her way closer and extended her tongue.

Krista watched as it lined her flesh, swirling around and around, causing her to twitch with need as it moved closer and closer to her swollen red clit.

"Yes," she hissed as the tongue found her, pressing and flicking. With her head craned back and her eyes fixed on the evening sky, she focused only on Erica's words. "You could charge people…"

"Yes, yes." She was finally feeling it. The tongue flickered and then pressed and then lapped. "Yes," she whispered, getting closer now. Rae's face resurfaced in her mind and she let it mingle with Erica's words. "Yes…*yes!*" she cried out as the idea took shape in the darkening sunset.

She laughed and threw her head back again. The answer was right there. Right there in the night sky, a star just waiting for her to reach out and pluck it. *I could charge people to work the ranch.*

She'd seen it on TV. Krista felt lighter suddenly, like she could just float right up off the car. Erica laughed along with her, her mouth barely lifting from Krista's aching flesh. As the pressure increased again and a desperately needed orgasm built, Krista closed her eyes and allowed the handsome face in her mind to remain. She wished with all her might that it was the one between her legs.

CHAPTER SIX

Your aunt's in a mood today," Sonja warned over morning coffee.

Krista chuckled softly and took a sip of the piping hot liquid. "I can handle it."

She was relaxed and at ease within herself. Finally, she'd figured out a way to solve their big problem. Finally, she'd gotten some much-needed sleep even though she'd got in late.

"I'm glad you think so." Sonja smiled. "Because she's waiting for you."

Krista poured coffee into another mug, then picked up her own to head down the hallway, wondering what it was her aunt had to say. She fought off a nervous yawn, remembering the night before. She'd come three times, calling out into the desert night while silently calling to Rae, a woman she didn't even know. It had been the only way she could find the release she'd needed, even if the climaxes were short-lived.

Feeling better than she had in days and hoping her aunt was as well, she said, "Knock, knock," as she reached the master bedroom. "Good morning, Aunt Judith."

She entered quietly, aware of her sleeping uncle in the opposite bed, and kissed her aunt on the forehead.

"Every morning I'm still here is a good morning," Judith teased, accepting the coffee with feeble-looking hands. "Well, maybe not for those around me."

Krista pulled up the chair that was resting against the wall. She sat and sipped her coffee as her eyes adjusted to the low light the one open set of blinds let in. The bedroom hadn't changed much over the years, with the exception of the hospital bed and beeping vitals machines. Her aunt's own artwork still hung on the walls. Bright watercolors of the surrounding mountains and valleys at sunset, cattle grazing next to large saguaros, a red-shouldered hawk sitting on a fence, all of it captivating and beautiful. Krista remembered watching her paint the one of the hawk. The bird represented the ranch, Judith had said.

Krista felt Judith watching her. The blue eyes were lively and penetrating. Judith took a long, loud sip before she spoke. "I'm disappointed in you, Krissy."

Krista rested her mug in her upturned palm. "Oh?"

"Taking off yesterday like you did. It was rude."

"I'm sorry, I—"

But Judith cut her off.

"I was really hoping you would talk with Rae. I'm counting on you. I thought at the very least you'd grant my last wish."

Krista let her finish and felt herself flush with emotion. She set down her mug on the bedside table and took her aunt's frail but warm hand. She had run out, too caught up in her own anger to notice anything else. It must've looked bad. "Aunt Judith, I'm sorry for leaving like that."

"And after all the bragging I did about you to Rae." Judith tsked.

Krista lowered her head, wondering what the vet must think of her. And then she wondered why she even cared.

"I'll apologize to her when I see her again." Which she hoped wouldn't be anytime soon. She didn't have time to have sudden feelings for anyone right now.

"Good, she should be here any minute now."

Krista tensed.

"I asked her to come over early this morning. So you two could talk."

Krista felt herself redden. "Damn it, Judith, I don't need any help."

"You watch your tongue, missy," Judith scolded.

Krista started to explain, but they were interrupted by a soft knock. The handsome vet poked her head in and smiled a warm smile.

"Rae. Come in, come in," Judith welcomed.

Rae walked in, hands pressed to her side, wearing faded Wranglers, worn boots, and a fresh, tight-fitting white T-shirt. Dark, thick nipples showed off the braless chest. Her short dark hair was thick and wet, the strong scent of an arousing, spicy cologne resonating from her. She bent and kissed Judith on the cheek, her forearms flexing as she carefully embraced her.

Krista swallowed against the rising lump in her throat, fighting both resentment and attraction and then hating herself for each unwelcome emotion.

"Krista was just telling me how sorry she was for running out on us yesterday." Judith raised her eyebrows at her niece.

Krista met Rae's deep hazel eyes. Instantly, she thought of the previous night and how she had come courtesy of the same mysterious eyes. Her flush grew hotter.

"Yes, please forgive me for leaving like I did," she said, her pride hurt. Embarrassed at her physical reaction to Rae, she looked away.

Carefully, Rae sat on the foot of the bed and Krista could feel the woman looking at her.

"I'm not here to step on your toes," Rae offered, her voice low and sincere. "I want you to know that."

Krista met her eyes and sucked in a quick breath at the intensity she saw there. Never before had eyes melted her, had a face haunted her. She looked away quickly and patted her aunt's hand, anxious to escape from the room. This woman stirred her in more ways than she could handle. She'd felt attraction before, the intense want and desire for another woman. But this was different. This was more. She not only felt for Rae physically, she wanted to know her. What made her laugh, what made her smile? What exactly was it that swam in the depths of those eyes?

"I've got good news." Krista spoke in her most businesslike manner, desperate to hide her escalating feelings. "I've got a solution to our problem."

"Oh?" Judith seemed surprised while Rae sat in silence, waiting.

"It just came to me." Krista thought back to the exact moment when it had indeed come to her. She cleared her throat, embarrassed by her memory. "I've decided to turn the ranch into a dude ranch." She smiled, victorious.

Judith moved her thin lips but said nothing. She looked to Rae, still saying nothing.

Rae finally spoke, her eyes searching pools. "I don't understand."

"I'm afraid I don't, either," Judith said.

"It's simple, really," Krista said. "We charge people to come here and round our cattle." *You could charge people*... She shook the voice from her head. "We charge them to come help run the ranch."

Judith simply stared. She cupped her hands around the coffee mug and looked to Rae.

Krista placed determined hands on her hips. "It can work. I know it will. The guests can stay in the bunkhouses, they can ride our horses and herd our cattle. I've spent the past hour researching online, and from what I've read I know we can do it." She motioned to Rae. "You said yourself that you're willing to invest..." Even though she was desperate to get away from Rae, Krista needed to sell her the idea.

Rae looked to Judith and nodded. "I would have to know more of the details, but it sounds like a good idea."

Krista nearly collapsed with relief. She gave Rae her best smile and was surprised when the vet's cheeks darkened a little.

"I don't know," Judith said.

To their left Clinton was sitting up in bed. He slung his long legs over the side and stood in his white boxer shorts to slip into his jeans. "It's a good idea. The ranch would make money."

He buttoned his pants and slid his arms into one of his numerous, freshly pressed denim shirts. With his white hair standing up in the back, he straightened his shirt and walked out of the room, no further words spoken. All three women watched him go, stunned by his well-voiced opinion.

"Well hell," Judith proclaimed, "I guess if Clinton thinks it's a good idea and he's losing his mind, then it must be a good idea."

Krista laughed, happy for the first time in weeks.

Rae chuckled and stood. "I guess I better get to work." She kissed Judith again on the cheek.

"Not so fast," Judith said. "You and Krista need to talk about this some more."

Rae sunk her hands in her back pockets. "Sure."

Krista nodded, unwilling to argue any further. She too gave her aunt a kiss and followed Rae out into the hallway.

As they entered the living room, Rae turned to her and offered a smile. "I really do think it's a good idea. If your aunt and uncle want the ranch to continue on."

"It will work. I'll see that it does," Krista said, setting the boundaries.

Rae studied her a moment. "Okay," she said softly, obviously catching the hint. She was about to say more but Clinton walked into the room, hair still a mess, carrying a mug of steaming coffee, his face one of surprise.

"Krissy, when did you get here?"

Krista sighed, having gone through this countless times already. "I've been here awhile, *tío*."

His eyes remained widened in surprise but the neatly stacked fire logs against the wall caught his attention. Krista and Rae watched as he set down his coffee to rearrange the pile.

"Well, as you can see, I have a lot to take care of here, so I better get to it," Krista said.

"I love this ranch," Rae said seriously. "In many ways it's been like a second home to me. And I respect your aunt Judith, more than anyone else I know. She wants me to help you with the ranch and I want to grant her wishes."

Krista placed her hands on her hips. "I appreciate your loyalties, Dr. Jarrett."

"Please, call me Rae."

The request startled Krista, though she didn't know why. "Rae," she breathed. *Who are you? And why do you affect me so?* "Look, I promise I'll call you if I need any help."

Rae clenched her perfect jaw and nodded in obvious frustration. After a brief, silent moment, she brushed by Krista and walked out the front door, her lingering scent spinning Krista's mind.

❖

"Holy fuck, is that her?" Lindsay wanted to know.

Lindsay Cassidy was Rae's assistant and her best friend for as long as she could remember. Rae pulled her dually truck into the front gravel drive of Wyler Ranch. She briefly studied the freshly painted house and cattle pens and then, spotting Krista, she answered, "Yes."

"She looks like a hellfire. That auburn hair and an ass that won't quit."

Normally Rae merely shook her head at Lindsay's prowlings. But for some reason she wasn't in the mood to hear her friend ogle over Krista Wyler. "Easy, Lindsay."

"Sorry, boss." She grinned. "You into her or something?"

Rae brought the truck to a stop and put it into park. She rolled her eyes at the ridiculousness of the suggestion. Lindsay knew better. "Of course not."

Lindsay studied her a moment in silence, her face serious and distant, obviously reflecting on the not so distant past. "I'm sorry," she offered. "I didn't mean anything by it."

Rae nodded while avoiding her eyes, knowing her friend meant no harm. "Just don't get carried away. Remember who her aunt is." She switched off the Dixie Chicks and climbed from the truck.

Lindsay came around the front to her side. "So is she gay?"

They walked back to the rear and unlocked the horse trailer.

"Who?"

"Who?" Lindsay's eyes widened at Rae's indifference. "The hellfire."

"How should I know?" Rae didn't like the conversation and she definitely didn't like where it was headed. The feeling surprised her. For a long time she just hadn't felt at all. About anything.

Lindsay leaned against the trailer and folded her arms as she watched a denim-clad Krista Wyler talk with a group of people by the cattle pens. Rae patted her two horses on the rump and backed them out one by one, glad that she and Lindsay were only there to drop off the horses and to clear the other ones for work. Lindsay couldn't do much damage if they didn't stay long. Most of the time she was all talk anyway.

Rae climbed atop Shamrock, who was already saddled, and clicked her into place. She called down to Lindsay, who was still eyeing Krista. "Are you coming or are you drooling?"

"With her, I'd like to do both." Lindsay hoisted herself easily up onto the remaining horse, a beautiful brown gelding, and they trotted over to the stables where Dwight stood packing chewing tobacco into his cheek.

It was a sunny Sunday morning and Rae was pleasantly surprised to see the ranch bustling with activity. Around her, several people walked the property with Krista, one of them taking photos with an enormous lens, all of them looking a little out of place with their shorts and sneakers. Apparently, the ranch was ready to take on its first paying group. And it hadn't been that long since Krista Wyler had all but told Rae to fuck off when she'd offered her support.

She guessed Krista was right after all. Maybe she didn't need any help.

"Doc," Dwight greeted her, taking her horse by the bridle as she dismounted.

"Morning, Dwight." She bent to stroke Repeat, who licked her hand eagerly, tail wagging.

Lindsay followed close behind, bobbing up and down in the saddle, showing off her dressage skills, earning some looks of awe from several of the onlookers. "Hey, handsome." She smiled down at Dwight, pleased with herself when he blushed. She sat tall and proud, turning the horse, loving that all eyes were on her.

Rae rolled her eyes, very much aware that Lindsay was showing off for Krista. "She's not even looking."

"No, but that blonde sure is."

Rae searched the small crowd and spotted the stunning blond woman standing next to Krista. Built like a Playboy bunny and dressed as such in short cut-off jeans and a tank top, she stood out like a sore thumb against the backdrop of the ranch.

Lindsay smiled, returning the obvious stare, and pranced her horse. But the smile faded when the blonde's eyes never left Rae.

Lindsay whistled enthusiastically "You should go say hi."

Rae frowned, unamused. "Why don't you take the horses inside and get started on the others?" She patted Shamrock on the rump, encouraging her to follow Lindsay into the stables.

Lindsay did as instructed, her eager eyes back on Krista, hoping the auburn-haired woman would look her way.

She didn't.

Rae shook her head as her friend disappeared inside, then she walked up to Dwight, shoving her hands down into her pockets. "What's going on? Anything exciting?"

He glanced at his watch and clicked his teeth. "Well, let's see here. They're supposed to take these city folk out on a six-day adventure in about an hour's time."

"You're leaving today?" *Wow. Krista really was a miracle worker.*

"I ain't, no. I'm staying behind to look after things. I'll be preparing the meals and such and a wrangler will take the fresh supplies out to the group." He chewed on the wad in his mouth. "They're gonna ride about a day's journey out to the cattle and then circle them back to the ranch in a radius, making sure to only stay a day's ride out from the ranch."

Any small comfort in hearing the detailed plans dissipated when she realized that Dwight was staying behind. The thought of the rushed preparation and the absence of experienced hands only made her all the more concerned. Judith had called her yesterday, requesting two horses, but she hadn't mentioned when the group was leaving. Rae had assumed they needed the horses for the city folk to learn to ride a little before they set out. But leaving today? She studied the group of men and women, all in shorts, three wearing fanny packs, and all of them looking as green as grass.

Rae tried her best to mentally catch up to the situation. "Doesn't it seem a little too soon? Have any of these people ever been on a horse?"

"By the looks of things yesterday when Cody was helping them rope, I'd say no," Dwight confirmed. "We showed 'em how to team pen a little and they didn't do too bad. A couple fell off but they got right back on. But cowboys? No. They ain't no cowboys."

Rae's mind flew in a fury of disbelief. Even if they'd ridden before, they'd probably never had to chase cattle or ride and rope for real. Team penning and roping for fun were one thing. Doing it for real out in the harsh terrain of the desert was another. It sounded like a nightmare waiting to happen. "And Judith's all right with this?"

"Shoot, Judith don't know. This is all Krista." Dwight met her eyes briefly before refocusing on the group. "But don't worry. They won't be going anywhere until the other wranglers show up. They were due in yesterday and we haven't heard from 'em yet."

Rae still couldn't believe what she was hearing, that Krista was even trying to take these people out on the trail so soon. She removed her ball cap and slapped it against her leg as she walked along the perimeter of the pen to where Krista stood, talking and smiling.

When she saw Rae, Krista's smile vanished. Rae noticed, but it didn't change her focus on the seriousness of the situation. "You got a minute?"

Krista seemed a little embarrassed. "Please, excuse me." She walked a few steps away from the people she'd been speaking with and stopped in the shade of the stables. "How can I help you, Dr. Jarrett?"

Rae clenched her hat in her hand. "Rae, it's Rae." Flustered, she said, "There's no way you can take these people out on the trail today."

Krista's fiery green eyes flashed before she spoke. "I'm sorry, do you have a problem? Is there something wrong with one of the horses? Judith assured me that you were bringing another two."

Rae held up her hands. "This isn't about the horses."

"No? Then what's it about?"

"You can't take these people out into the high desert without teaching them how to ride and rope better first."

"Most of them have ridden before." Krista forced a smile. "They spent yesterday morning and this morning grooming the horses, getting to know them. Dwight and Cody showed them how to herd a few of the cattle with the horses. And I was just about to have Cody lead another brief course on roping before we head out." She checked her watch. "We've still got an hour or so. I've got it all under control."

A young cowboy walked up and tipped his hat, hesitant about interrupting the conversation. Rae recognized Cody and nodded a hello. He had worked the ranch off and on for about two years as Dwight's second in charge.

"Ma'am?" he addressed Krista.

"Yes, Cody?"

"Our wrangler just showed up." He pointed to a short, stout cowboy, knapsack tossed casually over his shoulder. Dwight was talking to the new arrival.

"Wonderful." Krista smiled at Rae, obviously pleased with herself.

"I'm afraid it's not wonderful, ma'am." Cody looked serious way beyond his twenty years. "He's the only one comin'. The other two bailed."

Krista kept smiling, her face set in stone. "Oh. Well, I'm sure it won't be a problem. Go on ahead and start the roping. We'll get it worked out."

Cody sighed and tipped his hat again. "Yes, ma'am."

"Well, now you can't leave." Rae almost sighed herself, relieved.

"If you'll excuse me, Dr. Jarrett, I have urgent business to attend to." Krista brushed past her, storming up to Dwight and the wrangler. Rae couldn't hear what was being said, but whatever it was, the tone wasn't good.

She made her way into the stables where Lindsay stood brushing down one of the Wylers' horses.

"What's wrong?" Lindsay's eyes were glued to Rae's face.

"Nothing. Everything." Rae positioned herself and bent to lift the horse's hoof and held it between her legs, checking its shoe. Normally she didn't do farrier work, but she made an exception for the Wylers, making sure all of their horse needs were met and exceeded. The service saved her longtime friends both time and money. She worked quickly, lowering the first hoof and lifting the next. "Let's just get the horses checked and get the hell out of here."

She wanted no part of Krista Wyler's hasty scheme. Couldn't she see how crazy it was to take a group of inexperienced strangers out into the harsh desert to rough it as cowboys for six days? And without enough real wranglers? She lowered the other front leg and moved to the back. As she examined the shoe, she pulled her clippers from her back pocket and began trimming the hoof. She thought of Judith and the promise she'd made her. Like it or not, she couldn't just walk away. At the very least she would have to go and talk to Judith. The sooner the better.

"Can you handle this?" she asked Lindsay, handing over the clippers. "I need to go see Mrs. Wyler."

"Sure, go."

Rae tugged her ball cap down snug and walked toward the house. She smiled broadly, her heart warming at seeing Mrs. Wyler sitting outside on the porch in one of the large rockers. "Hi there, pretty lady." Rae bent and kissed her hello. Her pale skin felt warm from the sunlight.

"Sweet-talker." Judith smiled. "Sonja finally let me out of that dungeon." She fingered her IV pole. "Still can't get rid of this damned thing."

Rae pulled up a neighboring rocking chair and stared with her off onto the property. She folded her hands and rocked a little, laying her elbows on the armrests. "A lot going on today."

"Yes, there sure is. It's nice to see the ranch this way again. Full of life."

"Yes, ma'am," Rae replied, not sure how to broach the topic of Krista biting off more than she could chew. "The house looks good."

Judith smiled up into the sun. "Yes it does. Krista said the bunkhouses are next."

The rocking chair creaked as Rae worked up her nerve. "Dwight says they're heading out on the trail today."

"Are they?" Judith looked delighted. "Well, good. I knew Krissy could handle things." She patted Rae's arm. "With your help I knew she could do it."

Rae started to correct her, but stopped short. What could she say? *I didn't help. I didn't follow your wishes?* Rae hung her head.

"I'm a little worried about them heading out so soon. They're short two wranglers and..." Rae stopped talking as Dwight and Krista walked up.

"Rae tells me you're ready to ride out today," Judith said excitedly.

Krista smiled, her eyes traveling over to Rae where they lingered with curiosity. "She did, did she?"

Dwight spit and leaned against one of the posts. "Mrs. Wyler, we're short two men and, as I was just telling Krista, there's no way they can head out."

Krista folded her arms in defiance. "The guests expect to leave today. They were promised six days on the trail. They've been wandering around here for two days already. There's no way I can tell them no. And there's no way we can afford to refund them. We need to ride out. Today."

Judith seemed to think a moment, all eyes on her. "Krissy's right, you can't tell them no. It would ruin the business we're trying to build." She looked to Dwight. "Can't you call in a buddy or two?"

"They're all working other ranches or are too far away to get here by today."

"There's no one?"

"No, ma'am."

"Well then, that leaves us with only one option." Judith's eyes fell on Rae.

"What's that?" Krista asked.

"You'll have to go along with them."

Krista's hands fell from her hips in utter surprise. "Me? No way. I'm not qualified—" She stopped herself short of admitting her inexperience. "I haven't been on a horse in years." Again she stopped herself.

"I know, I know." Judith held up a hand to calm her. "That's why I want Rae to go too."

Krista's mouth fell open. Rae was a little shocked as well.

"Mrs. Wyler, I don't know. I've got appointments..."

But Judith wouldn't hear any of it. "I expect both of you to go.

Since you both want to grant my wishes and all. Rae, I'm sure Lindsay could cover for you. And, Krista, it will do you good to go out on the trail. After all, you're the one that's going to be running the show from now on. You might as well learn how the show is run." Slowly, she stood and anchored herself on the back of the chair. "You girls better get busy, then."

CHAPTER SEVEN

Two hours later, Rae stood packing her horse, softly cursing to herself about the situation. "If she'd allowed me to help, we wouldn't be in this position," she grumbled, tightening her saddle.

She'd gone home right after their conversation with Judith and thrown a few days' worth of clothes and supplies together. She glanced at her truck, almost forgetting the one thing she valued most. Reaching into the backseat, she pulled out her black guitar case, and felt relief just by feeling it in her hands. Even though it was inconvenient as hell to bring it with her, she never went anywhere without her guitar. It had been her only comfort for a long time and more recently, her savior. The afternoon sun was hot on her back as she strapped the soft case to the horse.

"You sure you don't need me to go along?" Lindsay stood next to the truck, one hand on her hip.

Rae squinted into the sun as she looked over at her. "Yeah, I'm sure. You'll be plenty busy covering my appointments."

"I don't know, Dr. Jarrett." Krista's voice chimed in.

Rae looked to her with surprise as she walked up.

"Maybe your assistant should go. That way I could stay behind." Krista returned Lindsay's eager smile.

Lindsay took Krista's hand with confidence and shook it long and slow. "I'm Lindsay Cassidy."

"Krista Wyler."

Lindsay still held Krista's hand cupped in both of her own. "I have to admit, Krista," she said in her best seductive voice, "I would only want to go if you were going as well."

Rae flushed at the blatant come-on. Krista kept smiling but she blinked a few times as if she wasn't sure what to say. Rae decided to settle it once and for all. "Lindsay is needed here. She has to cover my appointments."

Krista finally pulled her hand away, her smile slowly disappearing. Her eyes lingered on Lindsay a moment longer before finding their way back to Rae. "That's a shame," she said, her voice losing pitch. She tucked her hands into her jeans pockets and Rae thought she looked and sounded a little flustered. "I better get back to the guests."

She gave Lindsay a polite smile and strolled away, back to the pen where everyone was gathered.

"Damn." Lindsay laughed, her gaze traveling over to one of the cattle pens where two of the guests were slinging loose loops of rope over their heads, trying unsuccessfully to rope their wooden target. Some of the other guests were busy packing up their horses or trying their new cowboy hats on at different angles. "I wish I could go. Looks like fun."

"Be thankful as hell you aren't going," Rae said, shaking her head at the guests and their new denim wardrobes. They'd changed clothes, ready for the trail. "This is going to be a nightmare."

They both watched as the busty blonde they'd seen before shrieked with delight upon saddling her horse. The tall, thin man with the camera laughed along with her, snapping photos of her as she undulated on her saddle. She looked Rae's way and waved.

Lindsay whistled long and slow and then smiled. "Whatever you say, boss." She opened the door and climbed into the truck. "Whatever you say." She winked and started the engine.

Rae saddled her horse and watched Lindsay drive away. With a sigh, she tugged on the worn black Stetson she rarely wore and trotted over to the main pen. She counted six fresh and eager faces, all of them standing next to their assigned horses, all of them listening intently to Krista Wyler, who was introducing the wranglers.

Cody tipped his hat modestly as his name was called, unlike the short, muscular cowboy named Howie.

"Howdy," he grinned and removed his hat, eyes trained on Krista. A thick, weathered-looking hand held Krista's up to his sneering lips. "This trip is sure to be a pleasure with this pretty lady leading the way."

Rae slid off her horse, the urge to interfere almost getting the better of her. Seeing Lindsay do as much to Krista had caused some surfacing jealousy, but to watch this cocky cowboy try and kiss Krista's hand nearly overwhelmed her with rage. Rae told herself it was just protectiveness because Krista was Judith's niece, and she fought to let it go.

Krista jerked her hand away from the cowboy's, saving Rae the trouble, and she did her best to keep her composure. Howie slipped his hat back on, his grin intact. Rae stood between the two to settle her own racing heart as Krista introduced her.

"This is Dr. Rae Jarrett. She's our veterinarian and a close friend of the family's. We're very lucky to have her joining us on our first outing."

Rae nodded her hello and insisted, "Please, call me Rae."

The group said hello in unison, all smiles.

Krista continued. "We're already running a bit behind. So please, if each of you would please introduce yourselves, we can get going."

The young man with the camera around his neck spoke first. "I'm Adam. I'm from Phoenix." He looked handsome and chic, his button-down shirt purposely weathered and tucked into his tailored, fitting jeans. His smile was near perfect, and his eyes genuine. He ran a lean hand through his tousled blond hair. "And this is my good friend, Candace."

The busty blonde laughed and gave an excited wave as she stood next to her horse. Her breasts shook beneath the cotton of the tight-fitting tank top. The jeans she'd changed into were just as tight and led down to a pair of tasseled pink cowboy boots. Howie grunted his approval and Rae fought the urge to smack him upside the head.

Next, a middle-aged man with a thin white beard said his hellos. "I'm Frank and this is my wife, Jenna. We're from Boston." Frank was just barely taller than his wife and, with his infectious laugh, he reminded Rae of Richard Dreyfuss.

Jenna smiled from under her wide-brimmed hat, her hand fingering the Navajo dream catcher she wore around her neck. "We've always wanted to see the desert."

"Well, you've come to the right place," Krista welcomed.

"I'm Tom," said a quiet man near the back of the group. He looked to be mid-forties and an outdoorsman, his deep tan, athletic watch, and hiking boots giving him away. "I'm from Flagstaff and just always wanted to go on one of these."

The last of the group stood quietly by her horse. She wore new Wranglers and a stylish cowgirl shirt. Her white straw cowboy hat hid beautiful blue-green eyes that appeared to be pooled with sadness. She looked to be in her thirties and she had a quiet grace about her. Rae sensed the group breathe deeply at the sight of such stricken beauty.

"I'm Tillie. I'm here because I just needed to get away."

This time Howie spoke up. "Yeah, you're definitely in the right place."

Rae turned on him and upon seeing the disapproval on her face, his grin vanished. "What?" he asked, walking away toward the group.

"You know what," Rae mumbled after him.

At Krista's instruction, the group began mounting their horses. Most straddled their horses in one try but a couple struggled. Rae was holding on to Jenna's horse when she heard her name being called.

"Rae, Rae over here!"

Rae excused herself and stood alongside Howie at Candace's horse.

The blonde blinked her thick eyelashes at Rae. "I think I need some help getting up." Her gloss-covered lips spread into a smile. Rae wondered why she seemed to suddenly be having trouble. She'd mounted her horse just fine not long before.

"Well then, just give me your hand," Howie offered, stepping up to place a hand on her hip. Candace smacked it away and continued smiling at Rae. "I want Rae to help me. If that's okay?"

Rae flushed and cleared her throat as the color drained from Howie's face. He looked from Candace to Rae and back again in disbelief. With a look of scorned anger, he smacked his hand on his leg and walked away.

"Would you mind helping me?" Candace asked again, offering her hand.

Rae stepped up to help but said nothing. She held the blonde's hand and pushed up on her hip.

Straddling the horse, Candace smiled. "Thanks so much. You're very strong."

"You're welcome." It was all Rae could manage. No woman had shown interest in years, but it stung deep inside nonetheless.

Never again. Never again. I just can't handle it, she thought to herself as she walked away.

❖

Krista watched with a stone-feeling face as Rae walked away from Candace. She'd been green with jealousy at the flirtation, but she felt chilled and alarmed at Rae's reaction.

"All the more reason to stay away," she whispered as the rest of the group mounted their horses.

Six near strangers sat staring down at her, all of them excited and anxious to get on the trail. Cody and Howie mounted up and turned their horses to face the group, leaving Rae and Krista the only ones still standing.

"Where's your horse?" Rae asked Krista. If she thought she was getting out of this she had another think coming.

Krista refused to meet her eyes. "I don't have one yet," She held her voice low so the guests couldn't hear.

"Why not?"

"I haven't had the time." She waved at the group and then spoke to Cody, who had one of the supply horses tied back behind his own. "Go on ahead. I'll catch up."

"You sure?" He looked warily at Howie, who was already trying to talk to Candace again.

Krista nodded.

Cody whistled and kicked softly at his horse. "Let's go, folks!"

Several excited whistles followed and the group took off at a slow pace. Krista watched with her hand shading her brow and then turned to find Rae Jarrett staring her down. "Something keeping you, Doctor?"

"Yes. You."

Krista walked briskly into the stables. "Don't let me keep you. I can catch up."

"I'm sure you can. But I'll just stick around to make sure." Rae couldn't explain her reservations, but she was almost positive that Krista was going to try and weasel out of going.

Krista stopped abruptly, hands on hips, looking from horse to horse. There were two left. Frustrated, she turned on Rae. "Will you stop following me!"

Rae stopped, startled. She'd had enough of Krista Wyler and her rudeness. "Fine."

She turned and headed back out of the stables. *I'll just wait for her out here. And then when she's ready, I'll leave her ass.*

"Wait." The request was spoken softly. "Wait, please."

Rae stopped, unsure she'd heard it. She turned and met frightened green eyes.

Krista lowered her head. "Which horse…" She cleared her throat. "Which horse should I ride?" She lifted her head again, trying to keep her composure.

Rae approached slowly, hands sinking into her pockets. The fiery confidence was gone and Rae thought briefly about leaving her where she stood. But being rude wasn't her style, even if it was Krista's. "That depends. You've ridden before, yes?"

"It's been a long time," Krista confessed.

"How long?" The change in attitude was so startling Rae blinked to make sure she was still talking to the same woman.

"Over fifteen years."

"Well, as the old saying goes, just get back in the saddle."

"It's not that simple," Krista interrupted.

"Why?"

"Look, just point me to the most gentle horse." The green eyes were again full of fire.

Rae clenched her jaw, swallowing down the curse words that wanted so badly to surface. Instead, she brushed past Krista and opened the stall to where her beautiful brown gelding stood. Rae lifted a saddle onto him and strapped it on. She worked quickly, without looking at Krista.

"Where's your stuff?" She would help the woman pack her horse but that was it.

"Cody has it."

Good. The sooner they were on the trail, the better. She fit the bridle in the horse's mouth and led him out of the stall. With venom in her voice she offered Krista the horse.

"His name's Dollar. You two should be a match made in heaven."

Krista's eyes shot up to hers. "Just what the hell is that supposed to mean?"

Rae walked past her without looking back. "Nothing." She'd sized Krista up real quick upon first meeting her a few weeks back. Her car, her clothes, her attitude. Money and the bottom line seemed to be all she cared about.

Upon stepping back into the sunlight, Dwight nearly ran into her. "How did Krista do?" He sounded concerned.

"What do you mean?"

"Did she mount up?"

Rae studied him curiously. "No." She paused. "She's in the stables with her horse."

"You left her alone!" Panicked, Dwight shoved past her, running into the stables. He called back to her. "Go get your horse and wait for me!"

Rae stared after him, completely confused. *What in the world is going on?*

She sat atop Shamrock at Dwight's instruction, softly cooing to her as she waited. She'd tied on the remaining supply horse, her ears straining to no avail to hear what was being said in the stables. She looked out to the edge of the property and spotted the group in the distance moving at a good pace. A quick glance at her watch reminded her that they needed to get a move on if they were going to reach the designated campsite before dark.

Just as she was about call out for Dwight, the pair exited the stables, Krista atop Dollar with Dwight leading the way. Rae squinted into the sun and caught Krista's hand wiping away tears.

"Everything okay?" Rae asked.

Dwight forced a smile. "Everything's fine. Thanks for waiting."

"No problem." But Rae could see very clearly that there was a problem. Krista looked pale and shook up, her hands trembling on the horn of the saddle. "Is she okay?" Rae directed the question to Dwight.

"I'm fine, Dr. Jarrett," Krista nearly shouted.

Dwight shook his head. "As I said, everything is fine." He reached in his back pocket and handed Rae a radio walkie-talkie. Krista had a matching one on her belt. "Cody's got the first supply horse. I'll be the one bringing you some fresh ones in about a day's time." He turned and gave Krista a fatherly smile, patting her leg softly. "You two better head off now, then."

Rae clicked at Shamrock and took off slow and then led the horses into a trot. It took all of her patience as a good human being not to gallop off and leave Krista Wyler to fend for herself. She managed to ride at a slow pace for about ten minutes before the urge to turn her head overcame her. About a hundred yards back, Krista rode stiffly and slowly, her hands clutching the horn of the saddle for dear life, her legs swaying way too much. Their guests looked more at home on a horse. Rae sighed and waited for the other woman to catch up. When she did, her mouth once again battled Rae's good will.

"There's no need to wait for me, Doctor. I can assure you, I'm fine."

"Yes, you look fine," Rae countered. "Holding on to Dollar as if he'll spook any moment."

Krista glared at her. "I would prefer if you didn't wait for me."

"And I would prefer it if you didn't speak." Rae's chest tightened. She hated saying it but it was true. "I'm riding with you, so get over it."

"I don't need your goddamned help!"

"I'm not doing it for you!" Rae shouted back. She was doing it for Judith. She felt obligated to look out for Judith's only niece.

"I'm not a child! I don't need looking after!" As she shouted, Dollar stepped backward, growing nervous. Krista's eyes widened with sheer terror and she lost her balance and teetered to her right, falling off the horse. Rae jumped off Shamrock and helped to lift her from the ground. She was trembling, her foot still in the stirrup.

"My foot," she said, "Oh God, my foot." Her eyes were wide with terror.

Rae freed her foot and lifted her so she could stand. "You're okay. Your foot is fine," she said softly, trying to get her to look into her eyes.

Krista glanced down at her feet and then straightened her back and wiped away fresh tears. She noticed Rae's hands on her shoulders. "Please remove your hands."

Dumbfounded, Rae did so. Krista turned and hoisted herself back onto Dollar, her body still trembling. She didn't say another word. Not a thank you, not even a fuck you.

Furious, Rae galloped away, leaving Krista alone to fight against her tears.

CHAPTER EIGHT

Adam Burgess grabbed his own ass as he finished doing his assigned chore for the evening. The group had ridden for almost three hours, meandering through the high desert, watching as the setting sun nearly beat them to the campsite. It was their first night on the trail and they hadn't even caught up to the cattle, but his legs and ass hurt already. He eyed the tent he and his good friend Candace were to share, then went in search of some more firewood. Candace was stoking the fire while the more-than-macho Howie talked her ear off, stroking his prominent cowboy five o'clock shadow.

Adam rolled his eyes as he strode past them. Poor Candi. She loved and craved attention, but she was learning the hard lesson that she couldn't pick and choose when and from whom that attention would come. He had foolishly hoped this adventure would be relaxing and fun, but with an attractive female alongside a horny man, little of either was likely. But he would be damned if he was going to let a drooling caveman of a cowboy ruin their trip. He would still take his shots of Candi. She was counting on it.

He sighed, wishing at the very least an attractive cowboy had come along for him to enjoy. As he picked up a piece of dry wood, he heard hoofbeats approaching from the direction of the setting sun. Shading his eyes, he dropped the wood and admired what he saw, the androgynous cowgirl riding with the beautiful sunset as a backdrop. He lifted his camera, and his adrenaline pumped as he captured her, the face and arms tanned and coated with a thin sheen of sweat, her carved jaw clenched beneath the black Stetson. For a moment he almost wished she had a penis. She was amazing. Candi would die when she saw these photos.

Rae slowed her horse and lowered the brim of her hat. "Were you taking photos of me?" she asked, in no mood for saying "cheese."

Adam lowered the camera and acted as if he were cleaning the lens. "No, just taking some shots of the sunset."

Rae glanced behind her and slid off her horse. Her jeans were dark and covered with sweat along the insides of her legs. As she walked away, leaving the horses in Cody's hands, she stripped off her cotton button-down shirt, showing off her thick muscles in her sleeveless undershirt. Adam snapped more photos from behind, grinning as he did so. If only he could convince the cowgirl to let him use them. He could make a killing using her in a calendar.

A few minutes later, he was once again searching aimlessly for wood when another rustling noise disturbed him, and in the near distance he saw Krista Wyler astride a beautiful brown horse, walking very slowly up to the campsite. He raiseed the camera and zoomed in. Her face was bright red, having been unprotected from the sun. Her lips were dry and chapped, while mascara stains raccooned her eyes. It was obvious she'd been crying and she looked as if she was about to pass out. Adam lowered the camera and ran up to her. Hurriedly, she wiped at her eyes and cleared her throat.

"When did you guys arrive?" She straightened her hair and smiled, but she wasn't fooling anyone.

Adam offered his hand, taking her trembling one. Carefully, he helped her down and Cody took her horse.

"Thank you," she breathed, steadying herself against Adam.

"Don't mention it." He kept his hand on her shoulder as she bent over, obviously dizzy. "We got in about an hour ago."

"Oh?" She stood and began straightening her clothes, her eyes focusing on the heavenly ground. *Oh thank God, the ground.* She pounded her boots against the desert, making sure it was real. "How do I look?" She met Adam's eyes and smiled, doing her best to hide her pain. She shoved a trembling hand down into her jeans, hoping he didn't notice.

His eyes were sincere and concerned, but sparkling with humor. "Maavalus."

Krista laughed. She liked him at once. "That bad, huh?"

Adam took her arm as they walked toward camp. Cody offered the pair a concerned smile as he unpacked and watered the horses.

Adam was studying her. "We need to find you a cowboy hat and some sunscreen."

Krista kicked out her legs, in serious pain. "How's my ass?"

"Probably how it feels." He paused and lowered his gaze to her backside. "Tight and firm, but a sight for sore eyes."

Again Krista laughed and linked arms with the young photographer. "What in the hell have I gotten myself into?"

A few minutes later, just as some feeling was finally seeping back into her legs, a soft beep sounded from her waistband. Retrieving her cell phone, she saw that Suzanne had called. Anxious, and still hoping to somehow be able to work from way out here, she dialed her number.

"Suzanne?" She heard muffled sounds that made no sense. "You're breaking up."

The sounds muted into the static. Krista frowned with annoyance that she now had something else to worry about, and then flinched at the pain from her sunburn.

"Damn it!" How could she get anything done if she couldn't even use her cell phone? This was going to be one hell of an excursion. Deciding she'd try to text Suzanne instead, she walked into the camp with a forced smile on her face.

With the help of some aloe vera Adam had brought along and some fresh water, Krista calmed down and cleaned up as best she could. She changed into a fresh pair of jeans and a soft T-shirt and then busied herself alongside Cody, getting the group ready to spend its first night out under the desert sky. She was too tired to feel overly frustrated when her text messages refused to go through. She'd tried several times with no success and finally gave up, tucking the phone back on her belt.

After that, Krista allowed herself to watch Rae as she worked alone, double-checking the tents and supplies, and then preparing dinner. Rae avoided Krista altogether, and the blatant indifference panged in Krista's chest. But she knew she was better off without Rae's attention. She had a business to run. Two businesses to run. Still, her mind went back to the way she'd felt in Rae's arms. Safe. Secure. And the way she smelled, so warm and alluring. She shook the thought away. She and Rae were too different. It would never work.

❖

The campsite was warm and inviting as darkness settled in. Krista sat a ways back from the heat of the fire, due to her sunburnt skin. The burning mesquite smelled wonderful and rustic, soothing them just as the fiery colors of the sunset had done a bit earlier. Krista relaxed, enjoying the meal.

Rae had seasoned the rice and beans just right and Krista wondered how often she cooked and for whom. As she ate, she fought staring at Rae, who sat against a rock with her long legs outstretched and crossed. Her bare arms flexed as she held her bowl and ate. Her angled face looked breathtaking in the tickling firelight, and Krista found herself holding her breath as she watched her.

"Should I offer a penny for your thoughts?" Adam asked softly as he settled in next to her.

His messy model-blond hair was gorgeous, as was his smile, and she wondered how he did it. How did he manage to look that good out in the middle of nowhere? She let her eyes travel back to Rae, who was laughing at a comment from one of their guests.

Adam nudged her playfully as she sighed. "Oh, in that case, I'll offer a cool million." His gaze lingered on Rae. "She is something, isn't she? Candi's dying to get in her pants."

Krista jerked at the words. "What?"

Adam rolled his eyes and chewed his food. "Oh please, girl. Don't bullshit me. That is one sexy butch veterinarian." He paused, spoon in hand. "Think she's got a brother?"

Krista laughed and took a sip of her water. "I'm not into her, or anyone for that matter." What was she thinking, allowing someone to catch her staring?

"Uh-huh. And I'm straight."

"No, really." Krista turned to him, trying to convince him. Or was she trying to convince herself?

Adam merely raised his pierced eyebrow and she dropped it altogether. They sat in silence, leaning against one another as they finished their meal. She rose when everyone was finished and took Adam's bowl, determined to help Rae clean up.

But she was too late.

"Oh, I've got that," Candace said, giggling while handing over bowl after bowl to Rae, who was rinsing them.

Krista stopped and swallowed, straightening her back. She stepped up next to Rae and rinsed her own dishes. Rae glanced at her but said nothing, and Krista left the two of them alone.

Once everyone was finished cleaning up and their stomachs were full, Jenna brought out a large thermos full of red wine just as Adam was emerging from his tent.

"I brought along some music, to help get me in the game." He sat down the small, handheld recorder and pressed Play. A country music song began to play, upbeat and very catchy. The group cheered and took the offered mugs full of wine.

Eventually, Frank and Jenna embraced alongside the fire, swinging and swaying to the music. Candace sat on the rock behind Rae and began massaging her shoulders. Rae seemed to flinch at first and she voiced a protest, but Candace kept on, making high-pitched references to how strong Rae was.

Howie was watching closely, and his face tightened at Candace's words. Looking stern but determined, he stood and offered his hand to her, but Candace shook her head, declining the dance. He was about to protest when Tillie stood and pulled him away from Candace, dancing at a good arm's length from him. Krista breathed a sigh of relief and reminded herself to thank Tillie in the morning. Her heated gaze returned to Rae and Candace, and she downed the wine and hoped no one would notice that Howie wasn't the only one sending daggers their way.

❖

Rae closed her eyes and tried to relax. The firm hands on her shoulders were working magic, the music reminiscent, luring her to a place that seemed so far away. She raised the mug to her nose and thought about taking a sip. As she hesitated, she caught a whiff of the wine.

Her mind flew in reverse, back to a similar time, three years ago.

The wine and beer flowed endlessly, as did the loud country music. She laughed at Lindsay's joke and sipped her beer as she scanned the dance floor. Moving in tandem across the floor cowgirls clutched cowgirls, two-stepping to the twang of the slow song. One couple caught her attention and she clenched her jaw at the sight.

"What is it?" Lindsay asked, lowering her beer to turn and look. Following Rae's glare, she focused in on the dancing couple and shook her head. "Let it go, Rae, let it go."

"How can I let it go?" Rae swallowed the fire in her throat, wishing she had drunk at least enough to feel buzzed. "She's dancing with that cocky piece of crap again."

"She's just doing it to get a rise out of you." Lindsay reached across the small table and covered her hand. "You need to end this shit once and for all. She's no good, Rae."

Rae squeezed the glass beer bottle in her hand, fighting the urge to storm onto the dance floor and pummel the both of them. Lindsay was right, Shannon was doing it just to piss her off, to make her jealous. And damn it if it wasn't working. Lately anger, jealousy, and confusion were all she was feeling. She knew she should end it, but how could she? How could she end their relationship when she really cared about Shannon?

Lindsay gently squeezed her hand. "Rae, she's playing you, lying to you."

Rae shook her head. "No, you're wrong. She's just confused, immature."

"Come on, Rae. You're the smartest woman I know. Stop letting her treat you this way. You rescued her, you did a good thing for her. And now she's taking advantage. Playing head games with you."

"But I care." Rae slid her hand out from under Lindsay's.

"I know you do. You're a good person. Too good, if you ask me. But I know you well. And I know you don't love her."

Rae looked away. The fact stung. She had feelings for Shannon, she cared, she was attracted to her, the sex was great...but Lindsay was right. It wasn't love. She narrowed her eyes as the song ended and Shannon came staggering their way. A sloppy, mischievous grin spread across her face when she saw Rae.

"Hey, baby," she slurred, the scent of wine too strong on her breath. "Did you see me dancing?" She hung from Rae's neck, trying to force Rae to look at her.

"Yeah, I saw." Rae turned away from the kiss.

"I looked good, huh?"

"You looked great, Shannon."

Lindsay rounded the table and took Rae by the arm. Shaking

Shannon free, she eased Rae onto another stool and began massaging her shoulders.

Eyes full of venom, Shannon glared at the two of them and scooped her wineglass up. "Get your damn hands off my girlfriend!" She threw the near-empty glass at Lindsay but it smashed into Rae's forehead instead.

Shannon shrieked and rushed to Rae's side as blood ran down her face. "Oh, baby, I'm so sorry. So sorry." Lindsay offered a napkin and shoved Shannon away. "Why don't you just get the fuck out of here and leave her alone!"

Rae swung out her free arm to interrupt the ensuing shoving match. Around them women had left their tables to come offer help or just flat-out stare. Rae blinked through the warm blood in her eye. She held Lindsay back, not wanting any more trouble. "I'm fine," she whispered to her best friend. "Just let me take her home."

Lindsay stared at her like she was on crack, but Rae insisted.

"Let me take her home. I'm going to talk to her, okay?"

Lindsay caught the meaning and stood down. She lifted the napkin to dab at the cut. "You sure you'll be okay?"

"It's not so bad, is it?" Rae asked.

Lindsay sighed. "No, just clean it real good and use a butterfly bandage. I'll take a look at it again tomorrow."

Rae nodded and held out her hand to Shannon. The younger woman clutched her arm and gave Lindsay an eat-shit-and-die grin as they made their way to the door.

Rae blinked out of her trance as someone said good night to her. People were already stooping into their tents. She shouldered out from under Candace and found the blonde grinning at her expectantly.

"I think we should turn in," Rae said, standing to wipe the dirt off her backside.

"Yes, we should," Candace responded, moving closer to her. "Although," she whispered into Rae's ear, "I'm not all that tired. Maybe I could keep you company in your tent. Finish that massage."

Rae felt the chill bumps of arousal ignite on her flesh from the hot breath in her ear. Her body was responding after a long hibernation of celibacy and she considered the blatant offer for about a split second; then her eyes locked with the fierce green ones across the fire.

"That's a nice offer, but I'm beat. We'd better get some rest." She gave Candace a polite smile. "Thanks for the massage." As she spoke, Krista turned abruptly and disappeared inside her tent.

Jesus, why does that woman hate me?

Candace laid a lingering hand on Rae's bare arm. "Anytime, Doc, anytime."

CHAPTER NINE

Krista turned over and over again on the hard ground. Her thick sleeping bag and thin mat did little to cushion her, and replaying Candace's words only worsened the situation. The blatant flirting was bad enough, but what made her crazy was that Rae seemed to be responding to it. Krista was appalled that the vet had allowed Candace to massage her, even leaning back and closing her eyes in obvious enjoyment.

"Oh, Rae, you're so strong. I love the feel of your shoulders." Krista scoffed and flopped over onto her back once more. She winced as the pain in her ass registered. Unable to sleep and tired of turning endlessly, she sat up and slipped on her hiking boots. The fire was still burning, not nearly as bright as before, but enough for her to see by. She stood and inhaled deeply. She swore the moon ran a rake over the desert every night, stirring each and every plant, every grain of dirt. She could smell every tree, every shrub, as if they'd all opened themselves up in the darkness to enjoy the cool air.

Momentarily content, she decided to walk over to Dollar, to face her fear head-on. The horse blinked at her presence and she closed her eyes, trying to bite back the anxiety she felt in her gut. She reached out blindly and laid her hand on his firm, velvet snout. He made a soft noise, breathing and nodding against her. Krista blinked at the movement and Dollar stilled and stared back at her, eyes large and liquid coal. She kept her hand on his snout and then began stroking him.

"You're not so bad, are you?" She smiled a little, still nervous. His scent alone, one of dust and hay, made her heart hammer in her chest. The horse she'd ridden at fifteen, her very best friend, used to smell the same way. She moved her hands back across Dollar's powerful neck, feeling his muscles twitch, trying not to flinch at his harnessed strength. Breathing deep, she tried to calm herself, tried to get herself ready for sunrise when she would have to climb back on.

Her foot ached at the thought and she shook her ankle out, knowing it was her mind playing tricks on her. Dollar snorted again and another noise caught her attention in the distance. She searched the dimly lit campsite, at first convinced that it must be coming from Adam's recorder. But there was nothing there, nothing out by the fire. As she listened, she realized the sound was a guitar and it was coming from the trees. Krista retrieved a flashlight from her tent and crept away as quietly as she could, not wanting to disturb her sleeping guests.

About seventy yards out from the campsite, she stepped through the crisp-smelling mesquite trees and focused on a small area to her left. A single candle flickered on a rock against the diamond-strewn night sky. There, next to the candle on a large boulder, sat Rae, holding her guitar, strumming and humming a sweet tune. Krista couldn't make out the words but her skin warmed at the sight and sound.

She crouched down and killed the flashlight before Rae caught sight of it. The vet seemed as hypnotized by her music as Krista was with watching and listening. Rae's long lean fingers slid up and down the frets, pressing chord after chord. She was still wearing the sleeveless shirt, which allowed the candlelight to accent her muscles as she strummed. Her dark, thick hair was wavy and unruly, a few strands falling across her forehead. Krista held her breath, caught up in her beauty more than she was afraid of being heard.

Krista had no idea Rae was so talented. She'd obviously been playing for years. Right or wrong, Krista had assumed that Rae was a bit of a roughneck; she hardly seemed the sensual or artistic type. But as Krista watched her, she realized that there were many things about Rae she didn't know. She closed her eyes, listening. The melody didn't sound familiar and Rae would pause, as if searching for the next word or phrase. Krista felt her heart flutter when she realized Rae was writing a song.

The romanticism of that thought alone helped her drift back to camp. After crawling into her tent and removing her boots, she closed her eyes and imagined approaching Rae in the candlelight. She imagined her outstretched hand coming to rest on the angle of Rae's beautiful jaw, bringing her in for a soft, hot, long kiss. She imagined laying her down, sucking on her neck, making her sigh, then moving lower to under her shirt, going painfully slow over her bra and torso to unfasten her jeans. Tugging them down, she would kiss Rae's flesh through her panties, igniting wild pleasure. She would lick her hard, suck her hard, all without touching her flesh. She imagined what Rae's groans of pleasure would sound like, and how badly they both would want flesh to meet flesh. Panties finally torn away, she would kiss there, taste her, consume her, taking in all that was Rae.

It was then and only then that she was able to fall fast asleep.

Chapter Ten

Rae awoke early and lay blinking in her tent, listening to see if anyone was up and moving around the campsite. The predawn light was gray, the air heavy with a chill as she booted her feet and stepped outside. She stretched in the morning silence and slipped her bare arms into her flannel shirt, glad it was only getting down into the low sixties at night. Scratching her hair, she walked to the horses and gave them each a few pats. She pulled her ball cap from the saddle of her horse and walked off into the desert to relieve herself. Then after washing her face and hands, she got busy getting out what she needed to make a big breakfast. She started with the coffee, putting two kettles on to boil.

Even though the guests needed to be rising soon, she moved quietly, enjoying the sounds of the desert as it awakened. As she relit the cold fire, she thought about Krista Wyler. She hadn't been able to think about anything other than her the entire evening and into the night. The woman had even haunted her dreams. Krista's striking beauty had lured her, excited her, and then the mouth had opened, ruining it all.

She chuckled as she poured water into the large pot that sat atop the fire. Last night she'd admitted something to herself while she was playing her guitar. Krista Wyler was an attractive woman. Very much so. Rae didn't know why that was so difficult to admit but it was. Maybe because Krista had been nothing but rude to her from the word go. Maybe because she came off as a spoiled city girl, a hardheaded know-it-all. Rae sat down and waited for the water to boil. Given how little time Krista had available to get this outing organized, she'd done a fairly good job. They had plenty of food and water, and the campsite had been warm and inviting the night before. If only the other two wranglers had shown up, the trip might have been a big success.

Rae pulled off her hat and ran a hand through her hair, remembering the way Krista had looked at her across the fire after Candace's massage. The flames in her eyes had been evident, but what did her expression mean? *Does she really hate me? If so, how can I be attracted to someone who hates me?* Rae rubbed her eyes, stirred up and confused. A twig snapped and she looked up.

Krista stood watching her from the front of her tent. The flames in her eyes were gone but the intensity was still there, smoldering. Rae felt her own heart rate increase and she cursed it for doing so.

"Morning," she greeted, knowing they couldn't just stare in silence at each other all morning long.

"Good morning," Krista replied, more than a little groggy. She shoved her hands down into her jeans pockets and approached the fire. Her sunburn wasn't as red as it was the night before, but it still looked pretty painful.

"Sleep well?" Rae stood and made the coffee.

Krista seemed a bit uneasy in her presence. "Fine, and you?"

"Not so good," Rae confessed and then felt frustrated at herself. Honesty had always been her strong point, and she avoided putting on fronts, but why take the risk with Krista Wyler? The woman seemed to be dying to outdo her.

"Oh?"

As the scent of coffee started to stir her brain, Rae decided to be really honest. She took in Krista's shapely legs, poorly hidden under the worn denim, and the fleece shirt covering a soft, breast-hugging T-shirt. Then she met and held the eyes as green and clear as morning dew on grass.

"Because of you," Rae said.

Krista's eyes widened in what could only be pure shock. "I'm sorry?" She meant to sound strong and polite, but her voice quivered.

Rae repeated and poked at the fire, pretending she didn't notice. "I said I didn't sleep well because of you."

Krista blinked. A flush colored her neck and deepened the red in her sunburned face. Her lips moved as if she were searching for words. "Well, why?"

Rae retrieved the oatmeal, taking her time, enjoying way too much the reaction she'd gotten even though she had no idea what it meant. She poured the oats into the boiling water and sat back down, Krista's wide green eyes fastened to her. Crossing her feet, she finally answered, "Because I can't for the life of me figure out why it is you don't like me."

Krista just stared. As she was about to speak, Cody found his way out of his tent. His large smile vanished when he saw the look on Krista's face. It was obvious that he'd stumbled into a heated conversation. He beat his cowboy hat on his leg before placing it on his head.

"Mornin'," he said, lowering his head as if Krista were a rattlesnake about to strike.

"Morning, Cody," Rae greeted him.

Krista whispered a good morning, then said, "Please excuse me," and walked off into the desert.

"Everything okay?" Cody poured himself some coffee.

Rae shrugged. "As good as could be expected, I suppose."

Cody sat on one of the guest's camp stools and blew on his coffee. "How'd Ms. Wyler do yesterday?"

Rae folded her arms over her chest, curious. "What do you mean?"

Cody swung his head around, obviously making sure Krista was nowhere within earshot. "On the horse?" he mumbled.

"Is there some issue with her and horses?" The answer was obvious but Rae wanted to know.

Cody stared down into his mug. "Dwight says she hasn't been on one in fifteen years. Something happened. But I don't know what."

Rae cleared her throat as Krista reappeared. Her cheeks were a little wet and her eyes were heavy with moisture. Had she been crying? Unable to help herself, Rae asked, "You okay?"

"I'm fine, thanks." Krista held Rae's stare for a moment, then asked, "Can I help finish preparing breakfast?"

"Please do, because it already smells good enough to eat," Frank bellowed, stretching in the cool morning air. His teeth were as white as his beard as he smiled.

The rest of the group awakened shortly after Frank. They moved about with excitement, eager for another day on the trail. The oatmeal was flavored with brown sugar, thanks to Krista's help, and they had some dried fruit to go along with it. The coffee was good, strong, and plentiful. Tom offered lots of praise as he ate, while Adam primped more than the women, shaving with a travel razor and brushing and flossing his teeth.

Candace emerged from her tent looking almost perfect, her nipples erect and poking through the fabric of her thin bra and shirt. She pulled on a fleece pink jacket that went well with her pink tasseled boots. She gave Rae a thousand-watt smile over breakfast and insisted again on helping to clean up.

Howie was the last to rise, much to Rae's dismay, and he was obviously suffering from a hangover. His hair stood out on his head and he seemed to have an uncontrollable itch in his crotch area because he scratched for a good ten minutes straight. With heavy, blurry-looking eyes, he swished his mouth out with coffee and spat, coughed, and spat again.

He caught Rae eyeing him. "Something I can help you with, Doc?" His voice sounded like the rough skin of a Gila monster.

"Not especially," Rae countered. "But the guests could use help packing their gear."

He grumbled under his breath and set to work straight away helping Tillie. His broad grin gave away that he had switched his ogling to the quieter woman, although Rae still caught him glancing at Candace's backside from time to time. But the cowboy worked and kept his thoughts and hands to himself, and Tillie seemed good at giving him direction, so Rae let him be.

About an hour later, the sun had fully risen and the group had finished packing up the campsite. They saddled up and Rae replaced her ball cap with the Stetson. From the corner of her eye, she could see Krista still standing by her horse. Rae didn't say anything at first, but thought if she gave the direction to the group Krista might feel less pressure.

"We're going to run into the cattle today. Keep your ropes ready." She patted the side of her saddle where hers hung. "There's going to be more than a few strays." Several heads nodded. "Follow Cody, Howie, or myself when going after a stray. Do not attempt to go off on your own. Understood?"

The last thing they needed was a guest falling behind and getting lost while chasing a stray, or wandering into the middle of the herd and causing a stampede.

When everyone seemed in agreement, Rae tipped her hat. "Let's move out, then."

Cody whistled and Adam and Frank hollered their best "move outs!" Rae remained on her horse in the same position, watching as the small herd of wannabe cowboys trotted off. With her hands resting calmly on her saddle horn, she turned to look at Krista, who still had both feet firmly on dry ground.

"I don't need any help if that's what you're thinking," Krista said.

Rae merely smiled and looked straight ahead. "I wasn't thinking any such thing."

"Good, because like I told you yesterday—"

"Yes, I got it," Rae softly interrupted. "You don't need any help." She could feel the green eyes boring into the side of her face, but she remained calm.

"No, I don't," Krista reaffirmed.

"Good, glad to hear it." She didn't move.

Krista put her hands on her hips. "You can go."

Rae scratched her cheek, acting bored. "Nope, can't do that."

"Why not?"

"Never leave a man behind."

Krista scoffed. "This isn't the damned Marine Corps."

Rae looked at her directly. "No, it's not."

"Then go."

"Lindsay said you were a hellfire."

Krista sucked in a quick breath and Rae knew the fury was sure to follow. "Is that a fact?"

"Yeah, that's a fact." Rae met Krista's eyes. "And I'm beginning to think she was right."

"Is that what you and she do? Sit around, picking the manure off your boots and making up names for people?"

Rae fought off a grin. "No, just moody women."

"Moody!"

"Yep, Lindsay's always right too. Never once has she been wrong about a woman."

Krista's sunburnt face turned so dark red Rae thought she would burst like a balloon. "You, well, you're wrong this time!"

"Am I?" Rae raised an eyebrow.

Krista glanced down at herself and dropped the hands from her hips. "Leave. Leave now!"

Rae clicked her horse and trotted over to Krista, deciding she'd given her a hard enough time. At least for now. "I can't," she said softly. "You're not prepared."

Krista narrowed her eyes. "I'm not prepared?"

"That's right. It seems that you spent so much of your time readying everyone else for the trail that you forgot about you." Rae took off her Stetson and handed it over. Then she placed her trusty ball cap on her own head. "Go ahead, put it on."

Krista looked at the hat, startled. "But it's yours."

"Not anymore." Rae smiled.

"I can't, it's yours and—"

"Put on the hat, Ms. Wyler," Rae said firmly. She was still smiling.

Krista hesitated but placed the black hat on her head. It appeared to be a little large but she maneuvered it to where it fit best. "Well?"

Rae clenched her jaw. Krista looked stunning. Her auburn hair hung thick just below her shoulders, shining in the morning sun. The hat mischievously hid her penetrating green eyes, but fully showed off her high cheekbones and lush lips.

"You look…" Rae cleared her throat and glanced away. "It looks good."

Krista was staring at her again, Rae could feel it. She tugged on the bill of her cap. "Come on now, saddle up. Or we'll have to catch up, and you don't want to be stuck with just me again all day, do you?" She gave an easy smile, trying to lighten the heavy desire that had washed over her.

Krista's mouth tugged to one side. "No, we wouldn't want that."

Rae thought for a moment and then slid off her horse, tossing Krista a small bottle of sunscreen. "Don't want you getting burnt again today."

Krista seemed at a loss for words as she shook the bottle and squeezed out some lotion. She circled it into her skin, under her eyes and over her cheeks. Then she removed her jacket and rubbed some into her arms. Rae flushed at the sight of her ample breasts in the snug-fitting T-shirt. *Candace doesn't have a thing on you.*

Krista kept working, apparently not noticing Rae's preoccupation, and added some to her neck. When she finished she snapped the lid shut and returned it to Rae, who quickly tucked it in her saddle bag.

Rae was about to hold out her hand to help Krista in the saddle, but a white spot of sunscreen caught her attention. "You've got some lotion." Rae pointed to her own cheek.

Krista's hand flew up to her face but she couldn't find it. "Did I get it?"

Rae took a step closer, "No, it's…"

Hesitantly, she reached up and gently touched Krista's cheek. A soft breath escaped Krista, and Rae swore her skin heated under her touch. With her thumb, Rae smoothed out the lotion, and she swallowed back the lump in her throat. Touching Krista had sent her body into overdrive, and the feeling nearly knocked her to her knees.

Krista rubbed at her cheek nervously.

They stood in silence for a few moments, Rae trying to get her composure back and Krista unsure as to what to say. Finally, Rae held out her hand, the meaning obvious. Krista studied it a moment. Without a word, she nodded her acceptance of the offered help. She took Rae's hand and stepped into the stirrup. She reached for the saddle horn but her hand slipped and she lost her balance and fell backward. Rae held her tightly, catching her, their faces mere inches apart. She saw the spark ignite in Krista's eyes, watched her rose-colored lips part and beckon. Rae could feel Krista's warm breath mingle with her own. Both remained very still for what felt like an eternity.

No, it can't happen. Rae glanced away and allowed Krista to regain her footing. She then placed steadying hands on her shoulders but couldn't bring herself to look in her eyes. "Let's try again."

She offered her hand and Krista slipped her foot into the stirrup, this time gripping the saddle horn securely. With Rae's supporting hand on her hip, she pulled herself up.

Rae stepped back. "You good?"

Krista met her eyes fleetingly, a brush of color on her cheeks. "Yes. Thank you." The gratitude sounded genuine and not curt and firm like her usual remarks. "And just for the record, Dr. Jarrett…I *don't* dislike you."

Rae waited a moment to see if she would say more, but Krista stared straight ahead, her back erect. Feeling more than a little warm from their encounter, Rae pulled herself up onto Shamrock, and the two women started off the way the others had gone. Rae kept the pace slow. Krista still gripped the horn tightly and she still rode stiffly, but the fear had left her face.

Yes, you are a hellfire, Krista Wyler, Rae thought to herself. *A beautiful, beautiful hellfire.*

CHAPTER ELEVEN

The day was glorious by Arizona spring standards. The sky was vast and a startling clear blue, not a cloud in sight. But the mild, sunny air didn't do a thing for Krista and her aching ass and back. Careful not to let go of the reins, she twisted her wrist to glance at her watch. "Christ."

They'd only been riding for a little over an hour.

Rae Jarrett must have heard the curse because she glanced back. Krista lifted her hand to give a small wave, then quickly grabbed the saddle horn. She let out a long, slow breath when Rae returned her attention to the trail ahead.

She meant to concentrate on the surroundings and the need to keep constant control of her horse, but her eyes were trained on the tense muscles and tendons in Rae's arms, slick with sweat and kissed by the sun. Krista licked her lips, having felt their power firsthand. And the way Rae had looked at her a mere hour before. Was she crazy or had the vet been equally affected?

She thought back to Rae and Candace the night before, all cozy and erotic with the massage by the firelight. There was no way Rae was feeling anything for her in comparison to Candace. She'd only just voiced her concern over whether Krista even liked her.

God, what am I thinking? Krista wiped some sweat from her cheek. The Stetson was giving her face the ample shade it needed and she reminded herself to thank Rae again for letting her wear it. The gesture was very nice.

Great, so now I know for sure she's nice. The discovery didn't help the attraction factor in the slightest. *Why can't she be mean? A mean ole cowgirl who chews and has rough hands and a very prominent red neck?*

Krista continued to debate within herself as they traveled through the turned-up dirt from the group ahead of them. In the near distance, beyond the handful of manned horses, stood the Wyler cattle, spread rather thin with a few dozen strays off to the sides of the herd. Krista's heart rate kicked up at the thought of having to maneuver Dollar a lot better than she had been so far. She stared at Rae, riding a few yards ahead, and thought about telling the truth as to why she was so afraid. But just as quickly, she forced the urge back, determined not to show weakness in front of the strong veterinarian. Rae and her little assistant already had a nickname for her. What would they say if she shrank into the background while the guests rounded up the cattle? Krista could just imagine the new names they would come up with.

With brimming determination, she straightened her back and gave Dollar a soft kick. When he broke into a slow trot, she lurched forward and nearly lost her balance. With panicked hands she reached for the rein and tugged. Dollar responded at once, bringing them to a stop. Breathing hard, Krista had to wave Rae off once again. "I'm fine."

"You seem to be getting the hang of it, Ms. Wyler," Rae said, drifting back so their horses met side by side. "That trot looked pretty good for about two seconds."

Krista felt herself heat. "Think so?" Her only choice was to tease back, to take it like a woman.

"Absolutely." Rae chuckled, obviously enjoying the playfulness.

God, she's incredible. Krista let her grin widen. *I'll say anything to see her smile like that. Even if I have to fall off my damned horse.*

Around them voices whistled and called out to the cattle, the fun beginning.

Krista didn't want this moment to end. The way Rae looked, all strong and ruggedly handsome, smiling at her from her horse, the big blue sky behind her. Krista knew she should fight her thoughts and feelings but they felt too good. Too right.

"Call me Krista," she said softly.

Rae's grin tilted. "Sure thing. As soon as you start calling me Rae." With a wink and a tug on her hat, she gave Shamrock a gentle kick. "You fine staying back here for a while?" she asked as she rode toward Cody.

Krista nodded, too overwhelmed to even voice a response. What had just happened? *She winked at me, that's what happened. She winked and smiled and took my breath away.* She watched as Rae conversed with Cody and the two hollered out to the people who rode alongside them.

Cody brought the supply horse he was leading over to Krista. "Can you handle her?"

Krista swallowed, hesitant but unwilling to say so. "Sure." She took the offered rein.

The gray mare stared at her with blank eyes.

"Trust me, I'm not thrilled either," Krista told the horse.

She gave Dollar a kick and he nudged up past the mare and the two fell in line, with Dollar in the lead. Krista held tight and prayed that both horses would behave. She watched with envy as Rae and Cody began wrangling cattle. Howie had the remainder of the group out on the far right, pointing and hollering.

Soon enough the dust and smell of the cattle was so thick Krista was waving it away from her face. She used to enjoy this, but she had no idea why. Was the dirt and stench always this bad? Coughing, she took off her hat and waved the dust away. Loud laughter caught her attention and she put the hat back on and rubbed her eyes. Looking out to her left, she saw Candace trying to crawl up on Rae's horse. Rae said something but Krista couldn't make it out. Candace was determined and after a moment, Rae scooted back and allowed her up to share the saddle.

Krista watched in horror as Rae leaned into her, both their hands together on the rope. Rae raised Candace's arm and they swung the rope together in the air, Candace giggling like a schoolgirl.

"That's it," Krista declared to Dollar, tugging the Stetson on tight and releasing the mare to stand alone. "Let's go, boy."

She gave a soft heel and Dollar broke into a trot. Krista fought off a frightened moan as they began to gallop and she nearly lost her balance. But somehow, some way, she managed to hold on and stay on the saddle.

As she approached Rae, Adam met her on his horse, designer sunglasses covering his eyes.

"Hey, hot stuff," he greeted with a smile. "Looking good."

Krista brought Dollar to a halt, her eyes still on Rae and Candace, who were now tossing the rope out at a calf. "Thanks."

Adam followed her gaze. "She needs help roping," he half-heartedly explained.

"Don't we all."

Adam laughed. "Then let's go ask for some."

Krista trotted Dollar with fierceness in her chest, and while Adam stopped alongside Rae and Candace, she continued on, grabbing the rope that hung from her saddle. She slowed Dollar alongside a wandering calf and gripped the horn of the saddle tightly with her left hand while swinging the rope over her head with the right.

I can do this. I used to do it all the time as a kid.

With her jaw set, she swung and swung until the rhythm felt right and then she let loose. The rope hit the right side of the calf, and she pulled quickly to tighten the noose. The lasso fell just off the side of the calf's snout, missing by a mere inch.

"Damn!"

"Hey, that was pretty good!" Adam called out as he rode up to her.

Winding the rope, Krista said, "Not good enough." Damn, she'd really wanted to show up Candace. And to show Rae that she wasn't completely useless.

Adam began whipping his rope in the air, the calf still in front of them. His loop grew larger and larger with every swing. Krista flinched as it whacked her in the arm.

"Sorry." He laughed, hanging himself with the failed lasso.

"That wasn't half bad, Adam," Rae praised, once again alone on her horse. "Relax your wrist, you're too stiff." She offered Krista a smile but Krista was in no mood to return it.

Adam removed the rope from around his neck. "We were hoping you would offer some pointers." His eyes danced mischievously. "Can I crawl up on your saddle?"

Rae blushed considerably and put a fist to her mouth for an embarrassed cough.

"Yes, Dr. Jarrett, is that standard roping procedure?" The venom was back in her voice but Krista couldn't help it. She was seething with jealousy and the increasing fear that her attraction would never be returned.

"Not usually, no." Rae met her eyes.

Candace trotted up, all tits and no clue. "Rae's such a good teacher." She raised her rope and swung much better than before.

"Yes," Krista whispered. "She certainly is."

Unable to take much more, she rode off. Tom had waved a few minutes earlier, signaling that he had the mare, so Krista was free to try her roping skills again. She skirted the left of the herd and practiced her swing. She had it down immediately, her wrist falling into place from times long ago. But her aim was still slightly off and she had to endure watching Rae or Cody rope the strays she should've had.

After a few minutes, Rae made an attempt to offer encouragement, but Krista shot her a glare full of fire and she rode off. The morning flew by after that, with Krista so focused on forcing Rae Jarrett from her mind, she paid little attention to anything else.

At noon sharp, however, a whistle went out for lunch.

"Shit." She should've paid more attention; she was in charge of this charade and needed to help hand out the midday meal. Once again Krista felt like she was floundering.

Cody and Howie continued to ride ahead to keep the cattle in line while Rae directed the group over to the shade of the mesquite trees. Krista rode up and grimaced as she dismounted.

Adam welcomed her with a smack on the sore ass.

"Did that help?" he asked. "Here, do mine." He stuck his backside out and Krista couldn't help but smile. She smacked him firm and sharp. "Oh, harder, baby!" he cried.

Krista laughed, hitting him harder, stinging her hand. She shook it out as Candace approached.

"Yes!" the blonde pleaded enthusiastically. "Someone spank me!"

Adam grabbed Krista's wrist. "Don't even think about it, slick," he whispered playfully in her ear. He then smacked Candace on the rear and she ran away giggling.

Krista laughed. "I wanted to smack the tits right off her."

"Don't hit those things." He raised his hands in fright. "They'll fight back. They ought to, as much as she paid for them."

"I thought she was your friend!" Krista let out, bending over for breath.

"She is."

"Jesus, I would hate to be your enemy."

Adam pulled off his shades. "Trust me, I haven't said anything she hasn't heard before. And as far as Rae goes, Candi needs another lover like I need a hole in the head."

Leaning on each other in laughter, Krista and Adam limped sorely up to the group. Most riders were sitting on the ground, drinking from their bottles and canteens. Tillie had her hat off, pulling her dark curls into a fresh ponytail. Krista noticed her sparkling blue-green eyes and wondered what her story was. She was beautiful in a very natural way.

Krista helped Rae pass out the prepared lunches of granola bars, apples, and sandwiches, then settled herself next to Tillie. A gentle breeze blew the long limbs of the tree they were under. Krista spread out a little and fought the urge to grunt in pain as the tightness in her legs seemed to grip her rib cage.

"Having a good time?" she asked.

Tillie was chewing, quietly studying their beautiful surroundings. She held her sandwich gracefully and Krista noticed the pale band of flesh on her ring finger. Because her skin was a dark olive in complexion, the absence of a ring was more than obvious. "I am, yes, thank you."

"Good, I'm glad." Though Tillie was beautiful, Krista wasn't attracted to her in a physical sense. There was something different about her. A quiet intelligence, a deep sense of knowing, of living. Krista sensed that this woman had lived life and knew more than a thing or two. Again, she wondered about the unspoken sadness, about the scars that were hidden by her beauty but exposed in her eyes.

Krista swallowed a bite of her apple. "I wanted to thank you for putting up with Howie."

Tillie chewed and smoothed down the denim on her thigh with her free hand. "No thanks needed. Men like him are rather simple, really."

"I take it you speak from experience?"

"Unfortunately."

"You're a very beautiful woman. You must've put up with more than your fair share."

Tillie took a sip of her water, her gaze still focused on the different shades of brown and green the desert offered. "Since I was thirteen. But I learned real quick how to handle them."

"Care to share?" Krista chuckled. "Men are a complete enigma to me."

"It depends on the man, of course. Someone like Howie, for instance, who obviously thinks with his penis and is interested in nothing other than scoring." She shrugged. "You just have to take advantage of that. Talk to him, ask him for his help, and he's putty. I think mostly it's the attention he craves."

Krista sighed, worried about his tongue-wagging and tail-chasing. "I hope you're right."

Tillie met her eyes. "If he drinks, well, that's a different story."

"He won't be back for another outing," Krista said, imagining how much worse his behavior could get if he drank. "At least not for this ranch he won't. I just don't trust him. Anyway, thanks for handling him." She smiled. "So what about you? You married?"

Tillie started in on her granola bar and then lowered it as if she'd changed her mind. She narrowed her eyes out at the desert. "You know, I may have men like Howie figured out, but the rest of them, I'll never understand."

She looked once more at Krista, her eyes glossy and full of pain, then tossed the uneaten granola bar in her paper sack and stood, leaving Krista alone under the tree.

They finished lunch and relaxed for a short while, some talking low to one another, the rest silent, enjoying the afternoon breeze. Tillie spoke to no one, busying herself tending to her horse, adjusting the saddle and her gear even though Krista knew it needed no attention. Whatever the source of her pain, it remained a mystery.

Krista stood and stretched her sore legs as the annoying sound of Candace's laughter reached her ears. The blonde stood in front of Rae, comparing the size of their hands. Krista studied Rae's face, seeking any clue as to what the strong woman was thinking. But Rae caught her looking and lowered her hands to brush them on her jeans, calling out to the group.

"We better get a move on."

For a few seconds, she held Krista's eyes but Krista looked away, frustrated with the acid of jealousy eating her stomach.

The rest of the afternoon went by much like the morning. The group rode long and hard, following the direction of the wranglers and Rae, most too tired to keep trying to rope once evening began to settle in. Thankfully, they managed to keep the majority of the herd together and Cody rode off on his own to bring back the last one as they reached the campsite around six o'clock.

The group busied themselves unpacking their supplies and setting up their tents before it grew too dark to see. Krista erected her tent quickly, wanting for purely egotistical reasons to be the first one done. Hands on hips, seething with pride, she waited for Rae to notice and got a small nod of approval just as Candace declared, very Southern belle-like, that she needed help. Krista almost expected the blonde to raise a hand to her forehead and threaten to faint. *"I declare, Rae, I've got the vapors and I can't raise my tent without your help."*

Krista didn't know why she was trying so hard to impress Rae in the first place. Candace was always there to cry wolf just to get her attention. Krista tried to distract herself by helping Tom thread his tent poles through the weather-resistant fabric. As they worked together, she glanced across at self-satisfied Candace, who was standing back as Rae put up the tent for her. Rae's expression gave away none of her thoughts, and Krista wondered what kind of woman she was drawn to most, the kind that needed no help, or the kind that did. Whatever the answer, Krista knew she would never be the type to ask for help, attention, or anything else. She just wasn't the helpless type, and she wouldn't pretend otherwise.

As fatigue took hold of first her body and then her mind, Krista focused on other things. Like coffee, for instance. There was something about the way coffee smelled, the way it woke and stirred her senses first thing in the morning and then calmed and relaxed her in the evening. It was a mystery, but one she was very thankful for. She sipped from her mug and settled into a camp chair to watch Rae prepare dinner. The vet had politely fended off any help, preferring to make the meal herself. She set the big pot on the cooking rack over the fire, full of water, waiting for it to boil.

Krista knew that Rae was about to cook pasta, having packed the supplies herself. She'd kept to dried, nonperishable foods, mostly, thinking they would be easier to handle. Anything perishable was kept in one of two medium-sized coolers. These were packed to the brim with ice and would only stay cool for about two days. Then they would be replaced with newly iced coolers, brought out on fresh supply horses from the ranch. All in all, with the way things were turning out, Krista couldn't be more pleased with the preparations she'd made.

She took another grateful sip of her coffee while Rae poured in the pasta. She stirred it with care, then rose to fetch the French bread and sauce. Soon the camp was smelling as divine as Krista's favorite Italian restaurant miles away in Phoenix.

"Rae, I'm going to take you back to Boston with me," Jenna teased. "To cook for us."

Frank chuckled and agreed as the group settled in around the fire. All were dressed for the cooler night air in long-sleeved sweatshirts or flannels. They snuggled down with their arms tightly across their chests, hypnotized by the fire. Soon Rae had dinner finished and all were enjoying their bowls of rigatoni and seasoned tomato sauce. The French bread was toasted and buttered, the remainder of the red wine a real topper-offer of a treat.

As the fire crackled, Howie finished his mug of wine before his meal and shared what was on his mind. "So, Miss Wyler." He grinned sheepishly. "Do you have a boyfriend?"

Krista nearly choked on her warm bread. She had noticed him staring at her as she was eating, but she hoped he'd soon shift his attention back to his favorite target. Candace was sitting next to Adam, wearing jeans and a tight white tank top, no bra. The chill in the air puckered her nipples and Krista was convinced that if she so much as breathed heavy, her areolas would pop above the edge of the cotton for all to see. She ate slowly, slipping the fork in and out of her lips in dramatic fashion, her eyes fixed solely on Rae.

Howie's eyes danced expectantly from across the flames and Jenna added to his question. "Yes, you know all about us, but we know so little about you." She smiled, sincere in her words. "Do you have a husband? Kids?"

Krista eyed the remainder of her pasta with sudden distaste. She dropped in the last bite of bread and laid the bowl down next to her. Around the fire all eyes were trained on her, including Rae's. Rae sat eating as she had the night before, leaning back against a large rock, her legs outstretched and crossed at the ankles. She'd slipped into a thick flannel shirt, but Krista could still see the muscles in her neck and jaw as she ate.

Krista disliked being the slide under the microscope, but she was hosting this adventure so she did her best to answer in a general sense, giving little detail. "No, I'm not married and I don't have any children." *There, that ought to do it.*

"Ever been married?" Frank asked.

Krista shook her head. "No."

Howie was watching her carefully, his eyes darting down to the swell of her breasts and back up to her face. "Well, do you have a boyfriend?"

She clenched her teeth. The nerve. Was he going to hit on every woman in the group? She decided to play on his blatant ignorance. "No, Howie, I've been waiting my whole life just for you."

The camp erupted in laughter and Howie looked around as if he didn't get it at first. As if maybe she'd really meant it. Then, as anger washed over his face, he tossed down his bowl and bread and stormed away.

Adam was nearly rolling around in laughter. "Did you see his face? I think you broke his heart."

"Broke his hard-on is more like it," Tillie said, causing more outrageous laughter.

Krista laughed until her insides hurt. It felt good to laugh. Especially at Howie's expense.

"Watch out, Jenna," Adam said still chuckling. "You're next."

"He wouldn't dare," she murmured.

"He better not dare," Frank declared, standing to adjust the waistband of his jeans.

"Then next it'll be Rae," Candace added.

"Me?" Rae looked surprised.

The group fell silent until Krista started laughing, unable to help herself. They all knew it would be a cold day in hell before Howie ever hit on Rae. Everyone laughed along with her at the absurdity, even Candace, though she seemed to have little clue as to what was so funny.

When they all quieted down again, Adam looked up from his bowl to focus in on Krista. "Aren't you going to answer Howie's question?"

Krista shot him a look, letting him know that he would "get it" tomorrow, one way or another. He merely grinned, putting the Cheshire cat to shame.

"No, I don't have a boyfriend." She decided to make it perfectly clear. "I don't have anyone."

There were some nods of understanding and she was pleased, thinking the questions were finished. But then, after a series of loud crackles from the fire, Rae asked, "Why not?"

Why not? Krista felt her body heat in anger. *Why not?* She was just about to smart off to her when Adam added, "Yeah, why not?"

All eyes were once again on her and she could almost feel herself squirm. "I don't believe in love. I don't believe it really exists." She nearly slapped a hand over her mouth. The response had come from nowhere.

"Don't believe in love?" Jenna sounded saddened.

Krista felt the need to defend herself. "No, I don't believe in love. I believe in lust, I believe in having a good time, but love…" She lowered her eyes. "In my opinion it doesn't exist. It's just what people fool themselves into believing, afraid of being alone." *Yet, I crave it more than anything in the world, wishing it did exist. I'm a hypocrite.*

"Then how do you explain the euphoria people feel when they fall in love?" asked Tom. "There's scientific proof. Quite a few studies have shown that a chemical change happens in the brain. There are increased levels of testosterone, estrogen, serotonin, norepinephrine, and oxytocin, to name a few."

Krista smiled. Tom was obviously an intelligent man and a nice man. She wondered why he usually kept so quiet. "Oh, I believe they really do feel something. It's called infatuation and lust. The honeymoon syndrome. Rarely does it last."

"So you're going to live your life alone because you don't believe in love? Have you ever given it a chance?" Adam seemed genuinely curious.

"Wait a minute," Tom interrupted. "You're mistaking the honeymoon feeling for love. It's my belief that there are two parts to love. Sexual attraction and attachment. One experiences chemical changes during both stages." His eyes narrowed at her in thought. "You've probably never felt the need for attachment. Have you ever actually felt anything close to love?"

This time Krista did squirm. She wasn't sure what to say. She'd felt lust and infatuation before. "I don't think so." She spoke the words softly, deep in thought.

"If you're not sure, then that means no," Tom clarified.

"Yeah, that's like saying you aren't sure if you've ever had an orgasm," Candace added, obviously pleased to be able to contribute to such a conversation.

All nodded in agreement and Krista felt frustrated and exposed. She was about to get up and excuse herself when Tillie asked, "Can we please change the subject?"

Her beautiful face was tight and stern looking. She stood and carried her bowl swiftly to the cleaning station, leaving an air of discomfort.

Adam and Candace collected everyone's bowls, including Krista's and Rae's. Frank rummaged through the supplies and held up a roll of biodegradable toilet paper in victory. In his other hand he turned on his flashlight and announced, "I'm off to take my constitutional."

Jenna smacked him on the arm. "No one wants to hear that."

Shrugging, he scooted off into the darkness, the thin halo of light leading his way.

"Who wants the last of the wine?" Jenna asked.

Krista held up a declining hand, as did Rae.

Jenna poured what was left in her own mug. As she settled into her chair once again, she said, "Rae, I see you brought your guitar. How about playing a little for us?"

"I don't know."

"Oh, come on," Jenna encouraged. "Entertain us a little."

Rae uncrossed her feet and rubbed her hands on her jeans in obvious nervousness. "I don't ever sing my songs in front of anyone."

Krista was moved by her modesty. She was incredibly adorable and didn't even know it.

Adam came to stand before the shy vet. He held out a hand. "Then sing someone else's songs. We'll all know the words and we can help you sing."

Krista smiled, reminded as to why she liked Adam so much. After a brief pause, and some more encouragement, Rae took the offered hand and stood, brushing off her backside as she walked to her horse. Past her, Krista spotted Howie in the near distance leaning up against a dead saguaro. His arms were folded and his face looked ragged and tired. She thought briefly about apologizing to him but then changed her mind. He needed to be called on his behavior, and she was the one to do it too, being the leader of the gang, so to speak.

By the time Rae returned everyone was sitting around the fire like schoolkids on a field-trip bus, antsy and excited, nearly bouncing up and down. She dragged a camp stool with her and entered the circle of firelight, shiny guitar in hand.

"This is so neat!" Jenna exclaimed. "It's like having a live concert right in front of us!"

Rae sat on the stool, her form lit up by the firelight. She had just finished tuning her guitar when Adam rushed to her once again.

"Wait, wait!" Quickly, he removed her ball cap and ran nimble, expert hands through her thick dark hair. He stepped back a half step to get a look.

Krista laughed softly and then very nearly lost her breath as Adam sat and her eyes fell on Rae. With the guitar resting on her knee, she looked like a goddess in the golden orange firelight. Her thick hair was dark and gorgeous, finessed strands resting on her forehead, helping the firelight to show off her hazel eyes. Her worn jeans were nearly threadbare at the knees and her boots were scuffed and dirty. She'd removed her flannel shirt, showing off her body in a soft olive T-shirt. The frequently worked muscles in her forearms stirred beneath her tanned skin as she started to play.

"I can do country," she said.

I bet you can do just about anything, Krista thought and then blushed.

"I like old school, though," Rae added.

"Like who?" Tom asked.

Rae stared into the fire as she thought.

"The Judds!" Cody exclaimed.

"Yes!" Tillie piped in. "I love them."

Rae looked up. "The Judds I can do." She smiled, obviously excited, and Krista felt her heart threaten to melt.

"My mom and daddy used to play them all the time when I was a kid." Cody's young face reflected his memories of times that seemed to warm his heart. He cocked his head a little as Rae asked him to choose a song. He thought long and hard before he chose one of their first hit singles, "Have Mercy."

Rae nodded. "Okay, but y'all have to help me sing." With a flick of her wrist and a clenching of her perfect jaw, she started in. The melody was right away infectious, and Cody and Tillie knew the lyrics and Rae followed, a sly grin on her face as she sang.

Krista gripped the sides of her chair as the next verse came and Rae sang solo, her voice deep and smooth and hitting all the right notes. The firelight flickered over her body like a lover's teasing touch. Krista thought about touching her like that, and her heart beat like mad in her chest and she thought she'd pass out.

Rae met her eyes and Krista melted to her chair. Rae's gaze flashed against the flames, full of music, love, and passion. She truly loved what she was doing. She loved making music. And Krista loved it for her. She'd never ever seen someone look so good doing what they loved. Rae's hand paused over the guitar as she gutted out some passionate lines; she then began playing again as Cody and Tillie chimed in on the chorus. By the time the song finished, Adam had a lighter high in the air, waving it back and forth.

Rae chuckled as they all applauded.

"I had no idea you could sing like that, Doc," Cody said, giving her a standing ovation.

Rae blushed and waved them off, her pick held between two fingers. "Let's do another one you'll all know."

Rae played on, picking her guitar to perfection. Adam stood, wanting to dance, but Krista refused, wanting to sit and stare at Rae instead. She even moved her chair when Adam and Candace and Jenna and Frank started to dance. Nothing was going to get in the way of her enjoyment.

When Rae began the third song, Krista had her eyes closed. As she listened to the first few lines of "Why Not Me," her eyes flew open, the lyrics hitting home. Whereas Rae had started off a bit shy, she now sang with certainty and a strong confidence, her gaze fixed on Krista. *Oh. My. God.* Krista gripped the chair, unmoving and very nearly unbreathing. Her skin burned hotter and hotter as Rae continued to sing. She began answering the questions of the song in her mind. *Why not you? I don't know. I don't know, why not you?* Panicked and aroused beyond anything she'd ever felt, she wiped away the sweat that was breaking out on her forehead. One of the dancers moved in front of her, breaking the intense eye contact, and she breathed a little easier.

By the time the group started singing the next song Krista was afraid to leave her chair. Wetness had soaked through her jeans, and with every deep stroke of Rae's voice, she felt herself tremble inside. *This was a crazy idea. Why did I encourage it? Oh, God. And this song too, why is every word hitting home?*

Krista stared past the moving bodies, unable to look away. Rae's graceful, strong hands picked the guitar with fluid expertise. The sight, the sounds, the emotion in Rae's voice and the passion in her eyes— moved like waves inside Krista, making her dizzy.

To Krista's relief, Cody requested a slow song as soon as Rae's voice died away. The good news was that her heart got a moment of much-needed rest. The bad news was that everyone had sat down to recover from their dancing and Rae was the sole focus. And Rae wasn't singing to anyone but her. Krista could feel everyone's eyes on her but for once she didn't care. She was busy praying she would somehow be able to resist rising to kiss Rae, when she suddenly stopped playing. Everyone stared as Tillie rose to her feet, her hands covering her face. She ran into her tent, crying loudly.

Rae stood up in alarm, her guitar idle at her side. "Is she okay?"

Krista rose and plucked her wet jeans away from her backside. She crossed the campsite to Tillie's tent and gently rattled the flap. "Tillie?"

Through loud sobs she heard, "Don't worry. I'm just a little upset. Sorry. Tell Rae I'm sorry."

Krista held on to the tent flap, concerned. "You don't have to apologize, sweetie." Had the lyrics of the music hit home with everyone else too? "If you want to talk, I'm here. We're here."

Tillie appeared, her eyes large and liquid. "I know. Thank you. I just need to go to sleep."

"Okay. Get some rest." Krista zipped up the tent. When she turned everyone had quietly dispersed to their own tents. Everyone but Rae. The vet stood looking like she'd single-handedly caused Tillie's broken heart.

"She okay?"

Krista nodded, unable to hold the intense, sensitive gaze. "Yeah."

Rae lowered her guitar and sighed. As she was zipping it up in its case, Krista paused at the door to her own tent.

"You're very good," was all she could think to say.

Rae looked up as if surprised and slightly embarrassed. "Thanks."

"No thanks needed." Krista smiled. She hesitated, unsure of what to say but completely sure of her feelings. More than anything she wanted to stay with Rae and look into her eyes all night long as she sang. She didn't want the night to ever end. But as Rae continued to concentrate on packing up her guitar, she knew the romanticism of the moment was over. "Night."

She disappeared inside her tent but not before she heard Rae whisper, "Night."

Chapter Twelve

The dark desert chirped and hummed outside Rae's tent. Once again she couldn't bring herself to fall asleep. And once again her restlessness was Krista Wyler's fault. She sighed and rubbed her fingers together. They were still alive and tingling from her hour of intensive playing. Her heart still beat like the fast-moving footfall of a horse. Singing and playing like that, in front of Krista, it had excited her in ways she'd never thought possible.

She'd felt connected to her, as if they'd been the only two there. When she sang, she'd sung to her, for her. And she'd meant every word.

Dang it. She turned over in frustration. Had she been so caught up in the music and the moment that she'd mistaken Krista's eyes as ones full of burning desire? Maybe she should've had some of that wine after all. This wasn't like her, the tossing and turning. These feelings, these worries. None of it was like her. She was used to working hard, keeping herself busy and then unwinding with the guitar. When her head hit the pillow at night she did what her body needed to do. She slept.

This…all these things running through her head…she sat up and clamped her hands in her hair. *What is going on?* Instantly her mind's eye pictured Krista sitting across the fire, hands gripping her chair, looking like she wanted to eat Rae alive.

Rae closed her eyes and dropped her hands. Oh, how she loved that look. She knew she'd never forget it. Defeat settled over her as she admitted her growing attraction to Krista Wyler.

Sighing, she lay back down and zipped up her sleeping bag. She wasn't the slightest bit cold but she knew she would be eventually. To her continued amazement her hand drifted willfully over her hardened nipples. Another sigh escaped her as the fingers lingered a moment. A twinge of approval spread up from between her legs.

What am I doing?

Her hand continued downward, slipping quickly beneath her waistband. She cried out softly and slapped her other hand over her mouth. She was wet. Wet and swollen.

With wanting.

With need.

For Krista.

Krista Wyler had done this to her.

Rae's eyes felt wide, staring up at her tent as she let her two fingers squeeze and slide up and down along her engorged clit.

"Ah." Hot blood rushed to her ears. There was a pounding, a steady loud pounding. It was good, so good.

"Hey, sexy,"

"Holy shit." Rae yanked her hand from her pants and sat straight up to her knees, shocked and appalled.

While she'd been distracted with thoughts of Krista, Candace had unzipped the tent and was now inside, zipping it back up. Grinning, she dropped to her knees and lifted Rae's hands to her face.

Her tongue sneaked out and licked the moisture from Rae's fingers. "Mmm, I see you were thinking about me," she whispered. "Baby, you taste good."

She leaned in and licked Rae's neck and then lowered herself to suck Rae's nipples through the thin T-shirt. Rae gasped. The feeling was wonderful.

"No," she whispered, her eyes drifting closed, her head unsure what to do.

Candace paid no mind. Her mouth fastened onto Rae's neck. Her hand swiftly slid into the unzipped jeans where she found Rae insanely wet and waiting.

"Oh, sugar," she purred in Rae's ear. "I bet you taste just like sugar." Her fingers worked Rae up and down, quick and hard and fast.

Rae's mind was spinning. She was losing control. She reached out to lean on something but nothing was there. She fell to her elbow and Candace gave a soft laugh.

"Lie back." Candace's tongu snaked in and around Rae's ear while her hand worked magic in Rae's pants. "Mmm. That's it. Let me make you come, sugar."

Rae was helpless. She started to sit up but Candace pushed her back down. Her breathing was rampant, the pleasure mounting. It had been so long, so long...she clenched her eyes and thought of Krista across the fire.

And then, opening her eyes in sheer bliss, she beautifully came.

❖

To Rae's dismay, she was one of the last to wake the next morning. She rolled over and crawled from the tent with a bitch of a headache. Good mornings came from around the campfire and Rae had walked past almost everyone before she realized her fly was open. Blushing, she zipped it up and meandered through the trees. As she relieved herself and felt the familiar tingle from her crotch, she cursed herself, remembering the night before. Candace had sneaked into her tent, and she'd allowed it. All of it.

"Damn." She felt sick at herself. And as she fastened her jeans and walked back to camp, this sickness grew. When she spotted Krista scooping up some eggs and bacon into a bowl, she realized the sickness was guilt. Cold and hard.

Rae nodded a thanks as Krista handed the bowl to her. She forced herself to take a bite and caught Candace grinning at her. Suddenly Rae had no appetite.

She was about to return the bowl but Krista said, "I know it's not as good as your cooking, but I wanted to let you sleep."

"It's good," Rae said, and continued to eat, hating herself.

She wasn't even attracted to Candace. How had this happened? She hadn't been with a woman for close to three years, and now all of a sudden she was having sex with one she didn't like while thinking about the one she did? Frustrated, she ate quickly, cleaned her bowl, took several large, burning gulps of coffee, and then took down her tent and packed the supplies. She spoke to no one and worked by herself.

When they finally headed out on the trail, she relaxed a little, thankful for the time alone. She rode ahead of the group alongside Howie, leaving Cody behind with the supply horses. All day long, she roped and rode, thinking about nothing but the cattle. When her mind tried to stray she roped it back in, just like a calf. A few times she slowed to help Tom and Tillie with their roping, glad to be of help. But she was sure to steer clear of both Candace and Krista. When lunchtime rolled around, she stayed with Howie, eating the sack lunch while riding Shamrock. The cocky cowboy had little to say and she, for one, was glad.

A little before three, whistles went out and she rode back toward the group, calling Cody on the walkie-talkie to find out what was going on.

He was short of breath. "They've found a rattler."

"Good Lord," Rae said, riding quickly to the bushes where the guests had clustered.

She slid off her horse and approached Frank, who was holding a long stick. The rattle warning was loud. Too loud. He was poking at the coiled snake at close range, encouraging it to strike. When it did, the group let out excited shrieks. Krista was beet red, yelling at everyone to be quiet, but her voice was hoarse and they were ignoring her.

When she saw Rae approach, she held up her hands, once again resisting help when she obviously needed it. "I've got this under control."

Rae fought back her fury and fear. "I can see that." She took the stick from Frank and advanced on the group, waving them away from the bushes. They all stepped backward, eyes fixated on the snake.

"Thank you, Doctor, but I've got this," Krista insisted, taking the stick as if it were almighty and powerful.

Rae glared at her. "Just do yourself a favor, and shut up and *listen*."

Krista's mouth clamped shut in surprise. Rae refocused on the group her anger finally getting the better of her.

"You see that?" She pointed. "That is a rattlesnake. A Western diamondback." She eyed it carefully. "Probably about four feet long."

They oohed in awe, which only annoyed Rae even more. "Do you know what this snake can do to you? Frank? Do you have any idea how dangerous it is?"

"I know it's poisonous."

"And yet you poked at it, tried to provoke it."

He nodded. "I was hoping to kill it. Take the fangs and tail home with me."

"Oh, Frank," Jenna let out in disbelief.

"What?" he cried. "These snakes are legends."

"They're legends for a reason," Krista said, coming to stand by Rae, almost as if she were finally okay with her presence.

Rae felt heat spread in her body as Krista brushed up against her but she was too worked up to care. "If this snake bit you, which by the way it could've if it had wanted to. They strike at a distance of over half their own length."

The group mumbled and took another step backward.

"You would've been in a very serious situation," Rae continued. "We're miles from town. Miles from a hospital. The venom it would've injected, a snake that large, you would have felt it right away. First the severe pain, unlike any pain you've ever felt before." She dug out her wallet and retrieved three folded pictures. She held them up for all to see. They were of a rattlesnake bite on the back of a hand. The skin around the bite was purpling and bubbling while the rest of the hand was swollen to three times its normal size.

As the group studied the pictures, she said, "Then there's the swelling and the funny taste in your mouth. And nausea, vomiting, and sometimes diarrhea. Then hematemesis, hematochezia, paresthesias, and syncope..."

"Para what?" Jenna asked, looking mortified.

Rae stopped her rant and noticed that all eyes were on her. Fear had drawn the blood from their faces. No one said a word.

"I'm sorry, I got carried away." She glanced back at the snake, which still sat coiled, probably way more frightened of them than they were of it. "Rattlesnake bites can cause weakness, fainting, blood in your vomit, blood in your stool." She spoke slower, emphasizing her points. "Your skin will start burning and tingling and you'll get a bulla, or a large blister, around the bite area. If you're not treated with antivenin fairly soon after the bite you can suffer irreversible organ damage. Sometimes even death."

"No shit," Adam said softly, staring at the snake.

"It's an awful way to die," Rae iterated.

Frank cleared his throat. "I guess I won't be taking any fangs home."

Rae clapped him on the shoulder and he jerked. "I wouldn't recommend it. Especially since the venom can remain in the fangs well after death."

The group slowly mounted their horses, mumbling amongst

themselves. They still cast wary glances at the snake, clearly afraid it would slither after them.

"I like you all way too much to have to helicopter you out of here," Rae told them. "Get back to the cattle. They're much safer."

She refolded the pictures and shoved her wallet back in her pocket.

"Wow, you really are a veterinarian," Krista said in a tone that Rae couldn't place.

"You thought I was, what, faking all this time?" Rae was about to mount Shamrock but she hesitated, waiting to see if Krista needed help.

"Let's just say the big words were impressive." Krista gripped Dollar's saddle and hoisted herself up without assistance. "I really did have it under control, you know. You didn't have to scare them like that."

Rae clenched her jaw. "Scare them?"

"You went on and on, exaggerating just a bit, don't you think?"

Rae stalked up to Dollar and took Krista's hand in hers. Krista tried to pull her hand away but Rae wouldn't let her.

"Look," she insisted, gripping her hand tighter. "Look at the back of my hand."

Krista stared down at the two scars on Rae's hand.

"Who do you think those pictures were of?"

Krista ran her fingers gently over the scars, causing Rae to pull away. "You were bitten?"

Rae hoisted herself onto Shamrock. "Absolute worst pain of my life." She clicked and Shamrock started to walk away. "Almost," she whispered, with her thoughts far away.

CHAPTER THIRTEEN

Krista smiled and breathed long and hard as they came upon Sidewinder Creek. Howie and Rae had stopped the cattle, so the group had to ride around the herd to reach the creek.

The evening sun was getting ready to fall beyond the horizon. Its awe-inspiring colors played like freckles on the surface of the water, and Krista felt a warmth in her belly as she stared down at the creek. It was just as she remembered, amberlike, clear and flowing between wild brush and salt cedars and mesquites.

As the cattle began to spread out and settle down, the group crossed the creek to set up camp, ensuring the herd wouldn't cross until morning. To Krista, the water looked glorious, reflective and tempting, sliding over the smooth, moss-covered rocks beneath it. She slid off Dollar and bent to scoop some up in her hands. It was crisp and cool, a godsend. She splashed her dust-coated face and grinned. Her dry mouth pleaded and her cracked lips begged. But she resisted, turning for her canteen of water instead.

Jenna came up beside her, pulling off her large brim hat. "I say after dinner, we jump in."

"I'm not sure I can wait that long." Krista sipped some water and glanced longingly at the creek she knew from her childhood. It was named after a sidewinder because of the sharp curve to the left, beyond the bathing pool. "It drops off and gets pretty deep down a ways. Perfect for swimming."

Jenna replaced her hat and rubbed at her face. "Can't wait."

The group unloaded their gear and supplies from the horses just as they had the two nights before. There were the groans of worn and sore bodies, but they worked without complaint, just eager to get the job done so they could relax.

The campsite was set up facing the creek, the cattle grazing on the other side. Howie followed Tillie like a lovesick pup, helping her build the fire and set up her tent. Adam and Candace worked together, talking like high-school chums while Jenna and Frank worked silently and in sync as a long-married couple would. Tom set up his tent alone, which didn't surprise Krista since he'd pretty much kept to himself thus far. She plopped her tent and sleeping bag down next to him.

Across the pile of logs Howie and Tillie were stacking, Rae was busy pulling out the pots and pans for dinner. Krista thought about offering to help but changed her mind, preferring to work on her tent instead. Maybe if she just stayed away from Rae Jarrett the jealousy and attraction would cease. As Candace's laughter shot up her spine, she sighed. *Three more days. Can I make it three more days without killing her?*

❖

Rae wrapped the potatoes in aluminum foil and nestled them in the hot rocks on the edge of the fire. She fetched the last bag of rice, waiting for the pot full of water to start to boil. As she stood up with more cans of beans, she looked out at the sunset and breathed in the scent of burning wood. Oranges, pinks, and blues brush-stroked the horizon and shimmered off the surface of the flowing creek. Tall and thick saguaros stood guard over the land, outlined in black against the evening sky. The breeze had slowed a little and grown cooler, swaying the branches of the trees.

Always moved by the sight of the desert, Rae silently said a prayer of thanks, grateful that she was alive to experience such grand, raw beauty. She swallowed back tears, as she often did when she prayed or gave thanks. The guilt never failed to squeeze her heart and creep up her throat. She looked up at the sky, at the twinkling of two eager stars, and wondered for the thousandth time why she was here. Why her? What did it all mean?

"You coming?" Candace stood a few feet from her, wearing insanely short cut-off jeans and a black bra. A thin towel was draped over her shoulder. "Some of us are going for a swim."

Rae couldn't help the burning in her cheeks. "You've got about a half an hour yet before this is ready."

Candace dropped her hand in obvious disappointment. "You mean you're not coming?"

Rae stoked the fire. "Can't." Inwardly she knew she would go in the creek, but not until much later.

Jenna exited her tent, wearing men's boxer shorts and a tank top. She touched Candace's arm. "Ready?"

Candace pouted. "I feel bad. She's working so hard. Doing it all for us." When Rae didn't respond, she said pointedly, "I'll make sure to give you another massage tonight."

Rae's face burned so hot she was sure the world could see it. But Candace merely smiled and ambled off after Jenna. Rae watched them step carefully over the rocks that outlined the creek, balancing their way down to where the creek widened. Tillie was already in the water up to her waist, her thick hair in a ponytail. She waved at the approaching pair and yelled something about the water being cold. Jenna and Candace tiptoed in to join her and soon their hollers and laughter swept over camp.

Rae grinned, glad they were having a good time and relieved to be rid of Candace for the time being. As she poured the rice into the boiling water, she wondered where Krista was. She had disappeared without a word after setting up her tent. At the unmistakable sound of hoofbeats, Rae looked up hopefully.

In the deep orange glow of the setting sun Cody and Howie came riding in, followed by a slower horse, pulling two others. Rae grinned, tucking her hands in her back pockets. "Well, look what the cat drug in."

Cody dismounted and took the reins of Dwight's horse. The older cowboy smiled, his cheek lopsided with a wad of chew.

"Cat? Hell, I feel like I been drug by a bull!" He slid off his horse and helped Cody walk the trio up to the campsite.

"Bull or not, you made it just before nightfall."

They shook hands heartily. "I'm always on time, darlin', always."

Rae slapped him on the back, enjoying that he was tired but in good spirits. The harder the drive, the more Dwight seemed to thrive. Repeat came trotting up, tongue and tail wagging. Rae greeted him affectionately.

Howie brushed past them, dusting off his chaps, his eyes scanning the campsite. "They went for a swim, did they?"

The beginnings of a grin started to tilt his face but he tried to hide it as Rae said, "The men are going in later."

Tom and Frank stepped out of their tents and joined in welcoming Dwight. They helped unload some supplies, then told Rae they were going off to explore for a bit. Content with the meal for the time being, Rae sat down with Dwight, who cracked open a cold can of beer.

"How long she been at it?" he asked, slurping. Somehow he managed to drink while keeping the tobacco in his mouth.

The thought of the tastes mingling made Rae cringe. She waved away an offered can as Howie helped himself to two and then wandered off.

"Who?" she asked absently, enjoying the wafting smells of their dinner.

"Krista." Dwight pointed beyond the campsite to their right. "I saw her coming in."

Squinting, Rae stood and focused on the figure with her arm in the air, swinging a rope. "She's roping?"

"Yep." Dwight lowered his beer.

Krista swung the rope over her head and then flung it out at what appeared to be a dead cactus. She hit her mark and tightened the noose expertly.

Dwight sighed. "Just like when she was a kid. She'd practice and practice. Until she got it down. Stubborn girl, just like her aunt."

"Stubborn," Rae said, seriously considering a beer for the first time in three years. "That woman just flat-out hates me."

Dwight looked at her and flicked the tab on his beer can. "No she don't, Doc. Krista ain't got a hateful bone in her body."

"I don't know. She's awful rude to me. Every time I try to help or—"

"Well, see now, that's your problem." Dwight pulled off his hat and placed it on his knee. "Krista won't accept help. Never has." He motioned out to where she was still throwing rope. "See that? I showed her how one time. One time. Then she went off on her own for hours, teaching herself. She didn't want no help. Even then."

Rae couldn't look away, caught up in the intensity she felt radiating from Krista. The black cowboy hat was tugged down tight, and her every movement showed fierce determination. A spark of fire ignited in Rae's chest, startling her. She was aroused, caught up by the sight of her. She stared at her denim-clad legs, gloriously shapely, the T-shirt clinging to her upper body, showing off the swell of her breasts. She watched the thick mane of hair sway against her shoulders, the sun setting off the fiery auburn.

Clearing her throat, she returned to her seat, unsettled by what she was feeling and for whom. Krista Wyler wanted nothing to do with her. At least that was how she behaved, not to mention how she spoke to Rae. But then there were the unspoken moments, the ones where Rae clearly could see the passionate fire burning in Krista's eyes. Dwight interrupted her, as if he knew she was still thinking about Krista.

"Don't give up on her, Rae. She'll come around." Dwight took another sip as Rae dragged her attention back to the food. She pulled off the pan and pots and set them to the side to cool a little. "To be honest with you, Rae, I'm worried about how she's gonna be when Judith finally goes."

Rae hated thinking about it. "How is she?"

"Took to the bed as soon as y'all left. Hasn't been up since. It won't be long now." They were silent for a long while. He examined his boots and rubbed his stubble. "Anyhow, how's Krista been doin' on the horse?"

"Just fine, thanks." Krista answered before Rae could comment. Walking briskly into the camp, she tossed her rope into her tent and then removed her hat to kiss Dwight on the cheek. "How was your ride?" She spoke to him directly, refusing to look at Rae.

"Not too bad. And y'all look like you're doin' just fine."

Krista ran her hands through her hair, taking the time to massage her scalp. As her eyes fluttered closed, the burning in Rae's chest spread and she forced herself to look away.

"We're doing great," Krista said. "Everyone's a real hard worker and they seem to be having a good time." She began organizing serving bowls and silverware. "You leaving in the morning, then?"

"Yeah, I'll ride out at first light. Take the horses back."

"How are things back at the ranch? How's Judith?"

Dwight took his time answering. "She's the same," he fibbed, rubbing his stubble over and over, the guilt obviously affecting him.

Krista didn't seem to notice. "Have I missed any calls?"

Rae didn't miss the wash of anxiety that suddenly swept over her face. There was no cellular service this far out and Rae knew the loss of communication had to be eating Krista alive. Every time she'd seen her back at the ranch, there seemed to be a phone growing out of her ear.

Dwight shrugged. "There's been a few. Some woman." He snapped his fingers, trying to remember.

"Suzanne?"

"Yes. That's the one."

"Shit." Krista fingered her temple. "Did she say what she needed?"

"No, she didn't. She just asked that you call her when you can."

"Shit," Krista said again.

Feeling wary of Krista's sudden mood change, Rae was just about to whistle everyone for dinner when a shriek came from the creek and she bolted as quickly as she could, panic surging her heart. Right away she breathed a sigh of relief as she slowed and made out the three women standing on the bank. No one was missing.

"What's going on?" Rae asked. Tillie pointed to the trees, fury on her face. "He took off."

"Who?"

"Howie!" Candace let out. "We caught him watching us."

Rae clenched her jaw, her anger for the cowboy boiling past even her highest point. She let her gaze roam the area, but saw no one.

Krista limped up from behind to stand next to Rae, breathless and cursing softly. "You see him?"

"No."

"Sorry we screamed like that," Tillie said, shivering in the breeze. "But he scared us. I wasn't even sure what it was at first."

Huddled in their towels, the women walked to Rae.

"What happened?" Jenna asked, pointing at Krista's knee where a dark stain spread through the denim.

"I fell." Krista waved it off. "It's nothing. Looks worse than it is."

Just then a figure stepped out of the brush. Howie walked up just as cocky as ever, chuckling to himself.

Rae stared him down and spoke without looking away. "Ladies, dinner's ready. Why don't you head back into camp, change into some warm clothes, and eat?"

The three women all agreed and started back to camp, but Krista was still by her side. "Ms. Wyler?"

"I'm not leaving."

"As you wish." Rae stepped up to meet Howie. Reaching out to his chest, she clutched his shirt and held him still.

He laughed and dropped the can of beer in his left hand. "What's the matter, Doc? I was just having some fun."

"Listen, you piece of shit." Rae could smell the beer on his breath and she wanted to knock the smirk right off his face. "You stay away from every woman here for the next three days or I'll rip your balls off. Understood?"

He raised his hands in mock fear. "Okay, okay."

"No more fun, Howie," Krista added. "Or I'll fire you right here and now."

He laughed. "What good will that do? You need me to stick around."

Rae eased her grip and he swatted her hand away and walked off toward camp.

"Hey!" Rae called after him. As he turned, she tossed his beer can at him. He caught it, anger on his face.

"He's right," Krista whispered. "We can't afford to lose him. But he's trouble."

"He is that." Rae picked up a rock and threw it into the creek, her anger still fresh.

"Thank you for not hitting him."

Rae was surprised by the comment. "I don't like violence." She opened and shut her fist and knew it would be sore in the morning from the tight grip she'd had on him. "But I was tempted. If he'd touched one of them—"

"I would've beat the shit out of him," Krista finished.

Rae glanced down at Krista's leg. "You better let me take a look."

Krista scoffed. "I'm fine. Just a klutz is all."

But Rae was concerned at the amount of blood. "Have you even looked at it?"

Krista started to say no and then thought better of it. "I'm sure it's fine, just a little scratch." She tried to walk but winced.

The look of pain on her face, coupled with her hardheadedness, bowled over Rae's self-control. "Come here," she softly demanded, scooping Krista up in her arms and carrying her over the rocks.

"Oh!" Krista let out, completely startled. She started to protest but stopped when she saw the look in Rae's eyes.

Rae reached even ground and knelt down. She lowered Krista gently, lost in the green-golds of her eyes and the parting of her pink lips. In the breeze, Krista's hair swept over Rae's face and Krista clung to her neck, seemingly unwilling to let go.

Rae fought for her voice, knowing she had to speak before she did something she would regret. "Let's take a look at that knee." Her voice was weak, mirroring her reserve.

Krista blinked as if she'd been in a trance and lowered her arms.

Rae, down on her knees, noted the small tear in the jeans and scooted Krista's pant leg up gently. Her throat closed as her fingertips skimmed the curve of Krista's calf, smooth and tight. Gooseflesh pimpled under her fingers and she heard Krista draw a quick breath.

"Am I hurting you?" Rae couldn't stop staring at the beckoning lips.

"No."

Rae forced herself to look down. The dark stain of blood steadied her mind as she folded the jeans up over the knee. The cut was relatively deep and about three inches long, just below the kneecap. The bleeding had stopped but it needed to be cleaned.

"Wait here." She got up and jogged back to camp. Her medical supplies were in her saddlebag. After finding what she needed, she jogged back and nearly slammed to a halt when she saw Krista. She was sitting on the hard sand, leaning back on her hands, her injured leg stretched out, the other bent. Her hair fell across her shoulders in fiery waves. The creek rushed beyond her, the vanishing sun washed over her in a brilliant orange glow.

"My God." It was all Rae could say, all she could think as she walked up to her.

"I'm sorry?" Krista asked. "I couldn't hear you."

"Nothing," Rae answered, once again stooping to her knees, avoiding the catlike eyes. She opened the bottle of peroxide and soaked a cotton ball. Twilight was setting in.

Krista flinched but remained silent as Rae dabbed at the wound. Once she had the layer of drying blood off the cut, she said, "This may hurt a little."

She placed her fingers on either side and pulled the skin apart. Again Krista flinched and this time sucked in a hissing breath as Rae poured the peroxide down into the wound. She repeated the treatment three more times before the bubbling stopped.

"I'm sorry," Rae said, hating the pain she'd caused. Seeing Krista hurt was like having an angry hand inside her chest, tearing at her heart. She dabbed the wound, drying it as best she could with a clean cloth.

A soft hand covered hers. "It's okay. Thank you." Krista said.

Rae heated and glanced away, and Krista withdrew her hand. Rae worked quickly, her heart pounding so hard she thought she'd pass out. She applied the triple antibiotic cream and closed the wound with butterfly bandages, then stood and held out her hand. Krista took it firmly and allowed Rae to help her stand. Her thankful smile disappeared when she tried to walk. Rae took her arm, cupping the forearm with her strong hand. For a brief moment she thought about scooping her up once again and carrying her into camp. The determination in Krista's eyes stopped her.

Krista grimaced but bit back her groans of pain. Leaning into Rae she said, "Come on, let's go eat."

As the two women approached camp, Dwight stopped mid-sentence with Cody and stared. Rae and Krista were walking slowly, their arms linked together, Krista obviously allowing Rae to help her walk over the rocks.

"Well, I'll be," he whispered.

"Looks like Ms. Wyler took a spill," Cody observed.

"Uh-huh. It sure does." Dwight rubbed his stubble, unable to hide the growing grin that was stinging his face.

CHAPTER FOURTEEN

With her injured leg straight out in front of her, Krista sighed, still wanting that swim she'd promised herself. But she was tired and she knew she shouldn't get her wound wet. She fixed her eyes on Howie. She'd been watching him for a long while. Dinner was warm, hearty, and welcome. Rae had baked the potatoes to perfection and Krista devoured two of them, almost groaning at the softness of each center mixed with butter in her mouth. Howie ate his meal quietly and laughed along with everyone else, acting as if nothing was wrong. In her gut, Krista knew he was trouble, but for the time being all she could do was keep a close eye on him. She'd asked Cody to search his horse and had him hide the two knives he'd found. She'd also asked Tillie to sleep in her tent tonight, wanting to pair up all the women with someone else just in case.

That only left Rae, but Krista's inner turmoil over the woman was already way too much to handle. She wasn't about to offer to sleep next to her. Besides, Rae was the last person Howie wanted to be near.

Krista sipped her beer and lowered her eyes from Howie, staring into the hypnotic fire. Her thoughts drifted back to the creek and how warm and strong Rae had felt against her, lifting her as if she weighed nothing at all. She wondered if Rae knew how badly she'd wanted her. That she'd been desperate for Rae to lay her down on the ground and kiss her long and hard, claiming her as her own once and for all. God, she'd wanted it. And the look in Rae's eyes…so tender, so vulnerable, so…hungry.

"Good night," Howie grunted as he stood.

Drawn away from her daydream, Krista relaxed as he left, glad he was finally going to bed. She thought about securing his tent flap with something from around the campsite, but nothing came to mind. The rest of the guests followed the troublesome cowboy, all of them tired and ready for a good night's sleep, and Krista reasoned and hoped that Howie would be fine.

"Well, I guess I'll turn in," she said softly. She placed a hand on Rae's arm and felt the slightest bit of reaction to her touch. She smiled, liking that and remembering the desire she'd seen burning in her eyes. Maybe she'd been wrong. Maybe Rae shared her feelings. Maybe she wasn't going crazy after all.

"Night," Rae managed in a raspy voice. She returned Krista's smile but then stared into the fire.

Krista limped to her tent and paused there to get one last glimpse of Rae by the fire. She seemed lost in thought for a moment, but then walked to her horse where she unlatched her guitar case. With what appeared to be a thick candle in her other hand, she vanished into the darkness.

Krista's heartbeat sped up at the thought of Rae strumming and singing just as she'd done the night before. She wanted nothing more than to steal away and listen to her, to watch her strong, lean fingers work the strings, just as she wanted them to work her own body. She jumped, torn from her thoughts by a polite question.

"You turning in?" Tillie peeked out of the opening of the tent.

"Yeah," Krista whispered. Her eyes were lost in the darkness that had swallowed Rae, and she wished that she too could be swallowed up along with her, just her and Rae and the night.

❖

An hour later Krista thought she heard the zip of a tent and the scuffling of feet. She turned over and held open her tent, looking expectantly across the fire at Rae's. But it sat empty, its flaps loose and open.

Shit. Krista was wide-awake and frustrated as hell. Her body was wound tighter than a top and she felt like she would burst into flames each time Rae's face came into her mind. Next to her, Tillie softly snored and Krista let out a long sigh, knowing she couldn't even stroke herself to bliss. *Not that it would help.* She remembered the third and last orgasm she'd had with the young woman from the bar who'd lapped eagerly between her legs. It had been short, hard, and less than sweet. And only obtainable because she'd imagined Rae was the one pleasing her.

"God damn it," she whispered, pushing herself up and quietly slipping into her hiking boots.

Careful not to disturb Tillie, she crawled from the tent and hugged herself against the chill of the midnight air. Her long-sleeved shirt and sweatpants weren't holding in much of her body warmth, so she stepped up to the dying fire and tossed on another log. She held her hands out as it flared up, and slowly stretched her sore leg. Dwight mumbled in his sleep from his sitting position against a supply bag, and she covered him with another blanket, then stared into the darkness. She knew Rae was still out there, having listened for her to return. The gentle swish of the creek lured her. *Come this way, come this way,* it seemed to say as it flowed in the direction Rae was walking earlier.

After debating with herself for a few seconds, she grabbed the flashlight next to Dwight and limped off into the black night. She moved quietly over the rocks and sand, eyes straining until she caught sight of the glowing candle. Switching off the flashlight, she crept closer. Rae sat playing her guitar in the same spot where she'd tended to Krista's leg. Krista recognized the tune she'd heard the night before last, and her lips parted in awe as she listened. The song was about love and pain. About a woman. A woman who had walked into the singer's life and changed things. Rae played longer than before, having written more.

Go to her, Krista's mind screamed. *Go to her.* She took two steps as Rae stopped, midsong, to write something on a folded piece of paper. Krista took two more steps, her mind made up, then stopped abruptly as a figure appeared, approaching Rae from behind.

"That's a real nice song," Candace said.

The candlelight played across her long, bare legs and she tugged her shirt off over her head, exposing round, full breasts. Then she inched down her cut-off jeans and stepped out of them. Rae sat looking up at her in awe, saying nothing. Candace reached down and moved the guitar to the side and then straddled Rae, wrapping her legs around her.

Krista covered her mouth as a whimper escaped her throat. She watched in heartbreaking horror as Candace held Rae's face in her hands and kissed her long and hard. *That's my kiss. That's my kiss!* was all she could think as her knees threatened to give and her gut wrenched with a pain she'd never felt before. Candace moaned and ground her hips, pulling her mouth away and grabbing Rae's hands.

"Touch me, baby," she said, placing the strong hands on her breasts and throwing her head back in pleasure.

Oh, God. Krista couldn't take anymore. Fighting tears, she made her way back to camp but bypassed her tent. Instead she stumbled over to Dollar, ran her hands over his snout, and upon seeing his large liquid eyes, she buried her face in his neck and cried.

❖

"Krista. Krista, darlin', wake up."

Krista stirred as her eyes fluttered against the pale light of morning. She groaned and grabbed her head. Dwight was on his haunches in front of her, a gentle hand on her shoulder. He held out a bottle of water and helped her stand.

Every fiber of her being ached and her mouth felt like the desert ground, dry, rough and gritty. She sipped the water gratefully, relishing its coolness as it coated her parched throat.

"Feel better?" Dwight stroked the thick black and gray stubble of his beard, his dark eyes concerned.

Krista nodded and then regretted moving her head. Groaning, she ran soothing fingertips over her temples.

Dwight bent and retrieved the empty wine bottle she'd slept next to. Without a word he placed it in the heavy supply bag that held all of their garbage. He would be taking it back to the ranch with him that morning. Krista winced guiltily as she remembered drinking the wine the night before, wanting to dull the sharp pain in her heart. At some point she'd passed out on the cold ground, using the saddle as a pillow, too damn hurt inside to care.

Dwight moved past her again, lifting the saddle to place it on Dollar's back. He strapped it on and then folded the heavy horse blanket and returned it to one of the supply horses. Krista didn't remember the blanket, so she assumed Dwight had draped it over her sometime during the night.

"Thank you," she said softly.

Dwight gave her a caring look and then embraced her with strong cowboy arms. "No need, darlin'."

Krista lightly hugged him, afraid to really let herself go and clutch him. Hot tears burned her throat and she knew she would completely break down if she wasn't careful. The older cowboy seemed to sense this and he pulled away.

"I'm already packed up, so I'm going to head out." He picked up his hat and placed it securely on his head.

Krista was sad to see him go. His presence was a great comfort, and suddenly she couldn't wait to get back to the ranch. "How's Aunt Judith?"

The pain in her throat increased, though the cause was different. She needed to hear him say her aunt was doing fine.

Dwight fidgeted with his saddle bags. "She's okay."

"She told you not to bother me with talk of her, didn't she?"

Dwight nodded, a knowing smile on his face.

"Give her a kiss for me, will you?" Her heart broke with the thought of Judith. And again the guilt of staying away so long ripped at her insides.

"I will." Dwight climbed onto his horse and tilted the brim of his hat. He changed the subject as his voice quaked with emotion. "I laid out the Egg Beaters and bacon, along with the tortillas." He pointed to the rack by the fire. "Y'all have two full coolers and I'm taking the empty ones back."

"Sounds good." Krista glanced around and took a mental note of the supplies. Satisfied they would not run out before Dwight returned, she gave him a wave. "Be safe."

"You too." He clicked to his horse and started off into the desert, the supply horses behind him carrying the group's trash.

Krista stretched her stiff body and heard her back crack softly. It was going to be a long, hard day with the condition she was in. She tugged up her pant leg and examined her wound. It was still a little sore but there was no sign of infection. Her gallivanting around in the darkness the night before hadn't exactly been the wisest thing to do. An image of a nude Candace straddling Rae entered her mind and she cringed, thinking just how unwise it had been.

Needing to think about something else, she looked to the horizon where the sky was turning pink with the rising sun. For several minutes, she watched the hot ball of light rise above the horizon. She didn't know if it was her peaceful surroundings or the fact that she'd cried herself to sleep with her body worn to bits, but she felt very calm at that moment and in tune with all that was life. At that moment she knew she could handle anything. Whatever came her way. And that whatever was meant to happen would.

Wanting to get a head start on preparing breakfast before Rae woke, she got the fire going and then placed out the pans. A few minutes later she was pouring herself a steaming mug of coffee, loving the smell and taste of it as it stirred her mind and body. Enjoying the alone time, she placed the bacon on the pan and sat down in the camp chair. The strong scent of coffee, the smell and sound of the sizzling bacon, the fresh raked smell of the morning desert, it all caused her to close her eyes and relax. She breathed deep. Her bones were liquid, as were her thoughts. For the first time in her life she was too damn tired to worry.

❖

Soon the campsite was bustling and everyone was eagerly awaiting the scrambling eggs except for Rae and Candace. Adam sat in his chair, avoiding Krista's eyes. Krista stirred the eggs and placed the tortillas in an empty pan to heat them up. The cartons of Egg Beaters were way more convenient than real fragile eggs, and she tried to give herself credit for the wise supplies. Even though she was very much aware of Rae's absence, she continued cooking, paying no mind.

Howie stepped into the morning looking like a horse had dragged him for miles. She knew he'd had a lot to drink the night before, but considering her similar hangover, she didn't feel she had the right to say anything. At the very least, he'd slept long and hard, unable to cause any trouble.

As the group each dug into their tortillas stuffed with eggs, bacon, and cheese, Rae finally appeared. Krista glanced at her fleetingly, noticing the wet hair and freshly scrubbed face. She'd been swimming, and her T-shirt and neck were damp from her hair. Krista forced herself to concentrate on her burrito but Rae spoke to her, ruining the apathy she was trying so hard to practice.

"How's the leg?"

"Fine." She handed Rae a burrito, hoping she would sit and eat instead of trying to talk.

Rae ignored the plate and didn't lower her gaze. "I should probably take a look at it."

Krista fought against the racing of her heart. Rae was wet, fresh, and goddamn near perfect standing against the rising sun. Just as Krista was about to agree, despite her misgivings, Candace appeared from the direction Rae had, equally wet but with less clothes. She breezed into the camp with a secret smile. Same cut-off jeans and shirt she'd worn the night before.

"Good morning, everyone," she said, brushing past Rae to take the plate Krista still held. "Thank you, I'm starved." She turned, causing Rae to step to the side to let her pass. She gave Rae a devilish grin and went to sit next to Adam.

Krista closed her eyes, focusing, talking herself down. She didn't care anymore. It didn't matter that Rae and Candace had probably been gone all night. That they'd made love until the sun came up and swam nude together in the creek. Or it could just be a coincidence. It didn't necessarily mean anything had happened.

She opened her eyes and watched Rae run a hand through her hair. Krista's breath hitched in her throat at first from the sexy sight of Rae finger-combing her wet locks, but then at the dark mark on the side of her neck. It was purple and uneven, just the size of Candace's mouth.

Oh, God. Krista swayed as the realization slammed home. How could it hurt this bad? She wasn't supposed to care. She felt her body grow heavy and numb as she stared and heard Candace giggle beyond them. She felt her own eyes deaden, the light from within dimming.

Rae was staring at her, obviously wanting to speak. "After breakfast I'll check that wound." She spoke as if everything were fine, as if the mark on her neck didn't even exist. She even smiled her caring smile.

Krista clenched her hands into fists at her side. "No."

Rae looked surprised. "No?"

"No."

Rae just stared, completely confused. "Okay," she finally managed, drawing it out. "Well, would you mind handing me that last burrito?" She motioned toward the cooler on which the last plate sat.

Krista ignored the request and brushed past her, refusing to say anything at all. Her heart was heavy as lead.

❖

Rae rode alone, preferring her own company for the midmorning. Around her the steady stampede of hoofs on hard ground echoed across the land. A hawk cried out overhead, gliding against the pale blue sky, its wings spread wide. She took a sip of water from her canteen and squinted into the rising dust. She rode near the center, bringing up the rear as the rest of the group rode about a hundred yards away along the sides.

Replacing her canteen, she eyed the black Stetson that rested on the saddle horn. The hat had been lying there when she'd mounted up after breakfast. Krista obviously no longer wanted to wear it, donning one of Cody's ball caps instead. Rae rubbed her neck, tired and confused. Everyone had noticed Krista's rude behavior toward her this morning, but no one had said a word. They'd merely gone about their chores, refusing to make eye contact. Everyone except Candace, that was. She'd laughed and giggled and carried on, just like always.

An image of her nude and voluptuous body came to mind, the contours lit up like gold in the candlelight. Rae shook the thought away, unwilling to let herself go there. She considered Krista's behavior again. The warmth Rae had detected in her had gone completely. Why? There was no way she could know about Candace. They had been alone, in the dark. But they had both been in the creek that morning; maybe that was what Krista was upset over. Was she jealous? Did she think it was inappropriate behavior, mingling with the clients? If so, why didn't she talk to her about it instead of just stomping off mad?

Rather than trying to figure out the meaning behind Krista Wyler's behavior, Rae focused instead on getting back home. She couldn't wait to see Lindsay and get back to her regular routine. She missed her home, missed the safety of its walls and the peacefulness of her land. The house was a quaint three bedrooms, quite a bit smaller than the Wyler house and not near as nice. But it met her needs and she'd been happy there over the past five years. Her thoughts clouded with sadness. Up until Shannon. Since then she'd used the house as a haven, a place to hide away from the world, leaving only for work, refusing to go out with Lindsay and friends. The house seemed to grow dark and lonely overnight. Her cave. She longed for that safe, isolated place now. The quiet place where she could be alone with her music and her land.

Up ahead she saw Cody riding to her from the front. The scene could have been a Western cowboy oil painting, a young cowboy on a glistening chestnut mare, dust rising around her hooves, beyond them an endless sky.

He slowed and eyed the supply horses she was pulling. "Time for lunch."

Rae glanced at her watch, surprised it was already past noon. They summoned the group and headed for the shade of the neighboring trees. They had crossed the creek, but they were lucky that the water curved and the trail continued to follow its course. The guests were dust-covered and quieter than usual, crawling from their horses with soft groans, wiping dirty sweat from their faces. Rae headed to the supplies to hand out the lunches, but Krista beat her to it, giving her a glare that said, for sure, she didn't want any help. Tugging off her hat, Rae sat on the ground a good ways from Candace. When they all had their lunch sacks, Tillie offered Rae one but she shook her head.

She wasn't hungry.

The group looked at her and then looked at Krista, who was not eating either. No one spoke. Krista sat with a numb look on her face, ball cap on the ground, hair thick and tousled and sticking to her neck. Her Western shirt was sleeveless and open, showing off a sweat- and dirt-stained tank top. Rae swallowed against the desire swelling in her belly.

She hates me.

Krista moved her leg and flinched, pulling up her pants leg to look at her wound. Rae watched intently, worried. She wanted to tend to her so badly it hurt deep inside. The wound was bleeding, or had bled, she couldn't tell. Either way, she knew it needed to be cleaned again to ward off infection.

Rising, she capped her canteen and approached, winning another rattlesnake warning glare from Krista. "I should look at that," she said softly.

Krista shoved down the pants leg, like a child hiding her candy. "Not necessary," she said, staring straight ahead.

Rae thought about arguing but she noticed the uncomfortable silence of the group. She remembered the fall Krista took off Dollar, and how she'd seemed embarrassed, wanting to act like it never happened. Maybe she didn't want to appear weak in front the group. Giving her the benefit of the doubt she said, "Okay, later then."

Before she returned to her seat, though, she fetched two cold bottles of water and gave one to Krista. She'd taken on more sun and Rae was worried about her staying hydrated. Krista held the water like it was poison at first, but as Rae sat down again and the group began talking, she opened it slowly and took little sips as if she were ashamed to do so.

Everyone was tired and in no hurry to get back on the trail. Adam and Candace lounged back to back and Jenna leaned on Frank's shoulder, her face hot and flushed. Tom had taken a seat next to Tillie and they'd shared some trail mix and fruit.

Unfortunately, there was very little breeze even though they were next to the creek. The heat hung heavy in the air until the wind wanted to tease a little, brushing against their cheeks and then vanishing. Frank tossed out some crumbs near a pored mound several feet away. A prairie dog popped its head out and waited for several moments, frozen and watchful. When no one spoke or moved, it made a mad dash for the bread and darted back into its hole.

Chuckling Frank spoke. "Are we the only married people on this shindig?"

Most everyone nodded. Jenna raised her head. "Really? No one else is married?"

Tom said he had been married, as did Candace, but they didn't seem willing to share the details.

Jenna squeezed her husband's hand. "We've been married thirty years today." Her smile said it all and Frank turned to give her a small peck on the lips.

"That's wonderful," Adam said. "Congratulations."

The group all followed his lead, giving their congrats in soft voices.

"Love is a blessing," Jenna added. "I hope you all find it someday."

The prairie dog poked its head out again and stood on its hind legs in anticipation, but upon seeing no more bread, it ducked back inside.

"Love is a curse." The voice was so soft and low, Rae looked up, wondering who had said it.

"A curse?" Jenna asked.

"A curse," Tillie affirmed, tossing bits of twig at the ground.

"Why would you think that?" asked Jenna, still holding Frank's hand.

"Because I've lived it."

No one said a word, waiting. Rae looked up as another hawk called out overhead, adding to the effect, a foretelling of Tillie's tale of doomed love.

"Tell us," Krista encouraged.

Tillie shook her head. "It's a long, sad story."

"I'm in no hurry." Adam offered her a sincere smile.

"Me neither," Candace added.

Tillie seemed to think for a moment and then began. "I met him my senior year of high school." She chuckled a little, remembering. "I was at a party, drinking with friends. It was March, graduation not far off. We were all excited, thinking we were all grown up." She stared at the ground.

"He walked in with some friends and I thought Adonis himself had entered the room." Some mumbles of understanding encouraged her to continue. "He looked at me but I could tell he was shy. A mutual friend introduced us. His name was Gary and he was in Phoenix for spring training. He was nineteen and had just been drafted by a major league baseball team." Adam let out a whistle that Tillie didn't seem to hear.

"He was a pitcher. Tall and strong and handsome. A Southern boy from the bayou. We fell hard and fast, crazy about one another. We went to my senior prom and I followed him that summer as he went from team to team, from double A to triple A ball. I met his family and fell in love with them too. He'd met mine and of course everyone approved. I changed my ways as we talked about marriage. I had been a real partyer, not caring about much. But I wanted a family. I wanted him. So I converted to Catholicism in order to have a big Catholic wedding.

"Even though my father paid for the wedding, we had the ceremony in his small town. The church was packed with family and friends. I didn't know most of them." She smiled, her eyes starting to brim with tears. "I was so nervous, I was rocking myself in the bride's room just before. But the ceremony went well. It was perfect. I can still remember that tight little red dress I changed into at the reception. You should have seen how his eyes lit up. We danced the night away with our friends."

"Sounds like it was beautiful," Krista said softly.

"Oh it was." She smiled. "We honeymooned in the Caribbean.

The best week of my life. We loved each other so much." She sighed. "Soon after that, the next season, he went to big league camp and got put into the starting rotation. He'd signed a pretty big contract and we started living like we had a little money. We spoke of starting a family and I got pregnant. We planned it so we'd have the baby in the off season, so he could be there."

"How long had you two been married at this point?" asked Frank.

Tillie thought for a moment. "Four years when we had Brandon."

Frank nodded and she continued.

"Brandon was our little prince. He was beautiful and perfect, and my lifelong dream of being a mom had come true. Gary cried with me when he was born." She paused. "But everything changed after that, in a good way, or so I thought. Our life was no longer about us. It was about Brandon. I thrived at motherhood and Gary was a good dad, always so happy when he returned from a long road trip. We would just lie in the bed every morning, Brandon sleeping between us. We would watch him, sleeping like an angel, and smile. We were happy."

Candace sighed, her chin resting in her hand. "I want that someday."

"Really?" Adam asked, surprised.

"Yeah, why not?"

"Everyone should have that at some point in their life," Jenna said. "It's what life's all about."

"That's what I used to think too," Tillie continued. "I thought we were happy. We had Brandon, our intimate life was still good, his career was where he wanted, we had it all." She shrugged. "So we got pregnant again. This time with a little girl."

Again Candace sighed, dreamy-eyed.

"I was more miserable this time around, but I made sure everything was taken care of, including my husband, if you know what I mean."

The group was silent for a moment, seemingly lost in thought. Then Adam piped up, "Oh, you mean," he bent his fingers, mimicking quotation marks, "taken care of."

"Yes."

"Ohh," Jenna said.

"So I thought everything was fine. Isabella was born in late October, and Gary was able to be there. She was as beautiful as her brother, and I settled back into baby mode, breast-feeding and rocking her at all hours of the night." She tossed another piece of twig. "At this point I started noticing some troubling signs with Brandon. He wasn't talking and he was doing odd things, like spinning objects for hours or lining up his toys rather than playing with them. He paid attention to no one else and he wouldn't even turn when called. It was very hard to do things with him, like take him to restaurants or to stores, because he didn't like the noise or crowds or sitting still. And run, he could run for miles."

Another long pause.

"Isabella had just turned one when they told us Brandon was autistic. It was devastating news but we were prepared. We'd been aware and worrying for months up until that point."

"That had to be hard," Rae said.

"It was. But you go forward and deal with it. I found a really good place for his therapy. He progressed so quickly the first few weeks alone. So things were okay, you know?" her eyes clouded over. "And that's when I realized something strange was going on with Gary. It was his sixth season in the big leagues and he was hanging out with the guys on road trips. He started gambling, losing huge sums of money to his buddies in a night. I would go to the bank for cash and the teller would say you can't, your husband has pulled out the ATM daily limit every day this week.

"Of course, that started some fights. I just didn't see how he could willingly gamble away five to ten thousand dollars every few days. It made me sick to think about it. Especially when he'd scrutinize my credit card bills, wanting me to justify every purchase. And he was drinking. A lot.

"We came home that September and he started acting like an ass. He stayed out all night drinking, not coming home until three or four in the morning. I told him I'd had enough and kicked him out. He seemed happy to go. He moved in at his cousin's house and he wouldn't discuss what was happening. I asked him if there was someone else, or if it was the drinking. All he would say is that he no longer wanted to play baseball and that he didn't know what he wanted.

"And then he disappeared. He gave me some lame excuse as to why he wouldn't see the kids for a few days. No one could get a hold of him and no one knew where he was. His family was worried, so I went to his cousin's house and searched Gary's Mercedes. I found a stack of missing cell phone bills in his golf bag and suddenly it all clicked. There was a phone number that came up over and over again."

"Oh, Jesus," let out Krista.

"Yeah," said Tillie. "I went home and got online. I found out her name, her age and occupation." She looked at Krista. "Gentleman's club entertainer."

Adam gasped. "No."

Candace looked ashamed. Everyone knew she was an exotic dancer, and there was no reason for her to feel guilty about another dancer's behavior, but she said, "I would never do something like that...a married man..."

Tillie held up a hand. "I know, Candace. But I'm sure you know the type that would."

She nodded. "Yeah, I know a few."

"I was furious," Tillie said. "I called him and threatened to throw his beloved bikes out on the street, all of his stuff. When he didn't rush over, I knew he was out of town." She sighed. "So I searched the house. I found a cruise brochure. He had handwritten *Continental IHA* on the bottom. IHA stands for Houston's airport."

"You mean he was on a cruise!" Jenna exclaimed.

"You got it. He was on a Caribbean cruise with this woman."

"What did you do?" Adam asked.

"I called a private investigator. He found out that the woman had no place of residence in her name for the past two years."

"Oh, my God." Jenna squeezed Frank's hand tighter. "He'd bought her house."

Tillie wiped away tears as she nodded. "When he came home, I backed him to a corner and got him to admit to it. He blamed baseball and the lifestyle and drinking. He said he wanted to quit the game because otherwise he couldn't stop himself."

"Bullshit," mumbled Tom.

"That's what everyone kept telling me," Tillie continued. "My mother flew into town to help support me and to help with the kids. I was a wreck. A complete wreck. Gary had always shunned his friends who cheated. He called it 'dirty' and swore he would never do it. It was like I didn't know him anymore."

She wiped away more tears. "But because I loved him, because of my faith, because of my children, I didn't run him into the ground.

I refused to see an attorney. I hoped against hope that God would somehow make things right. I clung to that for a long time."

The group was silent for several moments as she composed herself. Tom rubbed her shoulder, his face full of pain and compassion.

"And now I'm here. A year and seven months later. We're divorced. He married the thirty-seven-year-old stripper. They have a son. Gary just signed his biggest contract to date. Fifty-five million for five years with the Yankees."

"Gary Thibodeaux!" Frank gasped. "That's him! The bastard!"

Tillie nodded, tears staining her face.

"Are you all right?" Asked Krista. "Financially?"

Tillie sniffed. "I get enough to survive through child support. But just before I married him, his agent drew up a prenup."

"Oh, shit," said Adam.

"I was barely twenty years old, away from my family, so deeply in love. I thought if I didn't sign it, it would look like I was after his money. That coupled with the fact that I didn't strike first with a lawyer, it nearly killed me."

"So you get next to nothing compared to what he makes?"

She nodded. "I get child support. It's more than most women get. I put as much as I can away in savings for the future."

"But that's not fair. You were there through it all. Putting up with his shit. Doing whatever he wanted." Candace looked like she might cry herself.

"What about the kids, Tillie?" Rae asked. "Does he see them?"

"He saw them quite a bit for the first few months. Then it changed to him calling only once a week. But when she had her boy, he stopped altogether."

"What an...an...asshole!" Jenna stood and paced, disgusted.

"The new little boy..." Krista started, then stopped.

Tillie nodded. "Yeah, he's perfect."

Adam stood as well, kicking a rock. "Well, no wonder you're scorned on love. I hate love for you!"

Tillie laughed but then she started to cry, covering her face with her hands.

"Men are dogs," Candace said, grimacing, "just dirty dogs."

Tom wrapped Tillie's shoulders with his arm. "All men aren't like that," he said softly. "Some of us are good people." A tear slipped down his cheek and Rae knew in her heart that he was one of the good ones.

Frank too wiped his eyes.

Rae stared at the ground, her own throat tight. She wasn't the only one hurt by love, it seemed. *You're not alone, Tillie. You're not alone.*

❖

Solemn from Tillie's tale, the group climbed back on the horses and set out into the afternoon sun. Rae's heart bled in her chest, pained for Tillie and pained for her own loss. She watched Krista intently, noticing her change in behavior as well. After the heartbreaking story she seemed less angry and more sad. She kept to herself and started roping again.

Rae couldn't help but admire her perseverance and smiled when she finally hit her mark. Krista tugged back on the rope quickly and Adam whooped at her success. The calf struggled and Krista nearly fell from her saddle trying to get to it. Grinning, she removed the rope and hugged the calf.

"You're a stud!" Adam said.

Krista took off her ball cap and bowed, but when her eyes caught Rae's, their sparkle faded and her smile mellowed a bit. She tugged her hat down tight and limped to her horse. The wound on her leg was bothering her and Rae's concern was growing. Krista's jeans were dirty and a stain had started to spread on the knee. Rae knew she would have to insist on cleaning it later that evening.

As her thoughts and eyes remained on Krista, Cody came riding up from the front once again. "Doc, I think there's something you should see."

"What's wrong?"

He slowed his horse and squinted. "You better come have a look for yourself."

Rae waved Frank over. "I need you to pull the horses for a while."

"You got it."

She helped him tie on the supply horses and then she took off, following Cody along the side of the creek to a heavy wooded area close to the neighboring ranch's property.

"I was riding ahead," he said as she came up next to him, "checking the trail when I heard it. I couldn't figure out what it was."

They were off the trail now, and from the tall grass ahead, Rae heard the high-pitched whines of an animal. Cody drew back on the reins as the sound grew louder. He slipped from his horse and waited for Rae to do the same. They approached slowly, and by the sound, Rae knew what she would find nestled in the high grass. Rae could smell her but couldn't yet see her. "Where is she?"

"Over here." Cody moved along the fence several yards to a disturbed patch of grass. A female coyote lay dead, her foot held captive in a steel trap. Her pup, a dirty brown ball of fur, scampered away as they knelt.

"God almighty." Rae knelt, overcome with emotion. "If I've told them once, I've told them a thousand times. No more steel traps." She swatted away the flies and the stench.

"I didn't think it was legal to use those anymore."

Rae stood, scanning the surroundings for the orphaned pup. "It's not. But ranchers are using them to kill off bobcats and coyotes. Protecting their herd and animals at any cost."

She found the little coyote scurrying through the grass and picked him up. He yelped in fear, and she laughed as she held his writhing body up for examination. She checked his baby teeth and felt along his distended belly and prominent ribs. "He's malnourished, but otherwise healthy." A scar ran across his brow and the hollow of the eye socket. "He's missing an eye."

The wound was somewhat healed over so it appeared to have happened sometime before its mother was caught in the trap. She ran her fingers through the matted fur on his forehead. It looked as though he had been in the jaws of a predator and had somehow escaped with his life, losing an eye in the process.

"What are we gonna do with him?" Cody asked.

Rae held him close. "We can't leave him. He's too young to fend for himself, not to mention the eye." She sighed. "We'll have to bring him with us." She carried him to her horse, her nose curling up at the stench. The defenseless pup had obviously been rubbing up against and hiding under his dead mother. "Cody, hand me some water, will you? And I've got a small bottle of hand soap in the saddle bag."

They bathed the coyote as best they could. He drank for a while and then continued to lap at the water as they poured it over him. Beneath his fur Rae could better see the healing wounds he'd suffered from his encounter with the predator. For his age and size, he'd been through a lot. It was a miracle he had survived at all.

She took a blanket and dried him. His honey-colored fur was thick and healthy, his ears on the smaller side due to his age. He grumbled as she worked on him, then yawned and lay down, too weak to do much else.

"We need to get some food in him." She dug through her saddle bag for some soft jerky. Tearing it into small pieces, she fed him and was relieved to see him eat heartily. He chewed as best he could, moving his head as if the meat were alive and he was afraid it would fly out of his mouth.

Rae's insides warmed at the sight of the tough little guy. He was trying hard, seemingly unwilling to give up, but he was weak and undernourished. She'd address his wounds once they hit camp. The next few nights would decide his fate.

The wind carried the scent of decay to her once more, and she fetched the handheld radio she kept strapped to Shamrock. "Dwight, you there? Come back."

Static crackled for a long moment before he responded. "Go ahead, Doc."

"I need you to call the Singers and tell them they've got a dead coyote to bury just beyond their fence line at Sidewinder Creek. They should know exactly where. It's where they set the steel trap."

"Ten-four. Will do."

"Thanks, Dwight."

Of course she knew confronting the ranchers about the traps would do no good. They would just deny responsibility and the brutal practice would continue. She knew these particular ranchers well. They were older and set in their ways. She'd had this talk with them before, when she'd caught them illegally trapping and killing bobcats. The drought had affected the wildlife as well as the ranchers, causing the animals to seek food in places they normally wouldn't. The ranchers, low on funds and cowhands, took to the ultimate measures of protecting their livestock. It was a bad situation for all, but killing off the wildlife was no answer.

Frustrated, Rae returned to the dead coyote and shimmied open the trap with her knife. She removed it and wrapped its jaws shut with rope before placing it in her leather satchel. At the very least the ranchers would be down one trap. She had already made up her mind to report them to the authorities.

Rae returned to Cody and took the cub from him. She held the scrappy little coyote up, smiling at his puppy breath. His eye was drifting closed and she knew he needed his rest if he was going to battle through the next few days. She lowered him to the grass, then slipped her arms into a denim button-down shirt and fastened the buttons halfway up. Tucking the shirt in, she climbed up on Shamrock and asked for the pup. Cody lifted him to her and she placed him inside the denim to rest against her stomach. He snuggled close, enjoying the tight quarters, and then rested his head to sleep.

Rae and Cody turned their horses and headed back to the trail, the little coyote riding like a baby kangaroo in its savior's pouch.

CHAPTER FIFTEEN

K rista was still pretending not to care about Rae and whatever might be going on with Candace when the group stopped to set up camp for their fourth night. The sky was bright orange and pink with countless purple and white clouds stretching across the horizon. The evening brought the return of the cooling breeze, and she shivered as it blew against her sunburnt arms.

Rae had returned, and everyone's attention was on a mysterious bundle in her shirt. Seizing the opportunity to escape while her guests were distracted, Krista grabbed a towel and a change of clothes and walked a good ways down the creek. Thanks to her childhood days on the ranch, she knew the creek like the back of her hand and easily found a good place to cool off. When she was alone and out of sight, she pulled off her dusty clothes and waded into the water carrying bio-safe soap. Gasping at the wonderful chill, she walked out to where the water deepened, covering just above her waist. The wound on her knee stung sharply but she didn't care. She dunked her head and bent her legs so her entire body was submerged. God, it felt good to bathe.

After washing herself, she floated on her back beneath the gloriously colored sky. She was smiling in delight when something startled her, a sound that did not belong in the perfect tranquility of the moment. Krista planted her feet on the creek bed and narrowed her eyes, staring into the heavy brush beyond the bank. Because the light was fading fast, she couldn't make out anything specific, but she swore something moved in the shadows. Suddenly anxious, she waded from the water and dressed quickly in her sweats, eyes trained on her surroundings.

To her surprise and jealous dismay, when she got back to the camp she found the group still focused on Rae and whatever it was she held in her arms. Krista stayed away and busied herself setting up her tent. A few minutes later, Howie appeared and began to help her make the fire.

As he lit the logs, Krista was unable to pretend disinterest any longer. "What's going on over there? With Rae and Cody?"

Howie grunted and spit in the dirt, his dislike for Rae very apparent. "They found something out there earlier."

"An animal?" Krista could hear Candace declaring how cute something was.

"I reckon. Cody said something about a trap."

Howie's eyes traveled up and down her body and she hugged herself, aware and uncomfortable. When he grinned ever so slightly, she felt her body grow cold. *Could he have seen me?* Suddenly she felt sick, but he didn't seem to notice. He met her gaze and his blue eyes looked hazy and unfocused, as if there was no soul inside. Krista shuddered, unsure if she should confront him, but she didn't want to be near him any longer and walked away, leaving him to set up camp on his own.

Absently, she strolled over to Dollar. If the light was better she could practice her roping some more. She'd done much better today, managing to rope a few calves after many tries. She'd forgotten just how much she enjoyed it. The rough feel of the rope, the earthy scent of the cattle, the dirt on her skin; it all brought back memories of a world all but lost to her, and experiences she'd missed more deeply than she knew.

Krista ran her hand down the muscles of Dollar's neck and the horse responded by snorting softly. She rested her cheek against the warm fur and drew a deep breath. Things could be worse, she supposed. Whatever was going on with Rae and Candace, at least the guests were getting the adventure they'd paid for, and they seemed to be having a good time. She jerked her head up as she heard someone clear their throat.

"Dr. Jarrett." It was difficult to keep her tone businesslike but she had to keep her distance. Befriending the attractive woman had caused her a lot of pain.

Rae stepped closer and looked down at the little bundle of fur in her arms. "I thought you'd want to meet him."

Krista's breath hitched as she caught sight of the little animal asleep in Rae's arms. She let out a soft sigh of caring and her hand came up to touch her throat. "Is that a puppy?"

"It's a coyote. Come and meet him." Rae offered the pup to her in outstretched arms.

He was warm and fluffy and Krista held him to her face where she inhaled his soapy scent. "He's had a bath."

Rae chuckled, the sunset gleaming in her hazel eyes. She seemed pleased that Krista was once again speaking to her. Krista felt her face warm and immediately tried to keep her own smile in check. She wished Rae didn't have such an effect on her. Even though she was angry and jealous over Candace, she couldn't help being happy that Rae was standing there wanting to share something with her.

"Cody and I cleaned him up best we could," Rae said.

Krista held the pup on her forearm, allowing him to sleep, stroking the fur along his head and back. "You found him?"

"He was the only one left." Rae's voice lowered in sadness. "His mother had been caught in a steel trap and…"

"Oh, my God. That's awful."

"It was pretty bad. This little guy somehow made it through. I think he's been sleeping under the carcass, staying warm and sheltered that way."

"That's so sad." Krista wrapped him closer, moved by the feel of his soft breathing against her skin.

Rae reached out and touched the coyote, running her hands over his scabbed wounds. "He's beat up something awful. Missing an eye."

Krista felt the blood drain from her face. "He's missing an eye?"

Rae nodded. "See these wounds here?" Krista looked under Rae's fingers. "Something had a hold of him and he got away. He lost his eye in the process."

"Jesus," Krista breathed. Animal suffering was one thing she could not handle. On any level. The puppy stirred as it caught Rae's scent. He raised his head and started whining. Krista lifted him up, looking into his adorable face. The wound came down over his eye socket like a jagged scar. She held him to her chest and kissed him. "Shh, you're safe."

Upon feeling her heartbeat, he quieted and licked her chin. Laughing, she glanced up and caught Rae watching them, a powerful look in her eyes and a redness tinting her high cheekbones.

"Sorry, it's just that you're so good with him." Rae stared a bit longer and then glanced away. "Anyway, I was going to treat his wounds and thought I would take care of yours as well."

Krista allowed the slow grin to spread on her face. She could tell Rae was nervous at having spoken her true motives. "Very clever, Dr. Jarrett."

Rae returned the grin and seemed to relax a little bit more. "I thought so."

Krista put some direct pressure on her leg, feeling it out. She flinched at the pain as it shot straight up her.

"It still hurts, doesn't it?"

Krista thought about fibbing but decided Rae wasn't stupid. "Yeah."

"It hurts worse than before, doesn't it?"

Krista narrowed her eyes. "Does always being right and calling people on their fabrications give you a sense of satisfaction?"

Rae kept her smile. "Of course it does."

"I thought so."

Rae tugged at the strap across her chest and brought her medical satchel from her back to her front. "Let's sit over here." She led the way to a fallen log and Krista sat carefully, puppy still in hand.

"Go ahead and hang on to him," Rae said. "I'll do you first."

Krista was about to nod in agreement when she caught Rae flushing furiously. "What?" she asked.

"Nothing, I just meant I would look at you first."

Krista almost burst out laughing. "I understood what you meant."

Rae's embarrassment spread up to her ears, reddening them. "I didn't want to be rude. You've been so mad…" Her voice trailed off. "I just didn't want to be rude."

At that moment, Krista wanted nothing more than to reach out and touch Rae's face. The vulnerability she saw there overwhelmed her. The coyote whimpered in her arms, distracting her, and she calmly shushed him and rocked him gently. He settled down again as Rae bent and washed her hands and then pushed up the pant leg. Krista's eyes traveled up her lean, strong arms to her small breasts and then settled on the mark on her neck. Once again the hot rush of bitter jealousy stung her throat. She was about to confront Rae about Candace when Rae touched the wound.

"Ouch!" Krista cried out in astonished pain and jerked away, scaring the pup.

"Hurts that bad?" Rae looked concerned.

Krista calmed the puppy and set her jaw. "You surprised me is all. I'm ready now."

Rae wet the wound with clean water and gently started to wipe away the fresh blood. Krista watched her, doing her best not to wince. Rae inched closer and closer and blotted at the wound. She poured on more water and retrieved new cotton.

"When did you pull off the bandages?"

"Shortly after we started out this morning. It was hurting and they were loose."

Rae absorbed the information without expression. "When did you bathe?"

"About thirty minutes ago."

Rae was concentrating intently. "I need to clean this real good," she said. "It's going to hurt."

Krista nodded and held her breath. Rae went from blotting to rubbing, adding more water to reduce the pain. She blew on the wound as Krista clenched her eyes. The sensation startled her and even though she was hurting like hell, she felt aroused at the cool blowing of Rae's breath.

"What are you doing?" she managed, unable to control her racing heart.

Rae looked puzzled then embarrassed. "I'll stop."

Krista watched her. The confidence with which she held herself was gone, replaced by someone eager to accommodate and even apologize needlessly. "Why are you being so nice?"

Rae stopped the blotting, pausing. "I'm always nice. You haven't exactly given me a chance."

Krista laughed softly, knowing she was right.

Rae opened the bottle of peroxide. "I'm worried about you."

"Aha. See I knew there was an underlying reason. All to get at my leg." She laughed again. "Even bringing me a puppy. You're good, Doc. Very good."

Rae soaked the wound with the peroxide. "Whatever it takes." She wiped softly at first but then harder. "Hang on to him tight. This is going to be bad."

Krista clenched her jaw as Rae spread open the half-healed wound.

The whimpers came from her and not the coyote as blood and pus ran down her leg.

"Just as I feared. It's infected." Rae held the wound open and poured in the peroxide.

"Jesus, that hurts," Krista breathed, burying her face in the pup's fur.

"I know. I'm sorry." Rae looked at her, empathy pooled in her eyes. "I need you to be strong one more time. I need to wipe out the wound."

Krista nodded. She couldn't summon the breath to speak.

With clean, saturated gauze, Rae held open the red wound and wiped it out. Krista groaned in pain and she saw little white floaters drift in front of her eyes.

"Look at me." Rae held Krista's shoulders. "Are you okay?"

Krista focused on the hazel eyes. She felt light-headed. "Yeah."

"The bad part's over." Rae blotted the wound dry and applied antibiotic cream. Then she closed it with butterfly bandages and wrapped it all up with lots of gauze and Ace bandaging. She lowered Krista's pant leg. "I want you to wear sweatpants tomorrow. It'll be easier on the bandages."

Krista nodded, too drained to argue.

Rae once again cleaned her hands. "Okay, let's have a look at the little guy."

Krista held him out, a look of worry stinging her face. "You're not going to hurt him, are you?"

Rae smiled at the concern. "No. I cleaned the wounds pretty good while bathing him. I just want to apply some cream."

Krista stroked him as Rae gently applied the same antibacterial cream she'd just used. The pup barely moved, too tired and too comfortable to care. Krista smiled down at him, her hardened heart won over.

"Krista?" Rae said softly.

"Yeah?"

Rae looked so beautiful, so strong and alive, bronzed from the sun and dirty from the hours on the trail. Krista wanted to pull off her ball cap and kiss her, mark or no mark. She could love her better than Candace, and she'd prove it.

"I think you should head back to the ranch."

The words slammed the daydream from Krista's head. "What?"

"Your wound is infected and it needs to be cleaned and stitched."

Krista flicked a hand toward the medical supplies. "So stitch me up and give me a shot."

Rae removed her ball cap and ran her fingers through her dark hair in frustration. "I don't want to do that, Krista."

"Why not?"

Rae stood and said nothing.

"Why not?" Krista demanded.

"Because I can't stand to see you in pain, okay?"

Krista clamped her mouth shut, taken aback. "Oh," was all she could say.

"Just cleaning your wound is hard enough on me. You may not like me, but torturing others is not something I'm into."

Krista inwardly cringed at the words. "I told you, I don't dislike you."

"Really?" Rae stood and lifted the medical bag, her stoicism back full-fledged. "You mean you're that rude to everyone? Even people you like?"

Krista grimaced as she tried to stand as well. Rae had to reach out and grab her shoulders to steady her. Feeling dizzy, Krista nearly fell over. Strong arms embraced her and she caught Rae's scent as her nose touched her neck. It was the same scent she'd smelled the last time they were this close. It was Rae, all sweat, spice, and pheromones. Never before had the scent of a woman stirred her so much. This was raw, this was real, this was powerful.

"I..." Krista started.

"Hey you two!" Adam called out from behind them.

Krista's forehead was resting on Rae's shoulder and she cursed under her breath as she pulled away. Rae's eyes looked like a deep green-brown lake. One she could definitely drown in.

Adam and Candace walked together holding hands, swinging their arms. Adam had his camera around his neck and he gave Krista an apologetic smile for the interruption. Candace released Adam's hand and came bounding up to pet the puppy.

"He's so cute!" She looked expectantly at Krista. "Can I hold him?"

Rae answered for her. "He's really tired. He needs to rest."

Candace dropped her hands. "Oh, shoot. Maybe later." She smiled at Krista. "You know, you have really beautiful hair." She reached out and touched a strand and Krista was about to thank her when she caught the look of fire in Rae's eyes. It so surprised her that she nearly said something. *Is Rae jealous too? Is it because she wants Candace to herself, or because she wants...*

Adam spoke again, interrupting. "I thought we'd come over here to get some shots of Candi."

On cue, Candace stood at the log and removed her shirt as if undressing in front of an audience was the most casual thing in the world. She dropped the garment on the log, exposing her full, round breasts.

"Oh, my God," Krista turned away quickly and caught Rae flushing.

"Sorry, she just does that," Adam said, raising his camera. "We're trying to win a spread in a men's magazine."

"That explains it, then," Krista said, turning back to catch Candace in various poses. The exotic dancer took Krista's rope, which she had obviously found, and draped it across her chest while placing Adam's cowboy hat on her head.

"The lighting is perfect right now," Adam said, clicking away.

"Well, there goes my rope," Krista whispered. "I won't be using that again."

Rae seemed to have heard her, and they walked back toward camp in silence. Krista could feel the jealousy churning in her gut and she knew she wouldn't be able to sleep again that night. The image of Candace's nude body, a body anatomically perfect with full, round breasts—there was no way hers could compare. It stung and it hurt and she hated herself for allowing it to.

"Candace is a beautiful girl," she said, unable to stop herself.

Rae said nothing.

Krista couldn't help herself, intent on self-torture. "Don't you think so?"

They reached camp and stopped by the blazing fire. Rae met her eyes. "Not especially."

Krista stared, unsure she'd heard correctly. "Excuse me?"

But Rae turned away and got busy gathering the pots and pans for dinner. "Look, I really think you ought to head back to the ranch. I can call Dwight and he can come get you on the ATV."

Krista stooped in her tent and placed the small coyote in her sleeping bag, ensuring his warmth. Then she faced Rae and placed her hands on her hips. "I'm *not*," she emphasized strongly, "going back to the ranch. There's only two nights left, and I'm needed here."

She tilted her head a little at her own adamantly stated words. Just a couple of days ago she would've killed for the chance to go back to the ranch. Now all of a sudden she couldn't bear the thought of leaving.

"I'm worried about your wound," Rae persisted as she opened a can of beans. "And you could take the coyote back with you."

Krista laughed, thinking of how much she already cared for the small cub. "You really know how to get to me, don't you?" She groaned inwardly at the statement. *Oh, my God. What did I just say?* Rae was staring at her, looking just as flustered. Krista held up a hand. "I meant the—"

A series of screams echoed through the camp. Krista dropped her hand and stared as Adam and Candace came running toward them. Adam clutched Candace's clothes along with his camera, a look of horror on his face. Krista hurriedly tossed Candace a blanket to cover herself with.

Breathing hard, Rae encouraged Adam to focus. "What's wrong?"

Candace wrapped herself up and trembled as Adam spoke.

"It's Howie. I was shooting Candace out where you guys were, where we were sure of our privacy." He swallowed, still worked up. "And we caught him watching us from the trees."

Candace looked pale in the firelight. "He wasn't just watching…" She met Krista's eyes. "He was masturbating."

Krista nearly fell over. Rae clenched her jaw and stalked over to her horse, where she retrieved her rope. Her eyes flashed dangerously in the firelight.

"If he wants to act like a deviant then he'll be treated like a deviant." She stormed off into the darkness with Cody and Tom hot on her heels.

The rest of the group filtered in, all looking concerned.

"I don't like this," Jenna said. "I don't like this at all." Frank hugged her to him, trying to comfort her.

Candace dipped in her tent to re-dress and Krista did her best to try and remain in control.

The shock was finally wearing off enough so that she could think clearly. "Don't worry. We'll call Dwight and he can come get him."

But the quiet control she was trying to maintain all but shattered when Howie stumbled into camp with Rae pushing him from behind. He cursed and clenched his fist, turning as if he were going to strike her. But upon seeing Cody and Tom step up next to her, he seemed to change his mind.

His malicious eyes focused on Krista. "Tell your *men* to keep their hands off me."

Rae's face was set in stone and Krista knew Howie was lucky he hadn't ended up tied like a hog. Candace emerged from her tent, her face now colored with anger. Before anyone could stop her, she crossed the dirt and slapped Howie hard and loud across the face.

"You sicko!"

Howie's eyes widened in evil intent. He stepped after her but Tom grabbed onto his outer shirt, stopping him.

"Don't you dare touch her," Adam seethed.

Howie laughed, loud and sinister.

Adam refused to back down. "I guess spying on women and jerking off is all you can do with a dick that small."

In an instant, Howie turned and sleeved one arm out of his shirt. "You little faggot!"

He lunged at Adam, his right arm still caught. But he tugged it loose before anyone could reach him and ran, full force, skirting the fire. Just before he reached Adam, he tripped and flew forward, landing so hard the breath was knocked from him. For a few seconds, Howie lay in a lump on the ground, his right arm under him, the black log he'd tripped over near his boot. No one moved. No one spoke.

He stirred and the grunt grew louder. "Ow, shit." He groaned as he managed to sit up. Holding his right arm close to his body, he stared at it in the firelight. "My arm." He held it out a little, a grimace on his face. Krista saw the very noticeable lump in his forearm and knew it was broken. He glared at them all. His whines were childish. "You broke my arm!"

Rae moved to him and knelt to get a better look, but Howie turned away as if he were five years old. "Don't touch me. This is your fault, you...you dyke!"

"Suit yourself." Rae looked to Krista. "He needs medical attention. I'll call Dwight."

"No!" Howie shouted, struggling to stand. "I'm not going

anywhere with you people!" He stumbled in his stance, eyes wide, spit flying. "You can all go fuck yourselves!"

Rae stepped up to him and clenched the soft part of his shoulder tightly. He tried to pull away but she had too strong of a grip. "Sit down over here and shut up." She led him to a camp chair and pushed him down into it. She held him there, gripping tightly, making sure he wouldn't move. He slumped and winced from the pain she was inflicting.

Rae finally released him but wrapped her rope around his waist quickly, securing him to the chair. Panicked, he made a poor attempt to stand and nearly toppled the chair. "You can't do this! You can't tie me up!"

"I'm doing it for your own safety, you idiot. That way you can't break anything else." Rae released him and dug in her medical bag.

"Not to mention the fact that you tried to attack one of the guests," Krista added.

When he saw the small splint Rae had pulled out of her bag, he jerked his arm away and yelled, "Don't touch me! Don't fucking touch me!"

Rae lowered the splint. "It will probably help with the pain."

"No, I said no!"

Rae pressed her mouth closed and motioned for Krista to follow her over to Shamrock. "I'm afraid he'll try and run on foot. And if he does that he'll wind up getting himself lost or killed."

"I can't believe this is happening." She was disgusted. Their first official outing and the one wrangler that showed was a sexual deviant.

"Did you check his background? His work history?" Rae asked, searching her face.

"I checked with his previous employer, but I don't think they ever returned my call. And then there wasn't time…"

Sick with guilt over her failure, Krista was about to walk away when she felt a warm hand on her arm.

"Krista."

She turned and found Rae looking at her softly.

"This isn't your fault. His behavior isn't your fault."

Krista wanted to agree but couldn't. "This *is* my fault. I should've checked him thoroughly."

"Even if you had, there's no guarantee that he's behaved this way on other assignments. If he's worked strictly with cowboys, then no one would've noticed anything."

"Still…" Krista shook her head. "I should've checked." Her voice faded as she met Rae's eyes. "I should've let you help me."

Then she turned and walked away.

❖

Rae wiped her eyes and stared up at the bright moon, wondering why all of a sudden it had turned on them. The call to Dwight hadn't gone well. The old cowboy had been just about to call her himself. Judith was very ill. She'd slipped into a comalike state earlier that afternoon, and they weren't expecting her to make it. Rae had to tell Krista but she wasn't sure how. She returned the radio to its secure place on Shamrock. In her saddle bag she felt the hard plastic of her flashlight and pulled it out.

"Is he coming?" Krista approached.

Rae caught Krista's hand and said, "Come on. We need to talk."

To her surprise, Krista didn't try to pull away. Walking alongside her toward the creek, Rae relished the warmth of her hand and thought for a moment how in another time and place, this could've been a very romantic walk. But reality sank back in and with a heavy heart she led Krista to a large boulder. Setting the flashlight down, she placed her hands on Krista's hips, and said, "I…I'm just going to help you up."

She couldn't help but see the flash in Krista's eyes and hear the quick intake of breath. Flustered, Rae held her tight and lifted, helping her gently onto the rock. *She feels so right in my arms.*

"Thank you," Krista murmured, scooting back and nervously tucking loose strands of her hair behind her ears.

Unsure what to say, Rae hopped up next to her and killed the flashlight, preferring the light of the moon as it danced off the water.

"You have bad news, don't you?" Krista said, resting her hand close to Rae's.

"I'm afraid so."

Krista bowed her head and Rae could hear her breathing change. When she turned to face her, tears pooled in her eyes and ran down her cheeks. "Is she…gone?"

Realizing what she meant, what she thought, Rae felt terrible. "Oh, no. No." Rae reached out and cupped her face, wiping the tears with her thumbs. "I'm sorry, I didn't…she's not gone." Rae paused, searching for a way to comfort without hiding the truth. "But she's not well. She fell into a coma this afternoon. Dwight thinks you should go back."

Krista drew a ragged breath. After the briefest hesitation, she took Rae's hands in her own. "You should come with me. She loves you. Very much. I know she would want you to be there."

Rae felt her own hot tears swell and trickle down her face. "The group…"

Krista shook her head. "I'm not going without you."

River rocks clanged together as someone approached. Rae and Krista dropped their hands to find a fluttering halo of light.

"Doc?" It was Cody.

"Over here." Rae switched on her light to guide him.

The young cowboy moved quickly, balancing himself as best he could. When he reached them he was out of breath. "Sorry to interrupt." The innocence on his face was endearing.

"No problem," Rae said. "What's up?"

"I just finished talking to Dwight. He was calling for you, but you were gone." Cody sighed and shoved a hand into his pocket. "And I spoke with the group and…we all think that you two should head back to the ranch and take Howie with you."

Rae shook her head. "And leave you alone out here?"

Cody smiled. "I've got six wranglers with me, Doc. We know what we're doing."

Krista wiped her cheeks. "They *have* come a long way in a few days' time."

"Honestly, Ms. Wyler, I'd rather ride miles alone with these folks than I would a cowboy like Howie any day. He's lazy and rude. He doesn't follow directions well, not to mention the other stuff."

Rae was still unsure. She slid off the boulder and said, "I don't know, Cody. A lot can happen out here."

But he stood his ground. "We're only two days away from the end of the designated trail. And only a day's ride out from the ranch, if for some reason we need to return sooner. These folks know the situation and they're insisting."

Rae was uneasy but Cody had made a pretty good case. She said, "I guess we could discuss it."

"Will you be able to see the trail well enough to leave in the dark?" he asked.

"The moon's pretty bright. It'll be enough to get by. And if we have to," she looked up and noticed the clouds moving in across the moon, "we'll stop."

Rae was about to speak again, but Krista braced herself and slid to the ground next to her. Taking her arm, she said, "Sounds like we all need to talk."

When they reached the campsite, Adam was serving Howie a hot dog on a plate. He smiled at them as they approached.

"Mr. Grumpypants here was hungry. And I thought since he showed us his wiener…"

Tillie and Jenna laughed, and Rae saw Krista turn away with a smile.

Howie chewed but refused to look at anyone. Upon hearing Adam's statement he lowered what was left of the hot dog and refused to eat.

Krista stood in front of the group, pushed her hair back away from her face, and straightened, trying to show the brave front that Rae knew was faltering.

"Cody tells me that you all are willing to go on without us."

Jenna put down her plate. "We insist that you and Rae go back."

"You're sure?" Rae asked.

Tom replied. "Absolutely. This is a family emergency. We understand, and as Jenna said, we insist."

Adam stood, holding Howie's plate. "I'll take lots of photos so you won't miss a thing." He winked.

Frank spoke next. "Can you handle Howie?"

Rae clenched her jaw as she studied the slumping cowboy. "Oh yeah. I can handle him."

Howie didn't say a word, just stared into the fire.

"You're leaving tonight, then?" Adam asked.

Rae squeezed Krista's hand, leaving the decision up to her.

Krista raised her eyes and nodded. "Thank you all for understanding."

Chapter Sixteen

Krista gripped Dollar tightly as she and the other two riders meandered through the silver shrouded desert. A light, cool drizzle had started and large gray clouds smeared against the dark sky, drifting closer and closer to the moon. Ahead of her, Howie sat slumped on his horse; every once in a while his head would bob and then jerk as he fought off sleep. Ahead of him, nearly out of Krista's line of sight, was Rae, leading them quietly through the night. They'd left the group a few hours before and weariness was weighing Krista down. She supposed it was about time they stopped to get some rest.

Fighting off a yawn, she smiled as the lump in her jacket stirred. The little coyote was sleeping soundly, nuzzled up against her, sheltered from the crisp, cool air. When her thoughts drifted to Judith, Krista wished she could pull the tiny cub out and stroke his fluffy fur, a comfort she desperately needed. Her insides felt like balls of lead rather than individual organs. And whenever she thought of Judith, the balls would rub together and grind painfully inside her, sparking a heated panic. Instinctively, she would heel Dollar, urging him to move faster, wanting and needing to be at the ranch.

It was the goddamn waiting that was eating her alive. She wanted to be there, now. Judith was slipping away, and Krista's biggest fear was not being with her to say good-bye, to be able to tell her how much she'd always loved her and how sorry she was for staying away so long. She wanted to promise that she would sacrifice everything in order to keep the ranch up and running. Riding slowly toward the inevitable was like being trapped in a nightmare. One in which no matter how hard she tried, she couldn't run. The ranch was calling to her, needing her and she just couldn't seem to get there.

A tear slipped down her cheek, cooling nearly instantly against her already moist skin. The past few days had changed her. She no longer even cared about her own business back in Phoenix. The life she had been content living for the past fifteen years seemed foreign to her now, cold and lifeless. There was no love in living for a sales commission, especially when she had no one to share it with. No sense of goodness or enduring value, no sense of *home*. This was what mattered to her now. The beautifully harsh land, her family's land. The ranch and all that it entailed. The cattle, the stables, the horses, and now the task of making sure the spark in her aunt's blue eyes would always be there because she would not let go. She would make this work.

Krista felt her throat grow raw with emotion. Again she hated herself for staying away. She was starting in on herself when Howie stopped his horse ahead of her, and Rae turned Shamrock around and approached.

"I think we'd better stop here for the rest of the night. Dry off and get a few hours' sleep." She slipped off the horse and pulled down Howie's rolled tent.

Krista eased off Dollar and glanced around at the small area of flat desert ground, relatively free of trees and shrubs. Rae tossed her a large flashlight and quickly built a fire and then put up their tents while Krista shone the light for her.

"Leave my tent, Rae. I can do that." Krista felt bad. Rae didn't have to do things for her. She could manage.

Rae dropped the tent and grumbled lightly, "I know, I know, you don't need any help."

"That's right, I don't." But Rae kept working. Krista's frustration mounted. She felt so damn helpless. "Rae."

"Just hold the light for me." Rae seemed to be feeling the strain as well, and Krista clamped her mouth shut, not wanting to argue. Rae set Krista's tent up a good ways from Howie's, knowing she wouldn't want to be anywhere near him.

She glanced at the silent cowboy. He was still on his horse, his useless arm held up like a wounded wing, unable to do much of anything but sit and wait. At least he was sober and not causing a problem.

Steadily, the rain increased in speed and volume, tapping against the fabric of the tents. Krista threw another piece of wood on the fire, hoping its heat would hold out. She could see her breath when she exhaled and she knew the temperature had dropped considerably. This was their coldest night yet.

Tent erect and drumming with raindrops, Rae stood and brushed off her hands.

Krista offered a smile, truly thankful. "You didn't need to do that, but for what it's worth, thank you."

Rae stopped and looked at her as if surprised by the verbal appreciation. "You're welcome."

Her eyes shifted to Howie and the warmth in her expression vanished. She strode over to his horse and helped him down, allowing him to get his feet under him before she stepped back. He resisted her grip even when it kept him upright.

"Tell your *man* to keep his hands off me," he told Krista before disappearing into his tent.

"I don't know why he thinks calling me a man would bother me." Rae moved about Shamrock unperturbed. "I'm more of a man than he'll ever be."

Krista thought about that for a moment. Rae was right. "Me too," she said softly.

The coyote squirmed again and Krista unzipped her jacket and placed him on the ground. She kept him in the beam of her flashlight as he stretched and then relieved himself. Before the rain could penetrate his fur, Krista scooped him back up and took him to her tent, where she set him inside. Then she crossed to Dollar and retrieved her sleeping bag and mat. Once she'd made her bed, she stepped back out, intending to help Rae with her own preparations. But to her surprise, Rae was settling in by the fire, covered in a horse blanket, Stetson pulled down tight to ward off the rain.

"Where's your tent?" Krista asked, shivering in the dropping temperature.

Rae snuggled farther under the blanket. "Can't use it." Her tone was flat, as if she didn't want to talk.

"Why not?"

"It's got holes in it."

"What?" Krista caught sight of it on the ground next to Shamrock.

Rae lifted her head. "Someone put holes in it. Big tears, gashes. Like from a knife."

Immediately, Krista swung her head around to Howie's tent. "The son of a bitch. When did he do it?"

"I don't know. Probably sometime earlier today. Before the Candace fiasco." Rae pulled up her knees and wrapped her arms around them beneath the blanket. "He didn't like me confronting him last night."

"But I had Cody take his knives."

Rae met her eyes. "That probably only pissed him off more. I'm sure he has a pocket knife. One he keeps on him all the time."

"Bastard!" Krista marched to his tent and unzipped the flap. She'd had enough of this asshole. "Howie. Howie!"

He rolled to his side and squinted as she shone the flashlight in his eyes. He had a bottle of aspirin in his hand and what appeared to be a small bottle of brown liquid.

"Get out of this tent," she demanded. "Get out of this tent this instant! You can be the one who sleeps in the rain!"

Krista was about to step closer to him, but a strong hand gripped her arm from outside the tent. She spun around, her breath puffing angrily in the rain.

"Stop," Rae quietly insisted.

"But he—"

Rae held up a hand. "He's paying for it. His arm is very badly broken."

"But your tent, you can't sleep in the rain!"

"I'll be fine." Rae zipped up Howie's tent, adjusted the Stetson, and steered Krista away.

Her calm infuriated Krista. "No. You're sleeping in mine."

Rae began stoking the fire. "No. I need to watch Howie."

"Howie's weak and in pain. He's not going anywhere. You know it as well as I do." Krista shivered from the cold. "Rae, you're sleeping in my tent."

Rae tossed the stoking stick into the flames. "I'll be fine out here."

Krista nearly blurted out curses. Was Rae that repulsed by her? "I know I'm not Candace, but—"

Rae's head snapped up. "What?"

"Look, I won't touch you, I know you and she... You don't have to worry."

Rae straightened from the fire and the rain fell harder and faster. "What are you saying?"

Desperate, Krista crossed to Shamrock and unlatched the guitar. The case was soft and she knew the guitar needed shelter from the rain. Rae watched in silence as Krista carried it toward her tent. She paused at the flap and said, "Get your ass in this tent or you'll never see your guitar again. At least not in one piece you won't. Or," she stumbled searching for threats, "I'll leave it out in the rain."

Rae stared at her for a long while. Her expression was one of calm amusement.

Krista hugged the case closer. "I mean it."

Removing her hat, Rae chuckled and crossed to the tent to stand before her. She reached out and took her guitar. Krista was unable to hold on to it, too lost in the depths of Rae's eyes.

Softly, Rae said, "Okay. Get in the tent, Ms. Wyler."

Krista started to protest but Rae touched her lips with a cool, wet finger.

"Just get in the tent."

Krista felt her eyes drift briefly closed, moved by the gentle touch. When she stooped into the tent the coyote scurried to her feet. She moved to the back and kicked off her hiking boots, allowing the little guy to lick her hands. Rain beat down noisily on the tent and Krista switched on the flashlight as Rae's black-cased guitar entered inside the flaps. Krista took it quickly and tucked it alongside the wall of the tent. Then she watched with mixed emotions as Rae stepped inside, dripping with water.

Krista crawled over and zipped the tent closed and then reached for Rae's hat. "Please, sit," she said, nervous.

Rae was stooped like a soaking-wet giant, shivering. Without a word she sat across from Krista, mindful of the coyote who turned his attention to her, licking at her wet hands. Krista could feel the cold wetness resonating off her and she kicked in, acting without thinking. She tugged off Rae's wet jacket and placed it with the hat. Then she tried to remove her boots but they were laced tight, well-worn ropers. Rae just sat and watched her, face pale, wet dark hair sticking to her skin. She spoke.

"The guitar's sealed in a plastic cover."

Krista glanced up. "Oh." She felt foolish. "I never intended on doing anything to it."

"I know."

"I was just trying to get you to listen to reason."

"I know."

"You play beautifully. That song you're working on…"

Rae looked away. "It's not finished. I didn't realize anyone had heard it." Her face reddened.

Krista spoke quickly. "I didn't catch all of the words, but it sounds nice."

"What you said about Candace—"

"Don't worry about it." Krista focused on unlacing Rae's boot. "It's none of my business."

"You need to know."

Krista swallowed against a suddenly burning throat. "No, I don't." She didn't think she could handle hearing. Not with all the other heartbreaking things on her mind.

"You do."

"No, Rae. Really, I don't."

Rae's hand came to rest over hers, stilling her. "There's nothing going on between Candace and me."

Krista didn't speak. She couldn't. She nearly lost her breath at the intensity in Rae's eyes. Her mind flew and her heart raced. Finally her eyes settled over the dark mark that still bruised Rae's neck. "I don't believe you."

She tried to continue removing the shoe but Rae gripped her hands with both of hers. "I'm telling you the truth."

Krista shivered but not from the cold. Her body was suddenly feeling feverish under Rae's strong hands and intense gaze. She knew Rae was telling the truth, simply because she knew Rae wasn't the type to lie. And she could see it in her eyes. But still, what she had seen that evening kept replaying in her mind. "But I saw you," she whispered, confused.

"You saw what?"

"The other night at the creek. Candace was naked and you were playing your guitar."

Rae squeezed her hands. "No." She shook her head in frustration. "God, you saw that?"

Krista nodded. Rae was upset, but not because she had been spying. Krista sensed something else was bothering her. Seeking a distraction, she lifted the coyote to the head of the sleeping bag. He dug at the material and tunneled his way inside, lying in a fatigued lump under the covers.

"Candace came on to me." Rae's face was sincere and determined.

Krista looked away, hating the thought.

"But I turned her down. She's a guest and I would never do something like that."

"Did you want to?" Krista couldn't help but ask.

Rae reached up and touched just under her chin, turning her head to meet her eyes. "No."

Krista took in a shallow, ragged breath. "The mark on your neck."

Rae's eyes widened. "I have a mark?"

Krista reached out and gently touched the skin on her neck. "Yes, here."

Rae's skin pimpled at the touch and her eyes flashed like lightning. "She was on me, trying...she bit me."

Krista clenched her jaw.

"I had to push her off of me. She wasn't willing to listen at first." Rae looked away suddenly. "That's probably my own fault."

Krista watched her, knowing there was more. "What is?"

Rae rubbed her palms on her damp jeans. "That night I sang for the group. She came in my tent and I...I let her."

Krista felt her face heat with jealousy. "You did?"

Rae closed her eyes. "I was weak and it had been so long." Her voice shook as her eyes came back up under dark lashes.

Krista covered her own mouth with her hand as strange noises arose from her painful throat. "She touched you?"

God, it hurt. It hurt more than anything. To hear it hurt like hell.

Rae's eyes watered. "Yes." She grabbed Krista's hand. "I was worked up and she came in and started touching me and I just lost it."

Krista wiped away the tears that were suddenly there. "Did you touch her?"

"No. Of course not. I don't want her. Aren't you hearing me?" Again she tilted Krista's chin. "That night, the way you looked at me across the fire…I was in my tent and I couldn't get you out of my mind. I was thinking of you, Krista. You're all I think about."

Krista blinked, disbelieving. "Really?"

"Yes." Rae pressed her lips together in seriousness. "I can't sleep, I can't concentrate."

Krista watched her mouth form the words. She felt her warm breath and saw the swirling fires in her eyes and suddenly she knew it was true. All of it. "I've been thinking of you too." Her voice trembled as she let her feelings come tumbling out. "I can't stop. It's driving me insane. And then when I saw you with Candace…I…"

Krista's breath caught as Rae moved toward her, crawling up to her knees. Her strong hand cupped Krista's jaw and her eyes burned in dark green and brown flames. Krista took hold of the hand and kissed the scars from the snakebite slowly and gently, watching in wonder when Rae's pupils dilated.

"Krista," Rae whispered, her warm mouth suddenly covering Krista's.

The kiss was soft and gentle, hot moist lips searching and finding. And then, in an instant, there was a groan and a rush of heat, and the kiss became much, much more. Rae eased Krista down onto her back and lay atop her, suddenly hungry and frenzied. She kissed Krista passionately, tugging on her lips with hot desire and then thrusting with her tongue.

Krista fell back, consumed. Rae was on her, taking her, devouring her. Long and deep and dominant kisses. In her wildest dreams, her fantasy kisses couldn't have been this good. She kissed her back, their tongues swirling, hungry and daring. Krista moaned and clung to her, gasping at the feel of the raw muscles beneath her fingers. Rae tore her mouth away and fastened to her neck, making Krista raise her hips with need. Rae groaned and rubbed a firm thigh into her crotch, knowing.

"Your knee," Rae whispered, worried.

"Fuck the knee," Krista said right away.

Rae laughed against her skin and continued to kiss her.

"Oh, God," Krista rasped, loving the feel of Rae's mouth.

Rae sucked and bit and licked. "Krista," she whispered. "I can't get enough."

Krista clawed up her back and knotted her hands in the damp, dark hair. She inhaled the wet scent of her neck and let her eyes roll back in her head. It couldn't get any better. "You are fucking everything," she whispered, tugging Rae's head back to look into her eyes. The desire she saw stopped her heart. "So beautiful," she whispered. "So strong and fucking beautiful."

She held Rae's face, consumed by all that was her. So wild and free and raw. Rae said nothing, breathing hard, her heart hammering against Krista's chest.

"Kiss me," Krista demanded, unable to wait, lifting herself.

Rae again pushed into her, kissing her hard and deep and long. Krista cried out when Rae moved down her neck to her breasts. Her hands squeezed and pushed up under Krista's shirt and bra, pinching the nipples.

"God, Rae," Krista managed, lifting her head to watch Rae's hot mouth find her. Her long tongue teased the nipples just before her mouth consumed them, sucking and licking and nibbling.

"Oh, fuck." Krista clutched the head of hair and lifted herself again, needing, needing so badly to see.

Rae flicked her tongue and raised her head. Her hands worked furiously, opening Krista's fly. "I need to taste you," she said. "I need it now."

Quickly and a bit roughly, she yanked down Krista's damp jeans to just below her center. Hurriedly, and unwilling to struggle for more, Rae lowered herself and whispered, "Oh yes." She buried her face in the reddish hairs, eyes closed. "I can smell you. Sweet God, it's so good."

She rested her chin on the tight crotch of the jeans and stuck out her tongue for a taste. Again she groaned and opened her eyes.

"Krista," Rae said again, lowering her mouth to feed. She kissed Krista's flesh like she had her mouth. Long and hard, swirling her tongue around and around, touching as much as she could, ravenously claiming her.

Krista clung to her head, watching, breathing heavily. She bit her lower lip and tried to remain quiet, but she was lost in crazy, erotic bliss as Rae worked her flesh, drawing out the raw pleasure with her tongue and lips. She flicked her clit firm and fast and then held it captive, sucking. She worked her heavy and fast, seemingly unable to slow down, unable to get enough.

"Oh, ah, oh, Rae." Krista craned her neck, feeling the wave of pleasure thicken and rise and swell, looming larger and larger. It kept coming, better and better, and Rae wouldn't stop, groaning into her flesh as she fed. Krista gripped Rae's head and clawed at her hair, trying to pull her away. But Rae kept on, pressing herself harder to Krista's flesh. When Rae looked up from between her legs and Krista saw the fierce hunger in her eyes, she completely lost it. The tidal wave of pleasure smashed into her, and her hips were suddenly bucking and her hands were clawing and her soul was bleeding.

"Raaaaae!" she cried out from a strained throat. Lifting herself up off the sleeping bag she held tight, fingers knotted in dark hair, her body undulating, milking the last of the pleasure.

Rae never stopped, she kept on, fastened to her. When Krista finally stopped bucking, Rae tugged furiously at the jeans, pulling them down farther. With strong hands she pushed Krista's thighs apart and lowered herself again. Krista tried to speak, to tell her she was unable to take any more, but Rae merely reached for her hand and kissed it.

"I told you, I can't get enough." She held Krista's hand firmly as she pushed her mouth against her flesh once again. Krista jerked and cried out softly but Rae knew where she was sensitive and went lower, working her tongue down to her opening.

Releasing Krista's hand, she wrapped her own around Krista's hips and lifted her slightly, thrusting her tongue up inside her.

"Oh, my God," Krista rasped, her eyes clenching closed.

Rae swirled around deep inside her and then thrust her tongue harder and harder. Krista tried to keep quiet but the velvet pleasure was stroking her from the inside out. Her cries became wordless and strained as her head tossed from side to side. The drumming of the rain morphed into a steady pulse of a sound, beating like a heart in her ears.

She nearly screamed when Rae pulled away for a second, chin glistening, eyes flashing. "I want to you to come now, Krista. Come with my tongue inside you."

Krista didn't answer. She couldn't. Somehow a squeak escaped her and she nodded. Rae pressed her mouth into her again and then the long, slick, thick magic was back, moving around inside her. Rae held her tight, tongue-fucking her. Krista began to moan and whimper again as the pleasure built, this time on a different sort of wave. It started from her legs and worked its way up into her belly and then into her chest. Her entire body was beating with the slow rhythm of a drum.

Suddenly, as the drum sped up, she needed more, would kill for more. She clamped onto Rae's head and thrust herself upward. "Rae, Rae, Rae," she chanted.

Responding, Rae moved her mouth, maneuvering it so that she could suck all of Krista with her lips while her tongue kept fucking her.

"Oh my…um…" Krista could no longer make noise. Her throat was tight and strained, her whole being pulsing with intense pleasure. She held on to Rae's hair, totally unable to control herself. She thrust and she bucked, she strained and she clawed.

It kept coming and coming, closer and closer. And then she opened her eyes and saw Rae's and it hit. It burst in her chest and spread rapidly throughout her body, everything inside disintegrating, like the biggest, brightest fireworks she'd ever seen. She arched her back and opened her mouth, but no noise escaped. She rocked and rocked, her neck strained as if what was inside needed to drift up out of her mouth like smoke from a spent shell.

She remained like that for what seemed like an eternity. Eventually she stilled and collapsed back onto the sleeping bag. The rain still fell, but it sounded strange and distant. She felt Rae move up her body and she opened eyes that she hadn't realized were closed. Krista looked into her face and her heart ached for her lips. "Come here," she whispered.

Krista fingered Rae's thick hair and then gently pulled her in for a searing, wet kiss. Never before had she tasted herself on another. A lingering spark of hot light fired inside her as her taste mingled with Rae's mouth. Tugging her away, Krista looked into her eyes and felt her own well with tears. She was so moved and she couldn't understand why. Overwhelmed, her body warmed under Rae and she knew she never wanted to be anywhere else. Suddenly she understood. This was love. Rae was love.

"Rae, I…" and the tears tightened around the words. Rae's eyes too began to water and suddenly Krista felt her pull away. Krista tried to hold on but Rae gripped her wrists and pressed them down.

Her eyes were pained and her voice strained. "I can't. You don't understand but I, I just can't." She moved away and grabbed her jacket and hat. Stumbling up, she unzipped the tent and turned one last time to meet her eyes. "I'm sorry." And then she was gone, into the cold, wet night.

The hot, stinging tears flowed freely then as Krista pulled up her jeans and curled into a ball next to the coyote. She cried and cried, mirroring the patter of the rain on the tent. Feeling too vulnerable and hurt to go after her, Krista forced her eyes closed and did her best to close the wounds inside. Just when she'd thought nothing in the world could feel better, the earth had tilted on her, leaving her all alone with nothing but darkness, confusion, and pain.

❖

The gray light of dawn found Rae slumped near her horse, rain drizzling down her Stetson onto her shirt and jacket. The cold and wet had long ago turned into uncontrollable shivers that rocked her body every minute or so. She had stopped fighting the weather and the bleak emotions that had driven her out into it. Overwhelmed, she simply let the mist consume her until she felt dead and dark inside.

There were no more tears, only the raw soreness of her throat and the dull ache in her chest. Twenty different times she'd risen to go to Krista, to hold her in her arms, to tell her how she felt, to crawl into her soul and be sheltered there. But she couldn't. There was no shelter, no escape. Ever. Love was a mirage that could crumble and blow away in the breeze in the blink of an eye.

The feelings she had for Krista—they were insurmountable, and she feared that if she let them, they would eventually hurt her and take her to a place where this time there would be no coming back. She couldn't bear to lose again. The way she felt about Krista, if anything should ever happen to her, she would never recover. Ever.

Her breath hitched as she looked up into the pinpricks of rain, remembering that kind of hurt all too well.

It was raining, a steady fall that had softened into a misty drizzle. She held the vehicle door open for Shannon, the country music from the club a low drone in the near distance.

"I can drive, baby," Shannon slurred, leaning into Rae, trying unsuccessfully to plant a kiss on her mouth. "It's my Jeep."

Her teeth found Rae's neck and she bit a little roughly.

Jerking, Rae gently pushed her away, smelling the wine on her breath resonating through the heavy drizzle. "I know. But you've had a little too much to drink."

Shannon stepped up and collapsed on the passenger seat, laughing as Rae placed her feet inside. "I love you, baby," she told Rae with a sloppy smile.

Rae said nothing, leaning over to strap on her seat belt. Shannon

had been declaring her love for over a week and Rae never knew
what to say. She cared about Shannon but she knew it wasn't love.
Was it? No. She was certain it wasn't. Love was powerful, passionate,
and overwhelming. What she felt for Shannon was different. It wasn't
intense, at least not in the way it should be. Shannon was young and
aimless, sexual and wild. It had even been fun at first. But now, now it
was taking an unhealthy turn. She had to talk to her.

Rae closed her door and rounded the Jeep. She got into the driver's
seat, closed the door, and strapped on her seat belt. She brought the
engine to life and shifted into reverse. She hadn't driven the Jeep since
Shannon had purchased large mud tires. The Jeep now sat a good
two feet higher and Rae found that she liked the extra height as she
maneuvered out of the parking lot.

They drove in silence for a while until Shannon reached over and
grabbed Rae's knee. "I want you, baby."

Rae sighed. She'd learned that frequent use of the word "baby"
meant Shannon was plenty drunk. She removed the hand from her knee
and adjusted the windshield wipers as the rain intensified. "We need
to talk."

Shannon seemed to ignore her, leaning forward to turn up the
radio. She sat back and smiled and unbuckled her seat belt. "Shush,
baby." Her hands found their way back to Rae, cupping her breast and
squeezing her knee.

Rae swatted her away, trying to focus on the road. "I'm serious,
Shannon. I think we need some time apart."

Silence.

Rae stared through the slippery image of the windshield. She
switched off the radio and listened to the whine of the wipers as they
worked overtime.

"You're wrong." Suddenly Shannon was speaking very clearly.
Rae could feel the venom in her voice and the heat in her stare.

"I've been thinking about it for a while," Rae said.

"I don't care how long you've been thinking about it. You're
wrong." Shannon reached for Rae's hand, pulling it off the steering
wheel. "I love you."

Rae shook her head. "Shannon, you're young. This isn't love."

"I'm young, so what? That means I don't know what love is? I
know more than you, Rae."

Her voice was high and sharp, a warning. Rae couldn't take it *anymore. She couldn't bear one more fight, one more heated exchange of meaningless words. "You see? This, this is what's wrong. The fighting. We do nothing but fight."*

Shannon squeezed her hand. "You don't listen to me, that's why! And you hang around Lindsay, and she's just waiting for us to break up so she can get in your pants."

Rae jerked her hand away. "That's enough. Don't talk about Lindsay like that."

"I bet Lindsay put you up to this tonight. She did, didn't she?" Shannon clutched at Rae's head. "Look at me! Look at me, damn it!"

"Shannon, knock it off!"

"Pull over!" Shannon seized the steering wheel. "I want you to look at me!"

Shannon jerked the wheel to the right, and the Jeep whipped across the slick road as Rae desperately pumped the brakes and fought for control of the steering wheel. The tires shrieked and a powerful force threw the Jeep off balance as it collided onto the earthy bank on the side of the road. Shannon screamed as they flipped once, twice, three times. With a loud smack, the Jeep stopped rolling and shuddered.

Rae groaned, her eyes wide open. She was hanging, strapped in her seat, the Jeep upside down.

"Oh, hell." She hurt everywhere. She tried to move but her bones felt like mush under her skin. Her hand found her head, where she felt blood. "Help," she croaked.

She heard clicking and smelled the strong scent of spilt liquid on the hot engine. She smelled gasoline and coughed against the black smoke. Her head throbbed and she fought hard against the darkness that threatened to consume her. Shafts of light shone through the vehicle at different angles and she heard doors slamming shut. Someone was coming to get them out. She tried to yell but her ribs screamed back. Sobs racked through her, paining her even more. Frantically she stared at the passenger seat. It was empty. "Shannon!"

She coughed as the smoke stung her lungs. She heard keys jangling and then there was a man kneeling at the open passenger door, looking in, a large bundle of keys dangling from his belt.

"Are you okay?"

Rae tried to focus through the sobs and smoke, staring at the swinging keys. "Shannon," she finally managed, pointing.

"There's someone else?"

"Yes, please, find her."

"Can you get out?" He started to crawl inside but Rae snapped at him.

"I can get out! Please, go find Shannon!"

He disappeared outside the vehicle and Rae licked her bloody lip. Her head felt like it was about to burst. With trembling hands, she managed to release the seat belt buckle and quickly used her arms to break her fall. She groaned in pain and lay on her side while the blood rushed from her head down to her body.

Shannon.

She heard the man outside, yelling as more car doors slammed. "We need help over here!"

More slants of lights pierced the darkness and Rae could hear the rain pinging off the Jeep. Slowly, she crawled to the open passenger door. She made it to the wet grass and collapsed in pain and fatigue. Sleep. She just wanted to fall asleep. She blinked, fighting it. In the distance she heard more voices.

"How many?"

"Two. One conscious in the Jeep, the other here." "She conscious?"

"No. She's gone."

Rae trembled under her soaking-wet jacket, numbly aware of the sun rising to shine through the rain and the light changing the color of the earth around her. She watched Krista climb from her tent, holding the baby coyote. Her face said it all.

Love hurt. Always and forever.

CHAPTER SEVENTEEN

Krista gripped her saddle horn, frustrated and burned. She'd exposed herself, and the rejection hurt. With other women she'd always been in control, never giving pieces of herself, never letting anyone in. With Rae, she'd gone against all she believed. She'd let her in before she even knew what she was doing. Allowing her to kiss her, touch her, make her come like there was no tomorrow. So hurried, so intense, like Rae was dying to get at her. It was wonderful.

And then she was gone.

And now...Krista fought off tears. And now she was paying for it.

She glanced sideways at Rae. She was still soaking wet from her night outdoors and shivering occasionally as she rode. Her red-rimmed eyes and obvious suffering only made Krista more upset, and despite her own confusion and pain, she wanted so badly to reach out and touch Rae's face. She wanted to understand what was happening. Had she somehow caused this pain? If so, how? She'd thought their passion in the tent was mutual. She *knew* it was. She'd seen it. She'd felt it. She'd felt *Rae*.

But then, rejection. Rae had up and left, saying she couldn't. Couldn't what? Couldn't touch her? Couldn't feel anything for her? What could possibly be so awful that Rae would choose to sit out in the rain all night long rather than share Krista's tent?

Krista thought about all Tillie had gone through with her divorce. You just truly never knew another person. Something about Rae's behavior didn't add up, and Krista was determined to find out what was not being said. But now was not the time. Up ahead in the distance, the ranch was finally in sight. Her own hurt feelings and the strain between her and Rae would have to wait. Her aunt needed her.

Krista straightened her back and increased her trot to a canter. She felt a pang of guilt about leaving Rae behind, stuck with Howie, who could not ride single-handed at any reasonable speed. Even though Rae's behavior confused and hurt her, Krista still felt for her. Love, she was quickly learning, could not be controlled. Krista glanced over her shoulder as she gained distance from the other two riders, and tried again to dismiss her worries that Howie might have heard them making love. He was passed out when she'd opened his tent at first light, having finished the whiskey and half the aspirin in his bottle. No one could have stayed awake after swallowing all of that.

She leaned down and patted Dollar's neck, aware the horse was tired and had traveled a long distance over the past few days. She was asking a lot of him, having him complete the journey at a pace, but she dug her heels in and sustained the canter as they covered the final few miles to Wyler ranch. They were both breathing hard when she pulled back on the reins and slowed to a walk before halting a few yards from the house.

Krista led Dollar to the stables and made him comfortable. Relief flooded through her as she stepped out into the weak sunlight and rounded the long front porch. She paused there and took in the quiet of the ranch, so glad she was back. The rain had stopped and the dew sparkled like diamonds on the grass. Only the occasional call from Pepe the rooster shattered the calm. At her feet the little coyote hopped and scampered about, wide-awake and raring to go. Krista decided to call him Jagger. It fit with his jagged scar and the jagged tear she seemed to have in her heart.

She couldn't wait to kiss Judith on the cheek and sit next to her with a hot cup of coffee, letting her know all about the first cattle drive for their new venture. Her smile quickly vanished as she remembered what Rae had said. Judith was in a coma.

The darkness in her head only intensified as she stepped up on the porch and found Clinton snoring in the rocking chair. A half-empty bottle of tequila sat in his lap and his skin felt cold as Krista touched his cheek with the back of her hand. A loud creak broke the silence, and Sonja came hurrying out the front door, a thick blanket in her hands.

"Krista!" A warm hand closed around Krista's arm and Sonja gave her a long, thankful look. "I'm glad you're back."

"Me too." Krista hardly knew what to say. The kindness in Sonja's eyes threatened to make her break down entirely from exhaustion and sorrow. "Thank you."

Sonja tsked as she tucked the blanket in around Clinton and scooped up the tequila bottle to take inside. "He can't handle this," she said in a voice broken up with sadness. "Every time he sees her it's a fresh wound. It's hurting him terribly. Now he's taken to the drink."

They watched him snore softly, head back, mouth open. Krista closed her eyes as the pain swept through her. It would be so easy to break down, to crumple in a heap and pretend none of this was happening. Her mind drifted back in time to other mornings, when she'd risen early to do chores with Uncle Clinton. The fresh scent of the morning, the tending to the animals, the things he'd taught her, she recalled it all with a great fondness and wished she could go back in time.

Krista sighed. Forcing herself back to the present, she picked up Jagger and followed Sonja into the house. She sat the pup on the rug in the living room and he immediately began wandering around, growling and pouncing at objects that were strange to him.

"He's a feisty little fella." Sonja chuckled over her coffee mug. "I can fix some breakfast for you," she offered.

"No, thanks." Krista stared down the hallway, knowing her aunt was in her bedroom, in a coma.

She tried to swallow but couldn't. Her throat felt like a vise. She'd been anxious and had hurried to get to the ranch all night and well into the morning. Now she was here and her feet felt glued to the floor. She was afraid to go down the hallway. She was afraid to see her aunt lying helpless and unconscious in that bed. Judith had always been so strong and vibrant. To see her pale and withered away, caught in a world between this life and the next—Krista suddenly wasn't sure if she could face it.

Her fears were momentarily pushed aside when Rae and Howie walked in the front door. Rae closed it behind them and placed her duffel bag on the floor.

"What in the world?" Sonja smacked her on the upper arm. "Go take a hot shower before you catch your death!" She stopped Rae's mumbled protest with a pointing finger. "Don't even think about arguing with me."

Rae remained where she was, staring at Krista.

Sonja frowned, swinging her gaze suspiciously between the two of them. "Something I should know?"

They were saved from having to answer when Howie groaned loudly and clutched his arm like he was about to keel over. Sonja responded to this bid for attention by motioning for him to sit at the table. She set down her mug and rolled up his sleeve. Krista turned away from the prominent bulge under his skin.

"Looks pretty bad, cowboy," Sonja said. "How 'bout some coffee?"

Howie nodded. "Yes, please." Suddenly his manners were back.

Krista thought it was a good thing because Sonja would've knocked him clear across the room if he'd smarted off to her. Rae was on the phone in the kitchen, speaking too softly for Krista to hear. When she hung up, she said, "Ambulance is on the way. They're going to take you to the local hospital."

Howie didn't respond, just sipped his coffee.

Krista stared at the back of his head, unable to stand the sight of him, injured or not. She wouldn't be able to relax until she'd seen him get into the ambulance. "I will send you your paycheck, paying you for the work you *did* do," she said. "I will also be filing a police report on your behavior."

He whipped his head up but Rae closed her hand in on his shoulder, her jaw clenched. "I think you owe Ms. Wyler an apology for all the trouble you caused."

Howie seemed stubborn for a few seconds, but then relented. "I'm sorry."

Rae released her grip and crossed the room to collect her duffel bag. Krista watched her disappear down the hall and heard the soft click of the guest bathroom door closing. Still hurting and confused, Krista turned back to her coffee and found Sonja focused on her. She didn't speak but her eyes honed in on Krista's neck.

Krista raised her hand to her neck, remembering the aggressive lovemaking. She didn't know Rae had left a mark.

Sonja's mouth turned down and she sat down at the table. "Mmm-hmm," she let out, making Krista blush. But Sonja let her off the hook, at least for the time being, instead shifting her focus to the slumped cowboy. "So what's your story, John Wayne? I heard you can't keep your brain in your pants."

Howie narrowed his eyes. "I don't know what you're talking about."

"Isn't that just like a man? They want nothing more than for the entire world to focus on their penis, but then when they get caught whipping it out, suddenly they don't have one."

"I'm sick and tired of hearing all you women talk," Howie grumbled.

Krista glared at him. "Well, you're in luck. Because if you've got prior offenses, my little report will send your ass to jail, where there's nothing but men."

She didn't wait for a response. She'd allowed Howie to distract her long enough, and she was impatient with herself for procrastinating. She stood.

"You ready to see her now?" Sonja asked.

Krista looked down at Jagger and felt her eyes begin to water. She wanted to move, but her feet remained where they were.

Sonja touched her arm. "Go on, honey. You need to do this. Just go on in there and sit next to the bed. Hold her hand and talk to her. She can hear you." She paused, gazing deep into Krista's eyes. "She's waiting for you."

Krista nodded. Not wanting to cry in front of anyone, she walked quickly away, concentrating on putting one foot in front of the other. As she entered the hallway she passed by the guest bath where she could hear Rae showering, but she kept her eyes forward. The morning light drifted into the hall, seeping in from windows of the other rooms. Krista was surprised to find Judith's bedroom equally bright, the blinds open, the white light warming the room. She stood at the door for a long while, letting her eyes sweep around the familiar furnishings and colorful paintings. In her mind, she'd imagined a darker, sadder space, with a funeral feel to it. But the room was tidy and warm with fresh flowers on the dresser. It smelled like it always had, like Clinton's Stetson cologne.

Slowly, and fighting back tears, she released a shaky breath and allowed her gaze to settle on her aunt. Judith was lying on her back in the bed, covers tucked in around her, her long braid trailing down her shoulder. Her breathing was slow and steady, her skin pale but her face peaceful. She looked as if she were taking a nap.

Krista approached carefully, afraid to wake her. She covered her aunt's hand with her own and bent to kiss her. Her skin was soft and cool. Next to her, the IV machine worked like a silent guardian.

Krista whispered, "Hello, Aunt Judith." She pulled up the chair from the wall and sat down. Holding her aunt's hand, she said, "I'm back from the trail. Our first run is a big success." She smiled, trying hard to sound positive. Her voice shook as she fought off tears.

"The group, they're still out, Cody's with them and they've all done real well." She watched Judith's face for some sort of reaction but saw nothing. Pained, she rose and tucked in Judith's blanket. Keeping busy seemed easier than sitting and staring and...expecting. "I think the whole thing's going to be a success. It's really going to work, Aunt Judith. As soon as you wake up you can see for yourself."

The words burned her throat. She lowered the back of her hand to stroke Judith's face. The beautiful, sparkling blue eyes didn't open. The witty laugh didn't rise up from her throat. Krista fought back sobs. "You will wake up, won't you, Aunt Judith? You have to."

Krista broke down then, the sobs squeezing her ribs. Oh God, she was too late. Judith wasn't responding, she was already gone. Krista covered her mouth to try and stifle the sobs and sank down into the chair. She kept talking, desperate, hoping. "And I did just fine on the horse. I know we both had our doubts but you were right, all I had to do was climb back up in the saddle."

She brought Judith's hand to her face and closed her eyes. Suddenly, she could no longer pretend. She was scared. Terrified. "I need you," she confessed. "All these years...I've always needed you."

She squeezed the limp hand and remembered how strong it had always been. Hot tears flamed up from her belly to her chest to her throat. She held the hand clinging to life and cried so hard it hurt. All the guilt, all the regret, it came surging up out of her. She thought of her own life and how she'd realized she'd wasted it on moneymaking and material things. She had no one. No one to share anything with, no family of her own. And then she thought of Rae and the rejection and how she'd finally found the romance and sparks and love, and yet it wanted nothing to do with her. More sobs came, hot and sharp; they hurt, badly. She swallowed hard and breathed deep, unable to take any more.

"Oh God, Aunt Judith, I should have done so many things differently."

Her body shook with pain and she felt hollow and bruised from the inner exertion. She focused on Judith. The constant feel of the soft, cool skin against her heated cheeks comforted her enough to calm. She continued to control her breathing and examined Judith's hand, massaging the pale skin that slid easily over the bone. Brown freckles from the sun showed Judith's age, just as the scars and rough feel of her knuckles mirrored a lifetime of hard work.

Krista smiled slightly and kissed it. She linked their fingers and reached out with her free hand to stroke the loose hairs away from Judith's forehead. As she stroked her aunt's face she began to hum. The sound was comforting, so soothing that she nearly put herself to sleep.

The restless nights and hard days on the trail, the confusing emotions over Rae, and the stress over Judith—all of it suddenly seemed to have drained her. She was beyond exhausted, but still, she didn't want to leave her aunt's side. She wanted to be there in case Judith woke up.

With heavy eyes, Krista leaned forward on her elbows. Still holding Judith's hand, she lowered her head and closed her eyes.

❖

Sometime later Krista felt a hand on her shoulder.

"Krista, wake up." It was a whisper and Krista opened her tired eyes to find Sonja tending to her aunt, taking her pulse and examining her eyes.

Feeling heavy and sore, Krista pushed herself up. At some point her head had fallen to the bed and she'd fallen asleep, yet she couldn't remember it happening. "How long have I been in here?" She pushed back her hair and wiped her face, trying to stir up some blood. Judith lay sleeping quietly, looking the same as she had earlier.

Sonja wrapped her stethoscope around her neck and adjusted the wrinkled blanket. "Two hours or so."

Krista groaned. "I must've fallen asleep but I didn't want to leave her."

"She's not going to get up and run away."

Krista nodded, studying Judith's pallor and pressed faded pink lips. "I know. I just don't want her to…" The mere thought of the word tightened her throat, so she considered the other possibility. "I mean, what if she wakes up and I'm not here?"

Sonja sighed and lowered herself to a chair. She seemed to think for a long while before she spoke. "She's not going to wake up. Not at this point. She's comfortable now, and she will pass on."

Krista lowered her eyes, refusing to hear. "My aunt, she's a strong woman. She might wake up and I want to be here when she does. To tell her how much I love her, and to tell her I'm here for her now and that I'm sorry I stayed away so long. So very sorry." She covered her mouth as the words began to strangle in her throat.

Sonja folded her hands in her lap. "Krista?"

Krista met her eyes.

"You just told her. She heard you."

"But—"

"It doesn't matter, Krista. You have to say your piece now, while she's still somewhat with us, and then let her go. It doesn't matter that she's not awake. She's still here, and that's all that matters."

Krista said nothing. She just sat and allowed the tears to slide down her face. After a while, Sonja spoke again.

"Why don't you go get cleaned up and get some breakfast?"

Krista wiped away the tears. "I don't want to leave her."

"She's not going anywhere."

"What if she dies? What if she dies and no one is in here with her?" The thought terrified her. She wasn't going to let that happen.

Sonja stood and came around the bed to Krista's chair. She reached out for her hand and helped her to stand. "She's going to go when she chooses to go. She's comfortable, not in any pain, her family is here… she'll probably go very soon now. And she may slip away while she's all alone. Or she may wait and go with all of you by her side. There's just no way to know for sure. But you've said what you wanted to say. You're here and she knows that. She heard you and that's all you can do."

Krista felt like melting under Sonja's kind touch. She was so tired. So confused. So torn up inside. Sonja seemed to sense this.

"Go take a hot shower. Get cleaned up and get something to eat." She smiled. "Besides, you know darn well that Mrs. Wyler wouldn't want you in here clinging to her, wet and dirty from the trail, catching cold."

Krista managed a soft laugh.

Sonja patted her arm. "Go on, now. Someone else wants to see her, so she'll be looked after."

Krista nodded and bent to kiss Judith on the forehead. She gave her hand one last squeeze, then headed for the door. Just before she walked out, she turned and asked, "Who wants to see her?"

"Dr. Jarrett."

Krista felt herself twitch slightly at the name. "Oh."

Sonja seemed to have noticed something odd in her reaction. Her mouth lifted on one side as if she knew darn well that there was definitely something going on between them but she wasn't quite sure what. "Yes. She's been waiting all morning."

The information stung and Krista knew her emotion was evident on her face. "Why didn't she just come in, then?"

"She didn't want to disturb you."

Krista looked away, unable to speak. Torn between confusion and grief, she turned and slipped out the door.

❖

Rae listened carefully from the living room as Krista left the master bedroom. She stroked the little coyote in her lap and kept an eye on Clinton. He tossed more logs into the fire, talking to himself as he worked and occasionally even whistling, somehow managing to do so with the pipe in his mouth. He'd already forgotten that Howie had been taken away by the fire department in an ambulance. Every so often he asked where the surly cowboy had gone.

"Mr. Wyler, why don't you go with Dr. Jarrett to look in on Mrs. Wyler?" Sonja asked from the entrance to the hallway doorway.

"Sure." Rae placed the pup on the floor and stood.

Clinton turned from the fire and puffed his pipe. He looked dazed. "Judy's still sleeping?"

"Yes, Mr. Wyler." Sonja's calm expression sent a signal Rae recognized from her own work. Judith was probably going to go very soon.

Rae's worries surfaced again. She didn't know how well she was going to handle this herself, and she knew how rough the loss was going to be for Krista. As she thought about Krista and the powerful feelings she'd stirred, Rae suddenly felt like she might not be able to handle anything anymore.

Rae knew she'd done wrong by Krista. But she didn't know how to make it right or even if she ever really could. How could she tell her that she was afraid to love? Afraid to lose? Especially when Krista would soon be dealing with Judith's death.

Sonja crossed the room to the fireplace to snatch up one of the countless books of matches they routinely took from Clinton. They'd tried hiding the lighters and matches, but when he wanted to smoke he always found the means.

Clinton ambled after Sonja as she and Rae walked down the hallway. Rae gently pushed open the door and allowed Clinton to enter ahead of her. He paused when he caught sight of his wife, and Rae had to place an anchoring hand on his shoulder to get him to move again. He approached the bed quietly, as if he might wake her. When he looked at her face, a genuine look of surprise overcame him and he staggered a bit before Rae helped him sink into the chair.

"Judy?" He reached out and patted her hand. The concern, shock, and sadness in his eyes was almost more than Rae could bear to see. When Judith didn't respond he tried again. "Why won't she wake up?"

"Because she's ill. She needs her rest." Rae walked around the bed and took a seat opposite Clinton. She held Judith's hand and clenched her jaw to fight off tears. The hand was smooth and still and cool. Just like Shannon's had been by the time she'd managed to crawl to her. Cold and wet, lying lifeless in the grass.

Rae forced the thought from her mind and let her gaze roam from Judith to Clinton, asking herself what she could do for her close friends now, when she was most needed. Clinton puffed his pipe, confused, his eyes continually sweeping over his wife, searching for answers Rae knew he would never find. Why was her hair gray? When did she grow old?

"Mrs. Wyler," she croaked. "It's me, Rae. And Clinton's here too. We're going to sit with you for a while, okay?" Rae concentrated on controlling her emotions. It was difficult to see her longtime friend in such a state. Weak, almost hollow. Just skin and bones. And Clinton didn't look much better, wondering where his vibrant young wife had gone.

Rae breathed in and out, soothed by the slow, steady pulse in Judith's hand. They sat in silence for a long while until Clinton began to talk. He spoke directly to Judith, surprisingly as if nothing at all was wrong. Rae watched and listened and reasoned that to Clinton nothing was wrong. His mind was taking him to all sorts of places in the past.

He spoke of the ranch and the new 1962 Chevy he wanted. And did Judith ever make up her mind about how many chickens she wanted? And how they needed to finish the bunkhouses before winter.

Rae listened quietly, moved by his memories and by the life they'd had together. She thought of Krista, and then of Shannon, and then of Judith passing on. Her chest ached in horrible pain. Her head swam in thick darkness. Nothing could make any of it better. Nothing.

Frustrated, she wiped angrily at her tears.

❖

Krista stood at the door, unsure about entering. She'd done as Sonja suggested, taking a long hot shower and then eating some eggs and toast. She'd been surprised at her hunger and she already felt a little better just from having eaten.

"Go on in." Sonja placed a gentle hand on the small of Krista's back. "I was just about to check on her."

Krista hesitated. Rae had allowed her to spend time alone with Judith and she thought that maybe she should do the same. She also wasn't sure how she felt about having to sit near Rae, or speak with her. "I think they may want their privacy."

Sonja gave her a look that let her know she wasn't fooling anyone. "You can't avoid Dr. Jarrett forever."

Sighing, Krista followed Sonja into the room. Clinton was chatting away about the new pipe Judith had given him for his birthday. Krista's heart melted; it had probably been years since the gift. Judith had been trying to get him to quit smoking for some time. Rae stood to let Krista by and glanced nervously at her, but then offered a small smile.

Krista returned it, unsure what it meant, but she reasoned that Rae was probably being polite just as she always was. She waited at the foot of the bed as Sonja examined Judith.

"How is she?" Krista smiled at her own question, thinking for the briefest of moments that her aunt would open her eyes and sit up and say, "I'm just fine, damn it! Don't talk like I'm not here!"

Clinton finally realized she was there. "Krista!"

"Hi, *tío*." Her voice was low with pain and she didn't think she could hold it together long enough to explain once again how long she'd been there. "How's Aunt Judith?" she asked, trying to change his focus.

"She's sleeping," he said matter-of-factly. "But she'll be up soon. We've got an auction to go to." He began digging in his pockets. "I can't find my damn truck keys."

Krista lowered her head. "I'll help you find them later, *tío*."

Sonja straightened from listening to Judith's heart. As she rounded the bed, she patted Krista's shoulder and left the room.

Clinton stared after her, his expression one of confusion. "Who is that?"

Krista struggled for a response and Rae sensed this and spoke for her. "She helps to take care of Judith. Her name's Sonja."

Clinton looked back to his wife and his eyes once again clouded with the mist of confusion and sadness. "What's wrong with her?" He seemed so childlike, so innocent and naïve.

"She's ill," Rae whispered.

Clinton searched his pockets again, this time for tobacco. When he came up empty he went to chewing on his pipe. They stood in silence as Judith began to make soft sounds. Krista straightened, and she and Rae stepped up to her and studied her face. The noise continued, small whimpers that soon turned into words.

"Clint…" Her mouth moved but her eyes remained closed.

Krista gripped her hand and felt a small squeeze. Her heart fluttered with excitement. "Aunt Judith? Can you hear me?"

Judith's lips continued to move. "Kris…"

"Yes it's me, it's Krista!" Krista beamed down at her.

"Rae…Kris…Rae." The words were soft mumblings.

"I'm here, Mrs. Wyler," Rae said.

Judith's lips continued for a while longer but her voice never returned. She squeezed Krista's hand again.

Tears began to fall down Krista's face as her hope diminished. "Aunt Judith," she pleaded. "We're all here. Please, wake up."

"Judy," Clinton pulled the pipe from his mouth, "we've got to get to that auction."

A soft cry escaped Krista at his words. He moved from the bed and walked to the closet, where he changed his shirt and belt. Then he moved to the dresser, and when he saw himself in the mirror, his hands flew up to his head of white hair.

"My hair." A look of ashen shock transformed his face. He hurriedly scooped up one of his cowboy hats up off the edge of the mirror and placed it on his head; then he sprayed on some cologne.

Krista felt her insides burn as she watched him helplessly. Painful sobs ripped through her. Rae placed a hand on her shoulder and wiped away her tears with the other, her own hazel eyes brimming. Krista sucked in a shaky breath and then collapsed in her arms. Rae held her tight, whispering into her hair.

"Shh, it's okay. It's okay."

Krista clung to her strength, crying into her shoulder. Concerned, Clinton approached and Krista embraced him as well, not giving him the chance to ask any questions. The three of them stood holding one another and crying while just behind them, Judith Wyler passed away.

CHAPTER EIGHTEEN

The rain fell in fat drops and thunder growled in the distance. Rae stared out the window at the thick, dark gray clouds as a silent ambulance drove away from the ranch for the second time in less than forty-eight hours. She hated the sight of them. Hated the sound of them even more. She turned from the window, thankful that its lights and sirens weren't on.

Clinton sat quietly in the recliner, staring into the fire. He'd been there for hours, refusing to speak since Judith had passed the day before.

Rae and several friends from the fire department had eventually had to pull him away from Judith, and Clinton had even taken a swing at one of them. He'd stayed by his wife's bed all night long, holding her hand and talking to her. The ambulance couldn't make it out until the morning because of the storm and when they'd finally arrived, he wasn't ready to let go.

Sonja had given him something to help calm him. They'd all sighed in relief when he seemed to fatigue and sat down to stare into the fire.

As Rae studied him, she heard someone emerge from the hallway. Krista limped into the room, eyes pained, carrying the sheets and blankets that had been on Judith's bed. She had been working diligently around the house since Judith had passed, sleeping only a couple of hours, and Rae could tell her knee was troubling her.

Cautiously, she asked, "How are you doing?"

"I'm fine," Krista insisted curtly. "Just fine." She took the bundle into the laundry room beyond the kitchen and disappeared with Jagger chasing her heels.

Rae stared after her, worried. She had expected Krista to continue to cry on her shoulder, to go into her room and curl on her bed and cry herself to sleep, allowing Rae to care for her. But Krista had done nothing of the sort, pushing her grief down deep in a way that had truly surprised Rae. Apparently, they all had their own ways of dealing with pain. Or avoiding dealing with it.

Krista was also back to speaking to Rae like they were virtually strangers. She was firm, distant, to the point. Her coldness bothered Rae intensely, but she wasn't sure what to do about it, if anything. As for herself, the best she could manage was not to think too much about losing Judith. Yes, she'd been there when Judith passed, she'd kissed her forehead and held her lifeless hand. She'd felt one of the greatest, kindest souls she'd ever known lift and dissipate from the room. It had pained her tremendously, just as witnessing Krista's and Clinton's pain had. But she didn't want to think about it. She couldn't.

She heard the washing machine start and turned to stare out the window once again. The rain continued to fall and her mind shifted to the other seven people she was concerned about. They weren't due back until that evening, but she was worried about the rain, knowing they couldn't do much in this weather. Noon was quickly approaching and she hadn't heard from Cody. She wondered if they were trying to ride or if they were holed up in their tents.

Hard thumps echoed through the living room as Dwight opened the front door and stomped his feet on the porch, trying to rid them of mud. When he entered the room, Rae could smell and feel the cold rain on him. He closed the door and removed his hat and wet duster coat. He hung them and glanced around the room. At the sight of Clinton gazing listlessly into the fire he shook his head.

"I saw the ambulance on my way in." Dwight had arrived to pay his last respects shortly after Judith passed, then he'd excused himself and left.

"Dwight." Krista followed Jagger from the laundry room. "You're back soon."

He stroked his stubble and it made a noise like sandpaper. "I couldn't stay away. You're my family." His deep voice shook and Krista crossed to him for an embrace.

Rae flushed, wishing Krista would hug her, but the chances of that seemed remote.

Dwight backed away fairly quickly and wiped at his eye. He spoke to Rae, obviously wanting to change the subject. "You heard from them yet?"

Rae shook her head. "No, nothing."

"Did you try calling again?"

"All I get is static."

Dwight stroked his chin and gestured for Rae to step outside with him.

"Wait," Krista protested. "What's wrong?"

"Nothing," Rae said. Krista had enough to deal with. She didn't need to be worrying over the group.

"Don't give me that," Krista snapped. "Why can't you reach Cody?"

Rae retrieved the radio from her belt and handed it over. "It's the weather. We can't seem to get through to them."

Krista took the walkie-talkie and attempted to call. Static whistled in and she got no response. "Shit." She returned the radio to Rae, wishing again that they could get cellular service out on the trail so they wouldn't have to rely on the radios. "Why didn't you tell me? We need to go after them."

"They're heading in," Rae said, wanting to calm her. "I'm sure they're fine. They can't be too far away now."

Krista stalked over to the kitchen table where her laptop sat open. "Well, we can find out." She sat down and adjusted the mouse. "I left the GPS with Cody."

Rae wanted to breathe a sigh of relief. At the very least Cody could never get lost, despite the rain. "I didn't know you had one."

Krista's fingers worked furiously. "You didn't ask." She studied the monitor. "They're not moving."

Rae and Dwight bent to look at the monitor. The flashing red dot wasn't moving in any direction, which meant for whatever reason, Cody wasn't moving.

Puzzled, Rae said, "They should be way closer than that if they rode all day yesterday." She searched the map, focusing on the creek and where the ranch stood relative to the signal.

Dwight rolled the ball of tobacco in his cheek. "They didn't ride," he concluded.

Krista lifted alarmed green eyes. "If the signal's correct, they're not far from where we left them."

Rae tried to remain reasonable. She could feel the worry and guilt poring out of Krista. "I'm sure they're fine. They're just playing it smart and waiting out the storm."

Dwight cleared a nervous throat. "Doc, I heard on the radio that this storm isn't going to stop anytime soon."

"What do you mean?" Krista's fingers flew across the keyboard. "I checked the weather before we started out. There was a possibility of scattered showers only."

She brought up a Doppler and they all watched it in silence. The green graphic was enormous and moving slowly over the state. A warning ran across the bottom of the screen. Flash flood advisory.

Rae's face heated. Flash floods in Arizona were notoriously dangerous, and sometimes they seemed to come out of nowhere. Sidewinder Creek had flooded many times in the past. "Oh, no," she whispered.

Krista shook her head. "Where did this come from?" She grabbed her forehead. "God damn it, can anything else go wrong?" Eyes wide, she looked from Dwight to Rae. "We have to go get them."

Rae nodded. She was right.

"Cody's too young," Dwight said. "He don't know how dangerous that creek can be. If he knew, he would've already moved them away from it."

Suddenly surging with nervous energy, Rae crossed the room and pulled on her jacket and Stetson.

"Where are you going?" Krista asked.

"To get the horses ready." Rae glanced toward Dwight, who was already retrieving his own hat and coat. "Unless you want to take the ATVs?"

"They're not here," he said. "They're in for repairs."

"Damn." Rae slipped on her jacket hurriedly.

Krista closed the laptop. "Be sure to saddle up Dollar. I'll be out as soon as I can."

"Don't you want to stay here, look after things?" Dwight asked.

Krista placed her hands on her hips. "I'm the one responsible for those people. I'm going with you."

"What about Clinton?" Rae asked. Krista needed to stay behind, to look after her uncle and handle the arrangements. She didn't need to be out in the cold, crazy Arizona monsoon, chasing rookie wranglers. "It could be dangerous," Rae let out before she could stop herself.

Krista's eyes flashed. "I don't need protecting."

Rae held up a hand. "I know, I know." She just didn't want her to get hurt. She cared about her. Too much.

"Good, then it's settled," Krista said. "Sonja has already agreed to stay on to look after Clinton for a while, and I'm sure we won't be gone more than a day or two."

Krista held Rae's gaze, as if waiting for her to protest once again. When she didn't, she turned and headed toward the hallway to pack her things.

Dwight tugged his hat down tight. "She shouldn't be going."

"Then you be the one to try and stop her," Rae whispered, pulling open the door to inhale the cold, wet scent of rain.

"Hell no." Dwight laughed. "I wouldn't wish that on the devil himself."

❖

"Any luck?" Adam asked, sinking his hands into his jacket pockets as he glanced up at the leaking gray sky. Dark clouds loomed, heavy-looking and full. He hadn't lived in Phoenix long, but this didn't look like an average storm. He blinked as lightning shot through the sky, stabbing the horizon.

Cody sighed. "No, nothing." He returned the radio to his belt and visibly shivered inside his jacket.

"Think it's going to pass soon?"

"They usually don't last this long," Cody said, obviously troubled. Around them, several small tents shook from the wind and the pelting rain. "This should've already blown over."

Adam kicked at a mud puddle. The rain had yet to stop and it was coming down hard and fast. The desert seemed to be rejecting it, the dirt too hard and dry to absorb the excessive amount of rain.

"I don't think we should ride in this," he said, restating the group's decision to wait the storm out inside their tents.

Cody stared off into the distance. "We may not have a choice."

"Why?" Adam winced at another flash of lightning. Surely in few more hours the storm would move on.

Cody gestured toward the creek. The water had risen and it was flowing much faster than before. "I don't know how long the creek will hold out."

Adam followed his gaze, shocked. Most of the rocks had already vanished under the whipping water. The cattle too seemed concerned and had all moved away. If the creek continued to build and gain strength, the entire area could flood. He swallowed against the sudden lump in his throat.

"I think you may be right."

Cody stared straight ahead at the water. "Tell everyone to pack up."

Adam could see the fear on his young face. Yet he was trying his damndest to hide it, and Adam respected him for that. "You got it."

❖

Rae rode quickly, the cold rain smacking her lower face and neck. She could hear Dwight close behind her and she hoped Krista was with him. They'd left the ranch a few hours before and Krista had once again insisted that she needed no help. Unwilling to hear any more, Rae had left Dwight to tend to her.

Her feelings toward Krista were as mixed as ever, and she knew that she wasn't behaving any better. She'd made love to her, then run away. Then she'd tried to comfort her, holding her in her arms, wanting to be there for her. She didn't understand her own behavior, so how could she expect Krista to? Krista had every right to be angry at her.

Rae squinted ahead. As strongly as she felt for Krista, she knew it was best to stay away. Neither one of them could afford to be hurt again. Especially now that Judith had gone. It hurt too deep.

Rae turned her head, unable to stay focused. Krista was far behind, once again clinging to Dollar's saddle horn. Rae slowed Shamrock and Dwight caught up to her. Both horses walked, hooves sinking slightly into the hard, wet earth.

"Don't even think about it, Doc," he said.

"She's too far back." Rae wiped the rain from her mouth as it thumped onto her Stetson.

"Then we'll keep her in sight," Dwight said. "I'm telling you, don't go back there. She made it clear she doesn't want you to."

"Oh, she did?" Rae felt a stinging in her gut.

"I'm afraid so." He looked at her long and hard. "Whatever the hell you two got going on, I wish you'd get it straightened out."

Rae stared. "She hates me."

Dwight laughed as thunder echoed around them. "I don't think it's hate that's got her all worked up."

"What?"

He grinned "I think it's love."

Rae felt her skin heat despite the damp cold.

Dwight's smile grew. "And by the look on your face, I'd say I'm right."

Rae clicked at Shamrock and they sped up, plowing through the heavy, wet desert. Dwight was right at her side and his words ricocheted through her mind.

Love. Love?

No.

"You're wrong," she said loudly, making sure he heard.

"No, I'm not."

Rae leaned forward, increasing her speed again. It wasn't love. It couldn't be. Love was loss. Love was pain. God damn it.

"It's written all over the both of you!" Dwight called out, falling behind. "You can run from it all you want, Doc, but you can't run forever!"

His voice tapered off as Rae and Shamrock surged through the stormy desert. Even though she knew she'd left him far behind, his words still chased her.

❖

Krista's heart pounded in her throat, in her head, in her fingers. She clenched the saddle horn as tight as she could and jerked again when thunder cracked in the near distance.

She'd just turned fifteen that summer and she was out looking for strays with her uncle Clinton. Her horse Sonny was under her, her very best friend. He'd been hers for less than a year.

They were a couple hours out from the ranch when a wall of dark clouds in the distance moved in, preceded by a blowing wall of dust. It was a monsoon but she wasn't afraid, having been in many before. The freak weather condition was part of Arizona life.

Up ahead of her, Clinton called out for her to head back before the rain hit and she nodded, holding on to her hat. Turning Sonny around, she lowered her head as they moved against the biting, blinding dust.

Thunder cracked incredibly loud overhead and Sonny took off at a start, frightened. Krista tugged on his reins and soothed him, patting his neck, calming him. The heart of the dust storm hit them as they continued to walk, and soon Krista found it difficult to breathe. She turned Sonny around to put their backs to the storm, and she could feel the dirt assaulting her back and whipping her hair. Lightning flashed, followed by more thunder, and down came the cold rain. Sonny began making noises and stepping in place. Krista did her best to keep him calm but when lightning flashed again, the hair on her arms stood up and she closed her eyes, knowing it was too close.

A monstrous, insanely loud pop exploded directly in front of them. Sonny let out an awful cry and bucked her up and off, sending her flying through the air, landing hard on her side. A groan escaped her and her head pounded in pain. She moved slightly and felt the rock she'd landed on. Warm blood trickled down her temple. She screamed as Sonny continued to buck, out of control. His strong legs came pounding down on her foot. She heard and felt a snap. She screamed louder, tugging her legs up.

As he moved away she focused on her feet. One was turned at an unnatural angle. She shook with terror, shook with pain. What was once a large palo verde tree burned in front of her. The rain pelted the dirt around her, sending up wisps of dust. Her eyes grew heavy and her body grew cold. Lightning shot down again in the near distance, rattling the ground. She flinched, beyond terrified. "Lightning never strikes the same place twice," she repeated to herself again and again. As the pain continued to shoot up her body, Sonny came close to her again, out of control, whinnying and bucking. Trembling, she curled herself up into a ball and allowed the tunneling darkness to consume her.

When she'd awakened in the hospital the pain in her foot was all too real. It was badly broken in numerous places and took two surgeries, several pins, and many months to heal.

Her first day back on the ranch, the following summer, she'd used her cane to walk out to the stables to go check on Sonny. With her aunt Judith at her side, she'd reached out to touch him and tried to stroke his nose. His eyes went wide with fear and he reared back again, just as he'd done during the storm, this time afraid of her. She remembered the accident and realized that he did too. The crack and flash of the lightning bolt, the harnessed panic of her horse—it all caused her to jump with fright in the middle of the night, just as her horse did at her touch.

After that she couldn't bring herself to go near any of the horses. The memory of it all was as fresh as the rain.

Krista continued to cling to Dollar as she saw Rae take off at a fast gallop up ahead, leaving Dwight behind. A part of her was glad she'd been left behind. She didn't have to worry about holding her own or about staring at Rae's raw beauty, then feeling the sharp stab of rejection each time Rae looked away from her.

Her thoughts returned to Judith and her heart ached even more. Upset, she wiped her eyes and pulled her uncle's hat down lower. Thunder cracked again and she winced as if it had touched her. Maybe she should give in to her fear and return to the ranch. No one would think it odd. There were things to take care of, arrangements to be made.

She was seriously considering doing so when Dwight approached. He had an unusual fleck of mischief in his eyes that Krista had only ever seen when he drank with Clinton and beat him at poker. "How are you doing?"

"I'm fine." *Should I turn around and go back? Now's the time.*

"Of course you are, darlin'." He smiled.

"Why are you so damn happy?" She examined him carefully, unable to understand his high spirits.

He and his horse fell into step with Dollar. "I'm just thinking of your aunt is all."

"Oh?" At the mention of Judith, Krista's determination suddenly kicked in and she gave Dollar a slight kick, the thought of returning to the ranch long gone.

"She was always right, you know."

Krista nodded. "Always. Even when she wasn't."

Dwight chuckled. "Yes, sir."

"So what's she right about this time?"

Dwight didn't respond immediately; he spat and stared off into the distance.

"You."

"Me?"

"Uh-huh."

"What about me?"

"I swore I wouldn't say."

Krista scoffed. "Come on, Dwight. You can't feed me lines like that and then not expect me to bite."

Silence ensued, the rain, thunder, and wind the only noise.

Dwight looked up at the sky and turned his palm up to catch the drops of rain. "I can feel her out here," he said. "Like she's all around."

Krista too looked around and breathed deep. The earthy scent of the rain, the blowing trees, the bright colorful blooms of the wet wildflowers, all of it was Judith. "Me too."

Dwight continued, deep in thought. "She loved this land. Almost more than she loved Clinton."

Krista laughed. "Yes, she did." After another brief moment of silence she asked again, too anxious not to, "So what about me was she right about?"

Dwight glanced over at her. "I told you, I swore I wouldn't tell."

Krista sighed. Was she proud of her? Of how she turned the ranch around? Or was she disappointed? Upset that she'd stayed away so long? She had to know. Otherwise it was going to eat her alive.

"Did I not do something right?" Maybe it was the horse. After all, Dwight hadn't mentioned anything until he rode up and looked at her and Dollar. "It's the way I'm riding the horse, isn't it? Because I'm afraid again, because of the storm."

She felt ill, like she might throw up. Her aunt was gone now, and Krista had been a big disappointment.

"Of course not!" Dwight exclaimed. "She was always proud of you, Krista. Even when you were gone she was always bragging about you, saying how hard a worker you were and how successful you were. She was very proud."

Krista swallowed hard. "Even now?"

Dwight cleared his throat. "Especially now." He winked at her.

As a small flood of relief washed through Krista, they both caught sight of Rae streaking toward them. When she stopped she was out of breath and she and Shamrock were covered in mud from their gallop.

"They're just ahead," she gasped. "They're okay. They'd already started heading back."

Krista nearly collapsed with relief. "Oh, thank God."

Rae nodded, catching her breath. "They have most of the cattle, but there are a few strays not far behind." She looked to Krista. "I'm going to send the group on ahead to you. You and Cody can lead them back to the ranch. Dwight and I will go after the strays."

"No."

"What?" Rae squinted at her in disbelief.

"Dwight, you take the group," Krista said in a tone that did not invite argument. "I'm going with Dr. Jarrett. My aunt would do the same." After all the talk of how proud Judith was of her, she wasn't about to back down now. She felt she had to do this.

"Absolutely not," Rae countered.

Krista returned her stare. She wanted to argue but she knew it would get her nowhere. She was inexperienced and scared shitless of her horse, but she wasn't about to let that stop her. Judith was all around her, and Judith wouldn't allow fear to stand in her way either.

"Let's get to the group and discuss it there." Krista clicked and clung to Dollar as he gained speed.

Rae and Dwight rode alongside her, Rae talking quickly.

"There's nothing to discuss. The wayward cattle need to be brought in and you're in no position to do it."

Krista kept her gaze ahead. "Neither are you and Dwight. Not in this weather. It's not safe for anyone."

"It's too dangerous, Krista!" Rae bit out, her expression fierce. "I don't need your damned help!"

Krista turned her head sharply to look at her. "Now who's the one being stubborn?"

Rae closed her mouth and clenched her strong jaw. She clicked at Shamrock and rode on ahead to meet the group.

Chapter Nineteen

Rae offered the soaking-wet group of wranglers a smile as she approached for the second time. Shamrock slowed to a stop as she took in their tired faces and glistening hats and jackets. Each one of them returned the smile sincerely.

"How's Mrs. Wyler?" Cody asked tentatively.

Filled with regret, Rae said, "She passed away yesterday."

The group hung their heads in sorrow but they perked up again as Krista rode into sight.

"Look at us," Adam declared, waving his hat in the air. "We're real live bona fide cowboys now!"

Krista smiled but her eyes were pained. "I guess so," she said. "After all that you've been through."

Frank laughed. "This has been the most fun I've had in ages."

Everyone agreed.

Krista looked at each of them and for a moment Rae feared that she might cry. But she smiled once more. "Then you're all absolutely crazy."

More laughter.

When she spoke again she sounded professional and confident and she held herself erect, her head high. Rae respected her courage. "We're going to have you all ride with Dwight the rest of the way. You're only two hours out, so it's not far."

"Two more hours and I get a nice hot shower." Candace beamed.

"Sounds wonderful," Jenna agreed.

"And I wanted to take the time to thank you all again for your patience and understanding. You'll all be given free return visits should you choose to come back."

Adam whooped. "Hell, yeah."

"Not anytime soon," Tom said with a smile. "I need to get a new ass first."

Krista laughed, as did the others. She felt her stomach drop as she watched Rae interact with everyone but her. She was so friendly and easy; she'd been the same with the firemen who'd helped deal with Clinton. Apparently she had been a volunteer firefighter at one time, so they had something in common. An image of Rae in a fireman's uniform caused fluttering in Krista's chest, and she raised a trembling hand to her temple. Wanting Rae so badly and seeing how warm she could be made Krista's pain all the more real. She still couldn't believe Rae had rejected her after she felt so close. Rae had maintained a distance ever since and Krista knew she had done the same, to protect herself.

Getting over Rae was going to be the hardest thing she'd ever had to do. She felt her throat tighten. That kind of pain would even overshadow Judith's passing.

"We're sorry to hear about your aunt," Tillie said.

Krista nodded as her eyes welled. "Thank you."

Everyone bowed their heads in a long moment of silence. The rain fell all around them, mirroring the mood.

Rae watched in continued silence as Dwight tipped his hat to her and took off with the group, leaving her alone with Krista. She still didn't understand why Krista insisted on being the one to help. The progress she'd made on the trail with Dollar seemed to be all but forgotten. She was once again hanging onto the horse for dear life.

"Don't say a word," Krista said, apparently having caught the look Rae was giving her.

Rae spoke anyway. "I just don't understand why you want to do this."

They turned the horses and rode back toward the creek. Krista held on tightly and tensed her body, just as she'd done the first day out. "Haven't you ever done something just because you needed to do it again?"

"Like what?"

Krista looked over at her. "Like facing a fear."

Rae allowed the words to register. "Sure."

"Well that's what I'm doing. I know it may not make sense to you, but it's something I have to do."

"Actually it makes a lot of sense." Rae paused, working up the courage to ask, "There was an accident, wasn't there? With a horse?"

Krista stiffened. "Yes."

"You're very brave to face it."

"I don't feel brave."

"You are." Rae offered a smile.

Krista started to return it but then her expression changed and her eyes were guarded again. Rae sensed that the topic was closed so she pushed on, leaving Krista a little behind.

When she reached the creek, the sight of it nearly overwhelmed her. The water, an ugly muddy brown, churned and rushed with power. The bank of river rocks had disappeared, consumed by the rising water. She spotted several cattle, one of them on the other side of the creek, and a few more scattered between her and Krista.

"Shit," she whispered, knowing the one across the creek was lost, at least for now. The water was too deep and powerful to cross. They would have to wait and come back for the animal after the storm.

As she organized her thoughts, deciding which of the remaining strays to go after first, Krista barreled past her, riding Dollar right into the creek. Rae's heart leapt out of her chest.

"Krista!" she shouted.

Dollar hit the water hard, slowing with each step. Krista urged him on as Rae watched helplessly.

"She's crazy! She's out of her mind crazy!" Rae kicked at Shamrock, thinking right away of going after her. But when Krista turned and saw her, she held up a hand.

"No, don't!"

Shamrock had her two front hooves just under the whipping water.

"What?" Rae could barely hear over the rush of the creek.

"Stay there!" Krista yelled.

"But you'll get yourself killed!" Rae began going over a plan in case Krista fell. She could she throw her rope out to her. Hopefully, Krista was a good swimmer.

"Stay there! I know what I'm doing! I know this creek!" Krista faced forward again, urging Dollar on. The water swirled and shoved against the middles of his legs and Rae was surprised when it went no higher. Krista and Dollar walked slowly onto land, where Krista slid off him to rope the cow.

Once the rope was secure, she climbed back onto Dollar and moved him quickly into the water once again. They entered at the same spot and Dollar moved easier this time, more confident. Rae watched in amazement as Krista led them through the raging water. When she and Dollar reached the other side, Krista slid off her horse and came over to Rae. They both stared at the cow standing a few feet away, suddenly frozen in the middle of the creek.

"Great," Krista said.

They tugged on the rope but the cow wouldn't move, fright evident in its eyes.

"Come on," Krista said, limping into the water.

"Wait! Krista!" Rae stumbled in after her, not having time to think.

"Just hold on to the rope and you'll be fine," Krista called over to her. Rae did as instructed, the rough rope biting into her hand as she squeezed it. Soon the rushing water was pressing against her upper thighs and she let go when Krista did to lean into the cow.

Krista had her back to the surge and Rae had the protection of the large cow to stop the onslaught. Both of them pushed on the animal, which stood its ground, mooing in response.

"Damn it, move!" Krista yelled.

Rae smacked the cow hard on the backside.

Nothing.

Krista did the same.

Nothing.

Rae watched, puzzled as Krista set her jaw and moved to the stray's rear.

"I've only seen this done once, but it's worth a shot." Bracing herself against the water, Krista lifted the tail and shoved her hand up inside the cow. A loud moo erupted and the large heifer moved quickly.

Krista pulled out her hand and moved with her, reaching for the rope just as Rae did. But the sudden movement of the cow had dragged Rae off-balance. The water surged against her, knocking her feet out from under her. She clung to the rope but was at once sucked under by the current. Beneath the raging water, she kicked and fought to regain her footing, but the water was too strong. She tried to pull herself above the surface but could only manage to sneak a small breath.

I'm going to die.

The water raged around her, beyond her, uncaring and unrelenting. She could feel the cow moving and she knew she wouldn't be able to hang on long. Just as her chest began to burn and her vision began to tunnel, she felt a strong arm under hers and she popped up out of the water.

"Rae! Rae, hang on!" Krista hauled them both ashore, collapsing next to the stubborn cow. Rae coughed and turned over to spit up some water. She gratefully sucked in big, ragged gulps of air.

"You're crazy," Rae wheezed, glancing at Krista as she lay back on her elbows.

Krista pushed back her hair, breathing hard. "What happened to hellfire?"

Rae laughed and coughed. "That too."

Krista looked over at the cow. "Never leave a man behind."

Rae laughed even harder, rolling over to push herself up. She stood and offered Krista her hand. "Come on, cowgirl, let's get these cattle back to the ranch."

Krista took her hand eagerly and her breath caught as they stood close, staring into each other's eyes. Rae was drowning again, this time in Krista. No words were spoken. Just ragged breaths. The rain beat down around them, the water surged behind them, the sky cracked, and the lightning flashed. None of it compared to Krista.

Reaching out, Rae tugged Krista to her and pressed her mouth to her, tongue right away searching and seeking. She heard Krista groan and felt the soft wet of her tongue meeting hers head-on.

Feeling the rush of wet heat between her legs, Rae pulled away, panicked.

Krista stared at her, chest heaving. There were flames in her eyes. "What is it?"

Rae couldn't speak. She had no answer.

Krista continued to search her face. "Is it because I stuck my hand up a cow?"

Rae laughed softly. "No."

Krista reached out and touched her cheek. "This is the clean hand," she whispered.

Rae closed her eyes as the wet, warm hand stroked her skin.

"Tell me why, Rae."

Rae opened her eyes. Her heart was nearly beating over itself. "I can't." Her voice was tight. *I could never handle losing you.*

"Can't what?" Krista's eyes were sparkling green and soft with sincerity. "Whatever it is…"

Rae looked away. "It's not something that can be fixed. It's not something that will go away." *Death is inevitable.* She felt the hand drop from her face.

"Then why kiss me? Why make love to me?"

Rae couldn't answer. She had none.

"Look at me, Rae, please."

Rae sucked in a painful breath at the familiar words. Shannon's last words. "We need to get going," she rasped, climbing onto Shamrock.

With her rope in hand, she gently kicked the horse and galloped off into the rain, aiming at a nearby calf. Angrily, she wiped away the burning tears and remembered Dwight's words.

You can run, Doc. But you can't run forever.

❖

Krista followed Rae at a careful distance. Her body trembled but it was no longer from fear. Behind her, the cow they'd rescued trudged along, securely tied. But that didn't stop Krista from roping two others and getting them into line at the edge of the herd.

Overhead the thick clouds wept more rain and the chill of the evening began to set in. Krista fought off tears, fed up with crying. She had no idea why Rae kept reeling her in only to push her away, but she wasn't going to let it happen again. She held her head high and did her best to ignore the handsome vet altogether. The ranch was just ahead and there would be plenty for her to do to keep her mind occupied.

She rode Dollar to the stables as the whistles from the cattle pens echoed through the damp air. The group had already boarded their horses but they weren't inside warming up. They were sorting the cattle, following Dwight and Cody's instructions. They'd come a long way, and standing in the pouring rain in their weathered cowboy hats and jeans, they looked like real wranglers.

They are real wranglers.

Smiling, Krista absorbed the scent of wet hay for a few seconds more, then crossed to the house. She hesitated at the steps, looking back to see Rae at the entrance to one of the pens, head bowed, talking to Dwight. When she raised her head, Krista was shocked at the deep sadness in her face. For a split second she thought about running to her. But the stab in her heart brought reason screaming back. Her chest felt like it was going to split in two. Twice she'd been rejected by Rae. She would not invite a third time.

Hurt and confused, she climbed up to the porch and her boots echoed as she headed toward Clinton, who sat rocking near the edge.

"*Tío*," she whispered, placing her hand over his.

He stopped rocking and looked at her with surprise. "*Mija.*" He smiled.

Grateful that he seemed to remember her presence for once, she stooped and gave him a kiss, then collapsed in the neighboring chair, exhausted. "How are you?" she asked, flinching as she straightened her sore leg.

He held the bottle of tequila in his lap, the same one she'd seen earlier.

"I'm okay." He started rocking again, leaning his head back to watch the wranglers at the cattle pens. Whistles, moos, and barks from Dwight's dog Repeat filled the air.

"Your aunt Judy." He looked over at her and then looked down, wetting his lips in a nervous manner. "That woman in there said she died."

Krista squeezed the armrests on her chair.

Clinton's eyes began to water and again he wet his lips. "I don't remember her dying, *mija*. Wouldn't I remember something like that?"

The fragility of her uncle at that moment caused her to gasp. Tears ran down his face and he looked a million years old. Hair stark white, face tanned and weathered, his tall frame thinning so that his skin hung off him.

"I can't find her. She's not here. Is she…" He was so sad and so serious. "Is she really dead?"

Krista had to clear her tight throat before she could answer. "Yes. I'm afraid she is."

Clinton kept rocking. He wiped away another tear and twisted open the tequila bottle. He took a quick, harsh-sounding swig, winced slightly as he swallowed, and then did it again. As he screwed on the cap, he continued rocking and staring out at the cattle. He spoke to himself, not to Krista.

"I would remember if she died. I know I would."

❖

Sonja took Krista's hat and jacket as she stepped in the house. "You look like a drowned rat."

"Thanks," Krista said. "That actually sounds pretty positive compared to the way I feel."

"Everything turn out okay?" Sonja moved back into the kitchen where she removed the lid to a large pot on the stove.

"Yes, fortunately." Krista crossed the room to stand by her side. "Something smells wonderful."

Sonja grunted knowingly as she stirred. "It's my chili. Thought you all could use some after being out in that rain."

Krista placed a hand on her shoulder and met her warm brown eyes. "I owe you, tremendously, for everything." She meant it. Sonja had been a savior.

"I know," Sonja said with a laugh. "I'm keeping tabs."

Krista chuckled. "Good." She stretched and noted that the chili looked close to being ready. "I'm going to go take a quick shower and then I'll get started on setting the table for everyone."

Sonja set down the spoon and replaced the lid. "Oh, no, you don't." She walked to the laundry room and opened the door. Out came Jagger, tail wagging and little legs flying.

"Oh, my God," Krista bent and lifted his wriggling body up for inspection. "You're covered in mud!"

Sonja placed her hands on her hips. "He spent the afternoon chasing that damn rooster around. I couldn't catch either one of them so I just waited it out until they got tired. This little one finally came back and collapsed on the porch, worn out."

"Jagger," Krista scolded lightly, touching his nose with hers. "Did you get in trouble?" She scrunched her nose at him. "You smell worse than I do."

Sonja laughed. "I won't argue with that." She touched Krista's arm. "After your shower, I'm going to take care of that leg."

Krista nodded and gave a small smile. Holding Jagger close, she turned to head down the hallway. She kissed his head as she caught the lamplight spilling out from the master bedroom. Passing the bathroom, she approached the room slowly and peeked inside. The hospital bed was gone and Judith and Clinton's bed had been moved back to its original position, neatly made with fresh linens. The colorful flowers still sat on the dresser and the room still had its familiar smell. The bedside lamp was on and casting a warm orange glow. It felt the same as it always had. Like home.

She sighed and Jagger stirred in her arms.

Just before she turned, she whispered, "I miss you," and headed back down the hall.

CHAPTER TWENTY

Lindsay came flying up the muddy gravel drive with the stereo blaring in tune with the windshield wipers. Rae tugged down on her Stetson and walked over to her.

"Hey!" Lindsay greeted, killing the engine to hop out into the rain. She pulled Rae in for a hug and then held onto her shoulders. "You look hot in that hat. You should wear it all the time."

She smiled, full of energy. Rae rolled her eyes, glad to see her friend, but in no mood for humor. "You shouldn't drive like that in the rain. Especially when you're pulling the trailer." She walked hurriedly back to open it, impatient about loading up her horses and getting home.

"What's eating you?" Lindsay fell into step alongside her as they headed for the stables. Around them the ranch was quiet, save for the moos from the cattle in their pens. "How was the trail? Did it go great?"

Rae kept walking. "Nothing, fine, and yes."

Lindsay stopped for a moment, hoping Rae would do the same. When she didn't, Lindsay had to run to catch up. "What the hell? Why are you acting like a dick?"

This time Rae turned. "A dick?"

Lindsay didn't back down. "Yeah, a dick."

Rae shrugged. "Maybe I am a dick."

"What?"

Rae opened the stall door and led Shamrock out slowly.

"Something happened with the hellfire, didn't it?"

"No," Rae said sharply. But she couldn't hide the dark flush of her cheeks.

"You like her," Lindsay accused.

"No, I don't."

"Yes, you do." Lindsay could tell something had changed in Rae and she suspected it was Krista Wyler's doing. Rae's answers were too short, too clipped, and then there was the blush.

"Look, can we cut the chitchat? I'm tired and I just want to get home."

Lindsay shrugged, curious and confused. "Suit yourself."

As she readied the other horse to be led from the stable she realized she'd only ever seen her best friend and boss like this one other time. Right after Shannon died. Rae had holed herself up in her house, refusing to even make small talk with her friends and clients. She had died inside. Lindsay only hoped it wasn't happening again. The rain pinged off the truck and trailer as they loaded up the horses. Lindsay waited to see if Rae would ask for the keys. Each time it rained, Rae usually insisted that Lindsay drive. Lindsay always hoped that maybe one day, Rae would try to drive in wet weather again.

"You drive," Rae finally said, rounding the vehicle to the passenger side. Lindsay opened the driver's door and was just about to step inside when the front door to the ranch opened.

"Wait!" Krista Wyler came limping out, carrying a large food container. She hurried down the stairs as best she could and handed the covered bowl to Rae, who looked dumbfounded. "It's chili. Sonja and I wanted to be sure you had some."

"Thanks." Rae took the chili and placed it inside the truck, then pulled out a container of her own along with a bag, which she handed to Krista.

"I had Lindsay bring some powdered puppy milk for the coyote. Give it to him three times a day with the bottle in the bag. You can continue to give him soft food as well."

"Thanks." Krista's voice was soft. She seemed touched.

Intrigued, Lindsay walked over to them. She thought Krista looked gorgeous in her faded jeans and simple gray sweatshirt, her thick hair pulled back in a ponytail. She gave the auburn-haired woman a wave.

"Hello," Krista greeted with a smile. "It's Lindsay, right?"

Lindsay smiled in return. "It is."

Rae shot her friend a look but Lindsay ignored her, wanting to test the waters further. Her eyes found the mark on the side of Krista's neck in about two seconds.

"Of course, you're both welcome to join us inside for dinner," Krista offered. "I...the group wishes you would stay."

Lindsay was about to accept the offer when Rae spoke. "I'm sorry, but we can't. We have appointments."

"In this weather?" Krista's shirt was darkening from the rain and the sun had set a few minutes before.

Lindsay stared pointedly at Rae. It didn't do any good.

"Some other time," Rae said without emotion. "Tell them I said good-bye." She tipped her hat and then climbed in the truck.

Lindsay gazed after her, beyond confused, and embarrassed by her behavior. She didn't know what was going on, but the hopeful look on Krista's face when Rae had brought out the food didn't get past her.

"Listen, Krista," Lindsay started with a soft smile. She knew Rae could hear her, the passenger door still open. "Since we can't make it to this one, how about having dinner with me sometime?"

"With you?" Krista blinked, obviously surprised.

"Yeah."

Krista stared through the windshield a moment and then answered. "Sure. That sounds great."

"Great." Lindsay heard the passenger door slam shut, but it didn't erase her smile. "I'll call you." She gave Krista a wink and climbed in the truck.

They drove in silence for a few minutes, then Lindsay turned up the volume to the radio. Rae immediately turned it off and stared straight ahead. "Something wrong, boss?" Lindsay asked.

"No."

"Could've fooled me."

"Slow down," Rae snapped. "You're driving too damn fast."

Lindsay kept her current speed.

Rae whisked her hat off her head and slammed it onto her lap. "I told you not to mess with Krista Wyler."

"Why?" Lindsay was finally getting under her skin, where she hoped the truth lay waiting to come out.

"Because she's Judith's niece, that's why. They've been my friends and clients for years."

"Sweetie, Judith's gone. And if you don't want me seeing Krista for any other reason, all you have to do is say so."

Rae clenched her jaw. "She's a client."

"We're both adults, and her *uncle* is a client," Lindsay replied.

"She's probably going to take over the ranch."

"Well, if she does, I'll go from there. In the meantime, she's one hell of a beautiful woman and I would like to get to know her better."

"I said no." Rae's voice was deep and low.

"Why?" Lindsay gripped the steering wheel tightly.

"Because I said so."

Silence.

"Because *you* want to date her?" Lindsay felt the chill and then the daggers.

"No."

"In that case"—Lindsay accelerated—"I'm going to see her." She reached over and turned on the radio.

❖

"Rae's not coming?" Jenna asked as Krista reentered the warm house. The group was all settling in at the table, candles lit, burgundy breathing.

"Rae's not feeling well," Dwight said, surprising Krista. "She told me to tell you all how much she enjoyed your company and how sorry she is that she can't stay longer."

"Aw," Tillie said, "That's a shame. We all wanted to thank her for everything she did for us."

"Yeah," said Candace innocently.

Krista tried her best not to glare at her. She found it difficult even to look at the woman who'd touched Rae so intimately. Something Krista would never get to do.

"I'm sure she feels the same about you all." Krista stepped up to her place and lifted her wineglass. "To the best darn group of wranglers around."

Everyone followed her lead and raised their glasses.

"To the best darn group you'll ever have!" Adam declared.

Laughter sounded around the table as they toasted.

Krista remained standing, staring into the candlelight. "And to Judith Wyler, my aunt, the heart and soul of this ranch."

"To Judith!" Frank endorsed.

"To Judith," the rest followed, clinking their glasses.

❖

The sun shone brightly the next morning, almost as if it were making up for lost time. Krista squeezed Tillie tightly, a tear slipping down her face.

"Thank you," Tillie whispered, "for everything."

They pulled apart and Krista smiled. "Don't be a stranger."

Tillie nodded and stepped away, allowing Tom to hold her hand as they walked toward their vehicles.

"They're good together," Krista said, watching them.

"They are, aren't they?" Adam replied, shading his brow. "They're just friends for now, though. Tillie wants to take it slow."

"I can understand why." She turned to face Adam, dreading the good-bye. "But Tom's a nice guy. He'll treat her right."

Adam lowered his hand. "What about you?"

More good-byes were called out as car doors closed and engines started. Krista waved to Jenna and Frank as they pulled away.

"What about me?"

Adam sighed dramatically. "Do I have to say it?"

Krista focused in on Candace, who was packing a white Jeep Wrangler.

"Rae?" He nudged her. "What happened with you two?"

"Nothing." Krista's heart sank at the mention of her name. She still couldn't believe Rae had left without having dinner with the group. And all because of her. For some reason Rae wanted absolutely nothing to do with her.

"Right." Adam nudged her again.

Krista straightened her back, trying to put on a brave front. But Adam reached out to touch her neck and raised his eyebrows.

"She...we...we made love and then she pushed me away."

Adam cocked his head. "Why?"

"I have no idea. And then yesterday she kissed me..." Krista paused, lifting her hand to her lips, remembering the way Rae's had felt. "And then she pulled away and said she couldn't."

Adam embraced her, kissing her cheek. "I'm sorry."

Krista's chest shook as she fought off sobs. "I feel like it's me, like I did something wrong." She left out how she'd never felt this way about anyone before. How this was love, she knew it in her gut. Everything she'd ever dreamed about.

"Hey." Adam drew back to look at her. "It's not you, it's her. She's got issues or something. You." He touched her cheek. "You are wonderful. And beautiful and passionate and…"

Krista's laughter bordered on tears. "Are you sure you have to leave?"

He bowed his head. "I do." He looked back up quickly. "But I'll come back in a few days to show you the photos. I think they could do wonders for your marketing campaign."

Krista hugged him again. "Sounds terrific."

Adam stepped back and slipped on his designer shades. "*Hasta, chica.*"

Krista smiled and squinted into the sun as she watched them drive away.

"They were quite a group," Sonja said from behind her.

"Yes, they were," Krista agreed. "I was sad to see them go."

Sonja stood leaning on one of the porch posts, wearing dark jeans and a tan button-down blouse. Her skin looked dark and smooth, her brown eyes deep and knowing. "Think they had a good time?"

Krista walked up the steps to stand next to her. "They said they did. I gave them all free return trips regardless." She folded her arms over her chest to stare out at the ranch. "Jenna and Frank are already talking about next year. So that's a good thing."

"Mmm-hmm."

Pepe the rooster came flying up the driveway, having chased all the cars away. He slowed as he approached the porch. He was still covered in mud from the days before.

"Someone needs to squirt you off with the hose, little man," Krista said.

"You could always put him in the shower with you like you did Jagger."

Krista laughed, picturing the little rooster squawking, wings and talons flying. "I don't think so."

They stood in silence for a while, Pepe snooping around the porch, claws scratching as he walked. He lingered around the door and Krista realized he was probably looking for Jagger. "Well, I better get inside and feed the wild man."

She sighed, knowing she had much more to do after that.

Sonja looked after her but remained standing on the porch. "If you need help, I'm here."

Krista offered a tired smile and gently shooed Pepe away from the door as she entered. Jagger was waiting for her, tail wagging as she walked to the kitchen. He chased her feet and tugged at her shoelaces. She made his bottle and he eagerly followed her into the living room where he whined, wanting to jump onto the couch.

"Come here."

She scooped him up, spread a dish towel over her lap, and began feeding him. Even though he had only seen the bottle once before, he sucked hungrily, closing his eye as he fed. With him settled in her lap, she reached over and turned on the speakerphone, dialing Suzanne's number. As she waited for her friend to answer, she sighed with relief. She couldn't be more pleased with the decision she'd made to quit real estate for the time being.

"Krista, hey! How are you?"

Krista stroked Jagger's fluffy head. "I'm okay, how are you?"

"Busy. Thanks to my best friend, I'm beating clients off with a stick."

"Good, I'm glad."

"So when are you coming home?"

"I'm going to have movers move my things next week," Krista said.

"So you're going to stay at the ranch?"

"Yes."

"Well, when can I see you?"

Jagger suckled noisily and Krista couldn't help but smile at him. "That's why I'm calling. The service is tomorrow."

"Where?"

"I'll e-mail you the directions. It's at a small church."

"I'll be there."

"Suzanne?"

"Yeah?"

"Thanks again for everything."

"You got it, babe. Can't wait to see you."

"Me too."

The call ended and Krista tightened her arms gently around the one being in her life she could truly, truly love without fear of rejection.

Chapter Twenty-one

The church was small, white, and quaint. Rae crossed the parking lot and sank her nervous hands in her pockets. The sun had just set, casting pinks and oranges on the front of the church, as if Judith herself were signaling the way.

Rae breathed deep and glanced down at herself. Black dress slacks and a blueberry-colored dress shirt. It wasn't exactly fashion attire but she hoped it was good enough. She held open the door as several people exited, whispering quietly. She knew the service had ended and she tried to relax a little when she saw the red felt pews nearly bare. As she walked down the aisle, her chest tightened and she knew she never would've made it through the funeral service itself.

She approached the shiny oak casket with fresh wildflowers strewn across it. Judith's favorite. Surrounding the casket were several other large flower arrangements. Rae inhaled, and as their strong scent filled her head, she began to feel dizzy. Trembling, she rested her hands on the sides of the casket.

"Judith," she tried to speak clearly, to share what she felt, but the words escaped her.

Judith lay in the center of the white satin cushions trimmed with lace. Her face was thin and drawn, but not pale like before. She looked peaceful, like she was resting, her long braid draped over her right shoulder. A light yellow cotton dress covered her body and her hands were folded neatly over her abdomen, with her wedding ring reflecting the light from the stained glass windows.

A vision of Shannon laid out exactly the same way flashed in her mind. Shannon's mother screaming from the front pew. Her family glaring at Rae, blaming her. And Rae had let them. Taking on all the guilt. Tears welled in her eyes. It was all too familiar. First Shannon, now Judith. Death didn't make any sense. It seemed to have no rhyme or reason. How was she supposed to cope?

"Doc," Dwight greeted her softly, standing next to her, hands clasped in front of him. He looked nice in a dark blazer, bolo tie, and dark jeans.

"Dwight," she rasped.

"You doing okay?" He clasped her shoulder. His eyes were sad and sincere.

"Yeah." She looked away. Her breath shook in her lungs. Judith. Gone. Forever. She forced herself to speak, shoving her trembling hands into her pockets. "How is everyone? Clinton?"

Dwight looked around. "Not good. He uh, he got up and ran from the service. The shock of it, you know. Every time he hears it, he's shocked again."

Rae swallowed back more fire. Poor Clinton. Dear God, how was he going to get through this? "Krista?" she asked, unable not to.

Dwight cleared his throat.

"I've been better."

Rae turned. Krista stood a few feet away wearing an elegant but simple black dress and pumps. Her green eyes sparkled, but Rae could tell she'd been crying. Dwight squeezed Rae's shoulder and excused himself, leaving the two of them alone.

When the door to the church closed, Krista pinned Rae with a serious look. "How about you, how are you?"

Rae sucked in a breath to speak but no words would come. She felt her lips begin to tremble just like her hands. Krista's face softened and her eyes searched Rae's face hurriedly. Her hand, soft and warm, cupped Rae's cheek.

"Come here," she whispered, pulling Rae in for a strong embrace.

The feel of Krista in her arms, the scent of her, the strength of her—all of it opened the floodgates and Rae clung to her, crying. The pain was fire in her belly, in her chest, in her throat. She cried hard. Long and hard. Krista never faltered. She held on to her as if they belonged in each other's arms and she would never let her go.

The door to the church opened again and Rae caught sight of Dwight, who froze when he saw the two of them. "I'm sorry. I just wanted to tell Krista that Clinton's in the car."

Rae pulled away and ran down the aisle.

"Doc!" he called to her as she brushed by.

But she kept on. She ran to her truck and drove away as fast as she could.

She ran and she ran and she ran.

But the pain always managed to catch up.

❖

"This is incredible," Suzanne said, walking with Krista around the property. "I can see why you chose this over city life in Phoenix."

Krista smiled and eased her hands into her back pockets. "It is something, isn't it?"

They stopped along the front fence line and stared out over the lush desert landscape. The day was bright and sunny, with high purple clouds that looked like they'd been rubbed into the sky. Krista was enjoying the light breeze, thinking of her aunt, when Suzanne spoke again.

"So what's going on with you?"

"What do you mean?" Krista asked.

Suzanne's eyes were full of concern. "Something's the matter. At first I thought it was your aunt passing, but now I know it's something more."

Krista stared back at the blowing sage trees. "I'm fine."

"Bullshit. You're skinny and pale and depressed. And don't tell me it's stress. I've seen you handle stress, seen you eat stress for breakfast."

Krista pressed her lips together. Her eyes began to well. It had been days since she'd last seen Rae at the church, and she still couldn't wipe her from her mind. "I think I'm in love."

Suzanne blinked. "What?"

Krista laughed and wiped away a tear. "I'm in love."

"Well, that's wonderful." Suzanne smiled.

"No, it's not." Krista sniffled. "She wants nothing to do with me."

Suzanne studied her. "Who is it?"

"Remember the woman who ran from the church?" Suzanne and a few others had been in the parking lot when Rae had made her escape.

"The vet? Tall, dark, and running?"

"Yes," Krista breathed.

"Does she know how you feel?"

Krista started to answer but stopped. "I...I think so."

"You mean you haven't told her?"

"She runs from me before I get a chance. She makes love to me and runs. She kisses me and runs..."

"Does she give a reason?"

Krista shook her head in defeat. "All she ever says is that she's sorry and that she can't."

"I see." Suzanne stared out at the desert. "She's the one who made love to you, kissed you?"

"Yes."

"So she made the first moves?"

"Yes."

Suzanne folded her arms across her chest. "She's scared."

"Of what? Of me? Am I that awful?"

"No. No, of course not. It's something else."

"Like what?"

"I don't know. But if you really feel how you say you feel about her, you owe it to yourself to find out."

"I don't think I can. I can't handle another rejection. I mean, if she felt the same about me, she would come and tell me, right?"

Suzanne seemed to think about that. "Maybe. It depends."

They stared off into the distance.

"You always seem to have all the answers," Krista said.

"So what are you going to do?"

Krista sighed and thought of her upcoming date with Lindsay. "Try to forget her."

Suzanne chuckled. "Krista, if it's love, you won't be able to."

CHAPTER TWENTY-TWO

Country music blared and women laughed and kissed and held each other close. Rae sat slumped at the bar, staring down into her mug of beer.

"You ever gonna drink that, pumpkin?" the bartender asked, trucker hat on crooked.

Rae examined the white foamy head of the beer. "No."

The bartender slung her towel over her shoulder and moved away, shaking her head in wonder. Rae inhaled the alcohol and closed her eyes. She wished she could drink. She wished she could just wash all her pain away with a few deep swallows. But she couldn't. She hadn't been able to touch the stuff since the accident. The night her whole fucking life changed forever. Why couldn't it have been her? Shannon didn't deserve that. Shannon deserved better, way better. Shannon deserved someone who loved her.

Rae rubbed her temples, a headache coming on full force. Sighing, she removed her ball cap and scratched her head, turning to face the crowd. It was Saturday night and the place was packed with cowgirls in Western wear, along with those just out looking for a good time and a good woman at the local country bar.

As she looked from face to face, Rae allowed her vision to blur, not wanting to focus on anyone particular. Earlier a couple of glammed-up femmes had tried their hand at getting her to dance, but she'd turned them down, uninterested. She'd already found the woman she wanted and she'd already figured out that she could never have her. That no matter how much time she could have with her, it would never be enough.

Krista. Thick auburn hair. Voluptuous body. Fiery green eyes. Lips to die for.

Like her.

The one sitting at the table across the room.

The one laughing and drinking Miller Lite from the bottle.

The one with Lindsay.

Rae stood and nearly fell, suddenly feeling like she'd had not one but twenty beers. Her skin flooded with red-hot heat.

"You okay, pumpkin?"

Rae pushed away angrily from the bar. The woman could go fuck herself and her pumpkins.

❖

"You're cracking me up," Krista said, still laughing.

Lindsay twirled her straw. "I'm serious. She was a petite woman but I swear to God, she was huge. I never did find my wristwatch."

Krista burst out laughing. It felt good to laugh. Really good. "You are so bad!"

Lindsay held up a hand. "I'm just telling it like it is. Or was."

She wriggled her fingers and Krista laughed again. *Rae must laugh all the time with her. They must have a great time working together.* Krista stopped laughing at the thought of Rae.

Lindsay too quieted down, sipping from her drink. "So what about you? You have any funny stories?"

Krista shook her head. "Not like you."

"Oh, come on. Beautiful woman like you. I know you've had at least one thing stand out in your love life."

Krista took a sip of her beer, her mood altogether changed. "Actually, there was this one."

"Uh-huh." Lindsay leaned in, interested.

"I fought it at first, you know. The attraction I felt. She was goddamned gorgeous. Not like any of the women I'd ever dated before. She was different. Raw. Intense."

"Sounds like a hottie."

"Hot doesn't even come close."

"No?" Lindsay egged her on.

"No." Krista smiled, suddenly feeling aroused at discussing Rae.

She could say what she wanted, what she felt, without any worries. "She was incredible."

"The sex was good?"

"The sex was phenomenal. Frenzied, passionate, like she couldn't get enough of me…" Krista met Lindsay's candid blue eyes. "Actually, those were her words."

"Wow."

"Yeah. I'd never let a woman make love to me like that before. Ever."

"Why not?"

"Because I always liked to be the one in control."

Lindsay nodded. "I know what you mean."

"But with Ra—" Krista stopped herself but Lindsay didn't seem to notice. "It was different with her. I gave myself to her. I wanted to."

"So what happened?"

Krista rubbed her beer bottle. "She ran."

Lindsay cleared her throat and sat back in her stool. Her eyes were focused beyond Krista. "She ran," she repeated.

"Yes."

"Is that a fact?"

Krista looked at her and saw the serious expression on her face as her eyes traveled to the door. Krista turned but only saw the door swinging closed. "Is something wrong? Someone you know?"

Lindsay's eyes drifted back to her. "Just someone running."

❖

"Good morning, *tío*." Krista smiled with difficulty.

Clinton smiled in return and she kissed his cheek. He felt cold and she could smell the strong scent of tequila on his breath.

"When did you get here?" he asked.

Krista held his face, worried. She didn't know if he meant overall or from the trail ride, or from her morning chores. She'd given up trying to keep up with where his memory left off. "A few weeks ago," she said, stunned at how so much had changed in her life within the span of a few weeks, especially the past few days.

Clinton nodded, but she could see in his eyes that he had already lost track of their conversation. Instead, he dug in his back pocket for his pipe and began packing it with tobacco. Krista led him out to the porch and they sat. He lit up and puffed away. Krista inhaled the familiar scent and allowed it to comfort her.

She hadn't seen Rae since the day of Aunt Judith's funeral. *Rae.* The black ravens flapping their wings in her mind kept calling out her name.

She glanced down as something yanked at her foot. Jagger tugged on her shoelaces, growling ferociously. Krista smiled down at the fluffy little cub, thankful she had him at this time in her life when she most needed his easy love.

"Is that a coyote?" Clinton leaned forward to get a better look at Jagger who was lying on top of Krista's shoe, chewing a little too much.

"Jagger!" Krista bent to scoop him up. He licked her face, tail wagging. She stroked his head turned him to face Clinton. "We found him on the trail. His mother had been killed."

Clinton sat back and puffed. "I had a coyote once."

Surprised by his memory, Krista said, "Really?"

"Tall, skinny thing." He stared off in the distance. "Caught him in the chicken coop when we first started the ranch. I was going to shoot him but he sat down and stared at me. Looked me right in the eye. After that, we had an understanding. When he'd wander onto the property I'd feed him and he'd leave the chickens alone." Clinton chuckled. "Your aunt Judy, she hated that coyote. Called him a sneak. She didn't trust him. And he wouldn't go near her either. He knew. He only came around when I was here."

"I can imagine that." Krista stroked Jagger as he settled in her lap and closed his eye for a nap.

Clinton stared off, lost in his memory. Then he blinked as if awakening from a trance. "Judy's fine. Just fine. She'll be up any moment to make breakfast."

Krista nodded, her eyes welling with tears. They sat in silence, the smoke of the pipe drifting out into the warm midmorning air. Krista didn't have the heart to repeat what she'd been telling him ever since Judith passed. Somewhere deep within the labyrinth of his memory, he knew his wife was dead.

❖

"I told you, I'm not coming in." Rae held the phone tightly, her knuckles whitening.

"Why?" Lindsay sounded irritated but Rae didn't care.

"Because I'm sick."

"Bullshit."

"Don't talk to me like that," Rae nearly shouted into the phone.

"I can and I will. You're being a stubborn ass."

"I thought I was a dick?" Rae hadn't forgotten that little stab back at the ranch. She stood and began pacing furiously. Twelve years of dedicated practice and she'd never taken a day off for herself. Sick or otherwise. She was entitled to a break.

"Oh, dick was being kind."

"What the hell is your problem? If I want to take a few days off I'm goddamned going to!"

"My problem? I'll tell you what my problem is. It's you running. That's my problem."

"What?"

"When are you going to quit running and hiding, Rae?"

Rae clenched her jaw. "I don't know what you're talking about, but you better watch your tone."

"I'll talk to you how I damn well please. You may be my boss but you're also my best friend. Now tell me the real reason you're hiding away again."

"I'm not hiding away."

"Rae."

"I don't want to talk anymore. I'm hanging up."

"I know you saw Krista and me!"

Silence.

"At the bar, Saturday night. I saw you. And I know you saw me."

"So?"

"So that's why you're pissed."

Silence.

"You told me to stay away from her because you like her. Because you've fallen for her."

"No."

"Yes, Rae! You're angry and you're hurt."

"No. You can do what you like. I don't care."

"Rae, listen! It's not like that. Krista and I, we're friends."

"Good, whatever. I'm hanging up now."

"All she did was talk about you!"

Rae ended the call and sank down onto the couch, head in her hands. The phone call and the emotions it caused only strengthened her need to hole up in her house.

❖

"I don't know where he is!" Krista paced back and forth across the living room, Jagger chasing her. "He was here one minute and gone the next."

Dwight cleared his throat and rubbed his stubble. He'd just come in from searching the property. He didn't have good news. "His truck's gone."

Krista stopped and stared at him. "What truck?"

"His old Chevy."

"You mean it still runs?"

Sonja shook her head. "Oh, Lord."

"He hasn't driven it in a long time, maybe over a year, but yeah, it still runs."

"Where was it?" Krista asked. "I don't remember even seeing it."

"It was in the old barn."

"Why weren't the keys hidden?"

"Judith had them hidden somewhere and I'd loosened the battery cable, thinking he wouldn't mess with it to begin with. It's old and it doesn't run real good."

"Oh, God." Krista grabbed her forehead. "He could be anywhere."

Sonja moved to the phone. "I'll call the police."

Krista collapsed onto the couch. "It won't do any good. He has to be missing for twenty-four to forty-eight hours first."

"How long has it been?" Dwight asked.

"Since I last saw him?" Sonja said. "Two hours."

"Me too," Krista said. "Two hours ago he was sitting on the porch with me."

This time Dwight moved to the phone.

"Who are you calling?" Krista asked.

"Doc," he said simply, lifting the receiver.

❖

Rae allowed the phone to ring. She stared at it with anger, hating Lindsay's words, hating that her friend was right. Each ring was a reminder, a blade twisting the words into her heart.

When it stopped she breathed deeply, relieved. She jerked when the rings started again.

"Damn it!" she lifted the phone and was about to press the button and yell into it when she saw the caller ID. She stared. Long and hard. Should she let it ring? It was Krista. Should she let it ring?

It stopped. She set it down.

Another ring started. This time from her cell phone. She rose and plucked it off the kitchen counter. She answered, this time concerned.

"Hello."

"Doc?" It was Dwight.

Panic flooded through her. "What is it?" *Is it Krista? Please no, don't let it be Krista.*

"It's Clinton. He's gone."

CHAPTER TWENTY-THREE

Krista paced back and forth on the stone porch. Night had fallen but she ignored the chill on her arms, clutching the cordless phone. She'd prayed over and over again for it to ring. A call had come in from Dwight about an hour before, but she couldn't quite make out what he said. All she'd heard was her uncle's name and that they'd found the truck. Again she cursed the poor cellular service outside the city.

"Why don't you come inside and have some coffee?" Sonja asked.

"No, I can't." Krista held her forehead. "He could be anywhere. He could be hurt, or lost, or someone could've robbed him, taken his truck, his identification…"

"Krista, it won't do you any good to think like that."

Krista dropped her hand in frustration. "Then what am I supposed to do?"

Sonja motioned for her to step inside. "Pray."

Krista entered the house and scooped Jagger up in her arms. She held him up to her face and inhaled the scent of his fur for comfort. "I wish Judith were here," she confessed, tears in her eyes. "I've already let her down."

She stroked the coyote's head. His ears had grown larger and his fur was beginning to lighten. He was starting to look like an actual coyote.

"You're doing the best you can. Dwight and I were here too. We didn't hear him drive off either. The possibility never even crossed my mind."

Krista sat on the sofa, lost in thought. "He's upset. Confused." She met Sonja's eyes. "I've seen a big change in his mood since she passed."

"I have too. He's depressed now and grieving. Only he doesn't have the benefit of grieving like we do. To him the wound is fresh again every day. Sometimes more than once."

"What can we do?" She wanted so badly to help her uncle heal, but his condition was worsening, making the healing process all the more difficult.

Sonja sipped her coffee from the kitchen table and seemed to think long and hard before she answered. "We have to surround him in the safest environment possible. And we have to talk to him. Remind him frequently of who he is and where he is. Maybe even give him more chores to keep him busy."

Krista nodded. "That sounds like a good start." Now if he would only be found safe. She glanced at her watch. Rae and Dwight had been gone for two hours. She looked back up to Sonja, grateful for her presence.

"What about you, Sonja? Do you have a family?" Krista had assumed she didn't have anyone immediate waiting for her. She'd yet to leave the ranch or ask for any time off.

"I don't have kids, no."

"Anyone special?"

Sonja smiled. "No."

"Why not?"

"I could ask you the same."

This time Krista smiled. "When you do find someone, they'll be damn lucky. In the meantime, you've become like family to us. We would love it if you would continue to stay on full time. Move in permanently."

Sonja considered her words and then nodded. "I'd like that very much."

Krista grinned and glanced down at the phone. She was about to call Dwight's cell phone again when she heard the gravel crunching on the driveway. In an instant, she had placed Jagger on the floor and was at the door yanking it open. Sonja was right behind her as she crossed the porch and ran down the steps.

Rae's truck was in the lead, big headlights shining, and Clinton's truck followed close behind. Krista's heart raced as the driver's door opened and Rae stepped out.

"Did you find him?" Krista could wait no longer.

Rae strolled around the front of her truck as the passenger door opened and Krista's question was answered.

"*Tío!*" She ran to her uncle and embraced him tightly.

He raised his hands hesitantly to hug her in return. "*Mija.*"

She could tell he had no idea why she was so excited to see him. Krista pushed back tears, knowing he wouldn't understand. "I'm glad you're home," she said.

Clinton removed his hat and walked up the porch steps. "I ran into Rae and Dwight," he said casually. He stopped on the porch as he caught sight of Sonja.

"I'm Sonja," she said just as she had many times before.

"I know." Clinton held out a bag. "I brought you and Krista a burrito."

He walked into the house without saying anything further. Krista turned to face Rae as Dwight crawled out from Clinton's truck.

"He was at Roberto's," Rae said. "Having *menudo.*"

Krista's laugh was strangled by tears. She threw herself into Rae's arms. "Thank you. Thank you so much."

Rae stood very still at first, but Krista could feel the fluttering beat of her heart. Eventually Rae's arms came softly around her and Krista forced back her emotions, not wanting to cry in front of her. She didn't move, wanting to remain there forever, smelling her spicy scent and feeling her strength. But Rae drew back as Dwight walked up.

"Doc knew just where to look."

Krista offered Rae a grateful smile. "Thank God. I was worried sick."

Rae looked a little uncomfortable with the gratitude. "He used to eat there at least three times a week."

"We found him pretty much right away but he wasn't willing to leave. Said he had errands to run, so we went with him to Home Depot and to Checker." Dwight laughed. "He bought some work gloves and new battery cable for the truck."

"He had no idea we were there to get him," Rae said. "No clue that we were worried about him."

Krista faced Rae. "Will you please join us for dinner?"

Rae shoved her hands into her pockets. "I really should be getting home."

Krista lowered her head. When she spoke again her voice was soft and defeated. "Of course." She climbed the steps and wiped a stray tear as she passed Dwight to enter the house.

Rae opened the door to her truck to climb inside.

"What are you doing, Doc?"

Rae looked up at Dwight. "I'm going home."

"I mean with Krista."

Rae narrowed her eyes. "Nothing."

"I can see that." He descended the steps. "Don't you think it's about time you let someone in?"

"I don't want to talk about this with you."

"No, I know you don't. I wouldn't want to either. But I care about you. And so did Judith." He paused, seemingly for effect. "When I came back from the trail and told her I saw the two of you holding hands, she smiled so big it must've hurt."

Rae climbed in the truck, affected by the words she wanted to block out.

"She told me a secret then, one she made me swear I would keep as long as she was alive. She told me that she'd hoped you and Krista would find each other."

Rae held his gaze for a long silent moment. Then she closed the door and started the truck. Dwight stepped back as she drove away into the setting sun.

❖

Krista stood at the door with tears in her eyes when Dwight came through. He paused and she said, "I heard."

"It's true," he whispered. "She was happy to hear the two of you were growing close. She died in peace knowing that, with hope. She always worried about you both, didn't like that you were both alone. Why do you think she insisted you both go on the trail?"

"And this was what you swore you couldn't tell?"

He nodded. "But she ain't here to kick my ass now, and I figured the two of you should know."

Krista wiped away tears. "Thank you for telling me." She forced a smile. "I can't believe she set us up." As the realization sank in she shook her head. "But I don't think it'll make a difference. Rae doesn't want…"

Dwight squeezed her shoulders. "She's scared."

"Why does everyone keep saying that? Scared of what?"

Dwight sighed. "I'm not really the one to tell you." He looked deep into her eyes. "She lost someone a couple of years back. In an accident."

Krista gasped. "Who?"

Dwight looked uncomfortable and cleared his throat. "A lady friend."

"Oh, no."

Dwight lowered his head. "I'm only saying something because I can see something's going on between you. And I'm worried about her." He raised his eyes to hers. "Your aunt Judith was a smart woman." He gave her shoulders one last squeeze. "I think she's right about the two of you."

Krista stood absorbing the information as Dwight dropped his hands and took off his hat to walk by her. She was lost in thought when headlights and the sound of popping rocks under moving tires got her attention. She walked back onto to the porch and tried to focus on the darkening driveway.

"Hey!" A door slammed shut and Lindsay came into view.

"Lindsay, hi." Krista closed her eyes. "Shit, I totally forgot we had plans."

"That's okay." She crossed the rocks to the front steps. "How's Clinton?"

"You heard?"

Lindsay greeted her with a quick hug. "Rae told me."

"Oh. Well, he's fine. Thanks to Rae," Krista softly added.

Lindsay followed her inside. "Well, that's our girl. Always coming to the rescue. Unless it involves herself."

Krista couldn't miss the sarcasm in her voice and she was about to question it when Lindsay said, "Put on your shoes, we need to get going." She smiled.

Krista glanced down at herself. "I'm not ready to go anywhere."

Lindsay waved her off. "You look great. Jeans and a T-shirt are fine."

Krista hesitated. She wasn't in any mood for a date. Even a purely platonic one. Which she was sure this was going to be. She hadn't felt anything physical for Lindsay and up until this moment she thought Lindsay felt the same way.

"Lindsay, I'm sorry, I'm just not in the mood to go out. After Clinton and everything…" She left out what she'd learned about Rae. She needed time to think on it.

Lindsay walked toward her and took her hands. "No arguing. You're coming."

"But I…" She wanted to be alone, to examine her feelings for Rae, to think over Judith's words and final wishes, and what, if anything, she could do about it.

"Krista, please. I need you to come with me."

Krista gazed into her eyes. When she recognized the seriousness and intensity she moved to the front closet and retrieved her shoes. Slipping them on, she asked, "Where are we going?"

"To meet a friend."

"A friend?" Krista smoothed her hair back with her fingers and tucked in her shirt.

Sonja emerged from the hallway, giving Lindsay a friendly smile.

"Sonja, this is Lindsay," Krista said.

Lindsay crossed the room to shake her hand. "Pleasure, Sonja."

"Likewise."

"I forgot Lindsay and I had plans. Do you mind if I go out for a little while?"

"No problem. Clinton's already turned in for the night."

Lindsay was still smiling at the nurse. Krista watched with surprise as she leaned in to whisper something in Sonja's ear. Sonja nodded and Lindsay smiled at her once again.

"I'll be back shortly." Krista moved toward the door. "Try and call my cell if you need me."

Sonja waved, her eyes only leaving Lindsay's for a second to meet Krista's. "You two have fun."

"Nice meeting you," Lindsay said. "I'm sure I'll see you again real soon."

They'd only reached the end of the long drive when Krista asked, "Am I mistaken, or did you and Sonja hit it off?"

Lindsay chuckled. "Maybe."

Krista grinned. "I thought so. And what was all that whispering about?"

Lindsay wagged a finger. "That's between her and me."

Krista relaxed against the seat, and as they pulled out onto the main road she began to feel better about being away from the ranch. Maybe it was a good thing Lindsay had insisted she come along. She needed some fresh air away from the grief and the stress and the heartache.

"So where are we going again?"

"Uh-uh. No more questions." She turned on the radio and Krista sat back and enjoyed the ride.

By the third song Lindsay slowed her truck and pulled off the road. Krista sat up straighter to get a look. They drove up a short dirt drive and the headlights shone on a small log ranch home. A dirty white dually truck and two horse trailers flanked the drive.

"Isn't that Rae's truck?"

Lindsay didn't answer, she just kept humming to the music as she put the truck in park. She killed the engine and opened her door. When Krista didn't move she said, "Well, come on."

Krista opened the door, her heart already doubling its pace. "You didn't say anything about Rae."

They walked up to the front door and Lindsay knocked. "I didn't know I needed to."

Krista felt her face heat. Lindsay knocked again. Krista looked around. She could picture Rae living there.

"Come on." Lindsay walked briskly to the side of the house and soon they were in the vast backyard, following a footpath. Krista struggled to keep up with her in the darkness and was about to ask her to slow down when she heard music. Lindsay stopped ahead of her and took her hand. They continued slowly and quietly until Krista could make out a figure sitting in a large wicker chair in the middle of the yard. The song was familiar, the one she'd heard on the trail. A candle flickered next to the chair and beyond was a wooden fence, where the shadows of two horses could be seen.

Lindsay whispered, "I just remembered I have something to do."

"What?" Krista stared at her in disbelief, the small moon showing the poorly hidden intentions in Lindsay's eyes.

"I'm sorry, I'll come back for you in a while."

"You can't leave me here!" But Lindsay was already walking away. Krista attempted to follow but stumbled. "Shit!"

She turned back to look at the chair in the distance. The figure was standing, guitar held close.

"Is someone there?" Rae called out.

"Shit," Krista cursed again. "I'm going to kill her!" she said, thinking of Lindsay.

"Who's there?" Rae stood taller, her voice on alert.

Krista knew she had to come clean. "It's Krista."

The guitar lowered farther. "Krista?"

"Yes." She crossed the lawn, feeling awkward and embarrassed. "I...Lindsay brought me."

Rae met her eyes and looked beyond, searching.

"She just took off," Krista admitted.

Rae's eyes came back to hers. Krista could see the scars in them. It pained her, knowing how badly Rae must have hurt, how badly she must still be hurting, having lost someone close to her as well as Judith.

"I'm sorry," she offered. "I'll call Dwight and have him come get me."

Rae said nothing. She stood, holding her guitar wearing the same dark T-shirt and jeans Krista had just seen her in. Her feet were bare. "Come inside," she finally said, her voice weak. "I'll get my keys and drive you home."

CHAPTER TWENTY-FOUR

K rista followed silently as Rae led the way, carrying the candle. She blew it out before opening the back door to step inside. Krista brushed past her and immediately felt the warmth of the house. Her eyes adjusted to the low light emitted by two small lamps. The floor in the living room was dark cherrywood, the oversized sofa beige, and the leather recliner a deep burgundy. Unframed canvas paintings of horses decorated the wall above the sofa and the empty fireplace. The room felt comfortable and inviting, almost cozy, and she could imagine Rae spending a lot of her time there.

Rae closed the door and crossed the room to the kitchen counter where she retrieved her truck keys.

"Okay," she said, turning to face Krista.

"Oh, my God." The words came out in a strangle as the light revealed the secrets of Rae's pain for the first time. She was pale, her face drawn. She looked like she hadn't eaten or slept in days. Dark crescent circles shadowed her eyes. Krista reached up to touch her face but then dropped her hands when Rae turned away. "Rae," she whispered.

Rae slowly met her eyes. Pain and sorrow swirled in the hazel depths, taking Krista's breath away. Gently, Krista reached out for Rae's hand. She opened the fingers and removed the keys. Placing them back on the counter she said, "Tell me about her."

Rae's eyes flashed in surprise, but she said nothing.

"Please," Krista said. "Tell me."

Rae steadied herself against the counter. "What do you want to know?"

She seemed to have trouble standing and Krista quickly led her to the couch where she sat by her side. She held on to her hand. "What was her name?"

Rae stared into the lamplight across the room. "Shannon."

Krista could tell how difficult it was for Rae to speak her name. Her face had tightened and her eyes had filled with tears. "She was your partner?"

A tear fell down her cheek and Rae wiped it away with the back of her hand. "No. We were seeing each other."

Krista wasn't sure what to say, what to ask. "What happened?"

Rae's breathing shook. "We were in an accident. It was raining and we were arguing. She was trying to get me to look at her and she pulled on the steering wheel."

Krista squeezed her hand, tears welling in her own eyes.

"The Jeep flipped and she was thrown out. She was killed instantly."

"I'm so sorry." Krista touched her face. "I'm so very sorry. You loved her?"

Rae shook her head, the sobs coming. "No, I didn't. She loved me but I didn't love her. I didn't love her and she died."

Her face crumbled as the sobs overcame her. Krista pulled her close and held her tightly as she cried. Tears of her own slipped down Krista's face as Rae shook and shuddered into her. Krista was stroking Rae's hair when Rae inhaled deeply and pulled away, quickly gaining control of herself.

"I'm sorry." She wiped hurriedly at her eyes. "It's not like me to cry."

"Maybe it's what you needed to do," Krista said softly.

They sat in silence for a while, Rae regaining her composure and Krista watching, hurting for her. "Can I ask you something, Rae?"

A nod. Krista racked her brain, making sure she had the right words. "Is that why you keep running from me? Because you know I care for you and you don't feel the same way?"

It made sense. That was what had happened with Shannon, and Rae obviously felt guilty over it. If that was the case she wanted to know. Then they could both move on. At least Rae could, anyway.

"No." Rae's hazel eyes looked deeply into her.

Krista stared back, confused. "Then what is it?"

"I'm…I care for you."

"You do?"

"Yes, very much."

Krista's heart pounded. "But?"

Rae looked down. "I'm afraid."

"Of what?"

Rae clasped her trembling hands. "Of losing you."

Krista stared at Rae's hands. Her mind went over and over the words. "I'm not going anywhere, Rae. I'm not like that. The way I feel about you…"

Rae lifted her head. "That's not what I mean."

Krista searched her face and then whispered, "You're afraid I'll die."

Rae didn't speak. More tears streamed down her face. Krista moved closer and reached up, turning her face to look at her.

"Oh, Rae." Krista closed her eyes and kissed Rae's lips, softly pressing, softly caressing. She pulled away from their warmth only to speak. "I love you. I'm not going anywhere. Anywhere. Do you understand?"

Rae searched her face, so vulnerable, so frightened.

"Please don't run from me because you're afraid. We should be taking advantage of every minute, of every second we can. That way we'll have no regrets, no guilt, no words left unspoken." She didn't know where the words came from. She just kept picturing Judith and Clinton and what a wonderful life they'd had together. She couldn't imagine what their lives would've been like if one of them had been afraid to love. Krista wiped the warm tears away from Rae's cheeks with her thumbs. "Please, allow us to live. Allow us to love."

A weak sound escaped Rae as she nodded. Krista smiled and sniffed back her own tears as she leaned in and kissed her again. Their lips met and gently greeted. Soft and warm and gentle. Full of acceptance and promises. Krista warmed from the slight heat of the kisses, and her heart swelled with what she could only describe as love.

"Come on." Krista rose and took Rae's hand. Rae looked up at her questioningly but stood. Krista stroked her cheek. "Take me to the bedroom."

Rae led her slowly through the house. They bypassed the kitchen on the right and then another room, this one a sunken den. A cherry antique desk and another sofa and large reading chair filled the room. Though it was dim, Krista liked the feel of it and as they continued down the hallway, the scent she knew as Rae's grew stronger.

Rae entered and stood waiting by the queen-sized bed in the center of the room. There was a painting on the wall of a woman in different shades of blue that matched the midnight blue comforter. The night table was illuminated by a lamp and matched the heavy-looking dark wood dresser. Krista approached it and touched the large, aged photo of a young sailor.

"Your father?" she asked, seeing the strong resemblance.

"Yes."

"Do you see him often?"

Rae looked incredibly fragile, watching Krista as she ran her fingers over the top of the dresser. "Not so much. He lives in Montana, along with my mother."

Krista paused at the glass cologne bottle full of gold liquid. She held it up to her nose. *Rae.* "This is what you wear?" She knew it was. She'd smelled it every single time she'd touched her. Inhaling the scent of her now sent her heart into overdrive.

"Yes."

Krista raised the bottle to read the small label. "Safari by Ralph Lauren." She replaced the bottle on the dresser and picked up the thick candle sitting next to it, along with a lighter. Her eyes drifted to the adjoining bathroom. When she caught sight of the large claw-foot tub, she held her hand out for Rae. They entered together and stopped in front of the tub.

Dropping Rae's hand, Krista lit the candle and placed it on the nearby counter. The flickering light played off the mirror and danced throughout the room. Satisfied, Krista turned on the faucet. As water began to steam into the tub she rose and stood directly in front of Rae. Looking deep into her hazel eyes, Krista touched her face, then trailed her fingers lightly down to her neck and then her shoulders. Rae's breathing changed as Krista's hands drifted lower. When they reached her waist, Krista ran them up under the T-shirt very lightly, and lifted it up over Rae's head.

The body before her was glorious. Tall and thick-muscled, the breasts small and perfect. Rae's neck and forearms were bronzed from the sun. Gooseflesh covered the skin as Krista's eyes traveled over it.

So badly she wanted to touch it, to kiss it, but she fought the urge and continued.

Rae stood very still, breathing very hard. Krista unbuttoned the jeans and lowered them carefully, along with the white cotton panties. She helped Rae step out of them and she folded the clothes neatly and placed them on the counter. Then she turned and stared at the beautiful creature before her.

Her eyes traveled down from the strong shoulders and arms to the pale breasts, which heaved with the rapid rise and fall of her chest. The nipples were dark, and several freckles were sprinkled across her chest. Her abdomen was contoured and toned, leading down to the slight flare of the hips and the well-trimmed dark hair of her center. Below that were her incredibly long and powerful legs. Krista felt her heart beat in her ears as she studied her. She was unlike anything she'd every seen before. So strong, so beautiful, so raw and elemental. So *woman*.

Krista's breathing was labored as she raised her eyes, seeking Rae's. The hazel gaze was deep and dark in the candlelight but she could see the intensity within. It mirrored every short breath she took. Krista clenched her hands into fists, fighting the urge to touch her. Rae's eyes flashed, letting Krista know that her steady appraisal had indeed touched her. But beneath the rising heat of attraction, the vulnerability was still there, marked by days of unrest and undernourishment.

"Please, climb in," Krista said. The tub was nearly full.

When Rae hesitated, Krista reached up and cupped her jaw, smoothing her thumb over Rae's cheek. "Please, climb in and relax."

Rae took hold of Krista's wrist and moved it from her face. Holding on to it for support, she lifted her leg and stepped into the steaming water. She groaned as she sank into it. Krista turned off the water and opened a cabinet, pulled out a thick, folded towel, and moved to place it behind Rae's head so she could lean back comfortably.

"I'll be right back," she said once Rae relaxed.

"Where are you going?"

Krista swallowed back more desire at the sight of Rae's glistening upper body in the candlelight. "Don't worry, I'll just be a few minutes." She left the bathroom and exited the bedroom, working her way back down the hall. In the kitchen, she switched on the light and rummaged through the cabinets. Finding what she was searching for, she opened a can of soup and poured it into a large soup mug. While it was heating up in the microwave, she readied another mug for hot tea.

Her insides warmed at the thought of being able to care for Rae. She wanted nothing more than this chance to love her. And she would do her best to do just that. When the soup was ready, she grabbed a spoon and carried it down the hall.

Rae looked at her in surprise. "What's this?"

"Chicken noodle." Once Rae had hold of the mug, Krista handed over the spoon. "You need to eat."

Rae's eyes held hers. "Thank you."

Krista smiled. "I'll be right back."

She returned to the kitchen and heated the water for the tea. When it was ready she added two tablespoons of Southern Comfort and headed off back down the hall. Rae was finishing the soup when Krista walked into the bathroom.

"Is it okay? It's chicken noodle right out of the can, so I know I couldn't have screwed it up too bad."

"It's great. Thank you."

"My pleasure."

"I didn't realize how hungry I was."

Rae sat up straighter, the water ebbing just below the weight of her breasts, the nipples firm. Krista looked away, heat spreading throughout her body. Rae watched her for a moment and then handed over the mug.

"All finished?" Krista took it, glad for something to distract her. She placed the mug on the counter and handed over the tea.

"Something else?" Rae smiled, her eyes sincere.

"It's a hot toddy. Thought it might help relax you."

Rae held it to her nose and hesitated. "It's spiked?"

Krista nodded, pulling over a small vanity stool that had been covered with folded hand towels. "Some Southern Comfort."

Rae looked unsettled.

"What's wrong?"

Rae refocused on her as if snapping back from a trance.

"I haven't had anything to drink since before the accident."

Krista stood, startled. "I'm sorry." She offered to take the mug. "I'll make you another one."

Rae held up a calm hand. She gave Krista small smile. "Shannon liked to drink. A lot." Her voice trailed off and she sipped the hot tea. When she lowered the mug she smiled again. "Thank you."

Krista returned the smile and moved the stool to the head of the tub. She plucked a small bottle of baby oil off the ledge and squirted some into her hands. After rubbing them together, she brought them to rest on Rae's shoulders. Rae jerked slightly at the contact but then she groaned as the hands worked her thick muscles.

Krista closed her eyes as desire shot between her legs. She squeezed and rubbed and pressed into the muscles that were slick and firm beneath her hands. Rae took another deep sip of the tea and then set the mug on the ledge to lie back in the tub. Krista followed her, hands submerging in the hot water, moving over the shoulders and down to the arms. She could see that Rae's eyes were closed and she closed her own as well.

"That feels so good."

Krista ran her hands over and down Rae's chest, careful to avoid her breasts, but the movement drew a groan from Rae and she pushed upward. Krista's eyes flew open. Her slick hands fumbled with the shampoo bottle.

"Wet your hair," she whispered, squirting some shampoo into her palm.

Rae sank down into the water and then surfaced, short dark hair smoothed back against her head. Krista lathered the shampoo into her hair, liking the coconut scent of it. Rae groaned again as Krista massaged her scalp slowly and thoroughly. When she was finished, Rae dunked under the water again and Krista rose to meet her with an outstretched towel. Carefully, Rae stood and stepped from the tub, allowing Krista to wrap her in the towel.

She followed Krista into the bedroom, her beautiful face still drawn, but the color had returned to her cheeks. Krista could see the fatigue. "What do you sleep in?" she asked softly.

Rae smoothed the towel over her body, drying herself. "I sleep nude."

Krista swallowed. *Of course you do.* She approached the bed and pulled back the duvet and sheets. She held out her hand and Rae dropped the towel to move toward her and take it. They stood mere inches apart, eyes deep and intense, searching one another's souls.

Again Krista broke the silence. "Lie down."

Rae blinked slowly and sank down onto the bed. Krista covered her and Rae grabbed hold of her hand. "Don't leave."

Krista stared into her eyes. She smiled. "I told you. I'm not going anywhere." She knelt and kissed her lips.

When she pulled away, Rae's eyes remained closed. Krista went into the bathroom and hung the wet towel. Then she blew out the candle and dug in the dresser drawers for a T-shirt. She found a large, soft blue one and undressed to slip it on. She too normally slept nude, but she knew she wouldn't be able to next to Rae without wanting more than sleep. She walked to other side of the bed and switched off the lamp to climb in.

The sheets were cool and divine, the scent of Rae's Safari on the pillowcases. She snuggled up close to Rae but kept her hands up above Rae's breasts.

Rae stirred next to her, turning into the snuggle. "Why did you do all that for me tonight?"

Krista stroked her cheek in the moonlight. "Because I love you."

Rae pulled her closer, nuzzling into Krista's neck. "I love you too."

Krista fought back a soft cry, stroking Rae's cheek.

"I'm so tired," Rae mumbled, eyes closed.

Krista kissed her forehead. "Go to sleep." She brushed back her damp hair. "We have the rest of our lives."

❖

Rae awoke to the soft feel of Krista pressed against her. She blinked in disbelief into the darkness. Then the tightness in her chest eased as she remembered the bath and the careful attention. And then her chest warmed as she remembered the words *I love you.*

She turned slightly and pressed her face into Krista's hair. She could smell shampoo and the lingering scent of her perfume. She listened as Krista slept, breathing softly. Rae smiled. She felt better than she had in days. Like a huge weight had lifted off her shoulders. Her head was clear and her heart was light, thumping madly away in her rib cage.

Krista was here. She was lying right next to her. And she loved her. What more was there?

Remembering Krista's words about taking advantage of every

minute, of every second, Rae slipped her hand under the covers. She sucked in a quick breath when she felt the hot flesh of Krista's bare leg and the exposed skin of her hip. Krista stirred as Rae lightly touched her, lifting her hand up under the shirt to her breasts, where she barely skimmed the hardening nipples.

The memory of Krista's taste made her mouth suddenly water and her blood begin to beat loud and hot between her legs.

"Mmm." Krista stirred some more. "Rae?" Her eyes were open, blinking.

"Hey, beautiful," Rae whispered into her ear, her hand continuing its sweet torture up and down Krista's torso and around her breasts.

"Hi." Krista's voice was groggy and Rae smiled, nipping her neck. She rose to rest on her right elbow as she lowered the covers with her other hand. She ran her fingers up Krista's bare thighs. "I see you found one of my T-shirts."

"I hope you don't mind."

"Not at all." Seeing Krista in her bed wearing one of her shirts excited her in a way she'd never felt before. Rae stroked Krista's leg, mindful of the patched wound on her knee. "How is your leg?"

Krista sighed softly as Rae's hand moved upward. "Sonja took care of it."

Rae laughed. "I'm glad you let her." Again she inched up the shirt.

"You sure you don't mind about the shirt?" Krista asked.

Rae reached the light hairs between her legs. "As long as it comes off right now, I don't have a problem."

Krista laughed. Rae pushed the shirt farther up and bent to suck an exposed nipple.

"Ah!" Krista lifted, surprised, and then lowered, aroused.

Rae pulled away, sucking hard, then released it with a soft pop. She drew Krista up into a sitting position and yanked off the shirt to toss it into the shadows.

Krista sat breathing hard, the filtered white moonlight showing off her skin. "Jesus, what was in that soup?"

Rae eased her back down, pressing a gentle hand to her chest. "It's you," she whispered. "You do this to me." She leaned down and kissed her, soft and hard.

Krista moaned, knotting her hands in Rae's hair. Rae pushed her tongue in to taste all of Krista, to stake her claim, wanting it all. She ran her hand down the center of Krista's chest to her stomach, to the wet flesh between her legs. As she plunged her tongue inside Krista's mouth again, Krista opened her legs, inviting.

This time Rae moaned as her hand slid along the slick flesh, open and waiting for her. Hungry and eager. She stroked the sides of Krista's firm clit and felt her reaction in her mouth when Krista's tongue pushed forward, demanding.

Rae kissed her back, their tongues dueling as Rae rubbed her up and down, faster and faster. Krista's hand lowered to dig into her back. The kiss went on, deeper and hotter, tongues swirling around and around. Noise came from Krista, groans, short moans, and Rae kept on. She dipped her fingers lower, getting more of the slick wetness on their tips, then returned to her clit. Krista's reactions were so powerful Rae didn't dare to stray to any other part of her body. She wanted to pleasure her this way, to work her sweet and hard. To see just how much she wanted, how much she could take. The cleft was hot and full, pushing against her fingers as they squeezed up and down. Another noise from Krista and then nails clawed Rae's back. Krista's body rose up off the bed and she turned away from the kiss and cried out into the night.

Rae watched her neck strain, felt her body shudder beneath her.

"Yes," she whispered, the sight more beautiful than anything she'd ever seen before. "Come for me, baby."

Krista pulsed, the cries loud and long as Rae continued to milk the pleasure from her.

"Rae," she said over and over, her voice rough. Rae watched in amazement as the last of the orgasm shot through her. Krista stilled and opened her eyes. A grin spread slowly across her face. "Are you planning on waking me up like that every night?"

Rae stilled her hand and bent to kiss her on the lips, her own feeling swollen and tingly. "If you want me to."

Krista threaded her fingers into the dark head of hair. "God, yes."

Rae smiled. "This feels good."

Krista studied her and cocked her head. "Yeah?"

"Yeah."

"Good."

"Thank you," Rae whispered.

"For what?"

"For not giving up on me."

Krista tugged her in for another kiss. When they moved apart, she lifted her hand to touch her lips. "You're not someone who's easy to forget."

"I'm not, huh?" Rae raised an eyebrow and Krista laughed.

"No, you're not." Quickly and with strength that surprised Rae, Krista sat up and flipped her onto her back, pinning her hands up over her head.

Rae looked up at her, aroused beyond words.

Krista pressed her nude body down upon her, lowering her head to lick Rae's neck. When she reached her ear, she whispered, "Now I'm going to do what I've been wanting to do since I first laid eyes on you." She licked Rae's ear, sealing the statement, and kissed down to Rae's breasts. She lowered her hands and Rae watched in helpless wonder as Krista carefully avoided her nipples with both her mouth and her hands. Her tongue was long and agile, licking patterns all over Rae's skin, driving her insane each time she blew warm breath across her straining nipples and then lifted her mouth to go elsewhere.

"Krista," Rae breathed. But Krista wouldn't stop. She kept on, lower and lower, pushing down, maneuvering between Rae's thighs.

She bent and blew upon Rae's hungry flesh and Rae shivered, mad with desire. Her skin tingled where Krista had licked her, leaving her starving for more. Krista stared up at her from between her legs. Rae had never seen a lover look so hungry, so thirsty for her. Her legs trembled and Krista pushed them apart as she rubbed her face against Rae's flesh.

"Oh, uh." Rae clenched her teeth. The pressure had almost sent her over.

Krista grinned, extending her tongue to lick up one moist lip and then down the other.

"Krista, God, Krista." Rae clutched handfuls of auburn hair.

She wanted to watch as the tongue did it again, extending to lick her up and down, edging closer and closer to her clit. But the sensation was too much and her eyes clenched closed and her body bucked with frenzied need as the hot, wet tongue finally reached her.

"Jesus," she seethed as Krista's mouth found her and fed.

In and out, in and out, Krista was sucking her off.

Rae raised her head and forced her eyes open. "Agh..." She couldn't even form words watching as her clit was tugged in and out of Krista's mouth, the tongue massaging as the lips worked.

Krista stared into her eyes as she bobbed. She reached up and pinched Rae's aching nipples, tugging them along with her clit. Rae tensed and her body thrust. They were in a rhythm now, so good, so goddamned good. Rae clung to Krista's head, the feel of it moving back and forth adding to the pleasure.

"Oh God, oh Krista." It was coming. The pleasure. The orgasm. Coming hard and fast. Her head fell back and her eyes drifted to the ceiling.

She tried to stifle her cries but the white-hot pleasure consumed her all at once, slamming into every cell over and over again. Her body arched and she cried up toward the ceiling, her head lifting off the pillow, her hands holding Krista to her. She cried long and hard, cried for the pleasure, for Krista, for love, for life.

All of it was sacred and pure, worth everything she'd ever had.

When the last wonderful pang of pleasure finally left her soul, she collapsed into the pillow, her throat tight and sore. Krista stilled between her legs and crawled up to straddle her waist. Rae could feel the hot slickness of her pussy.

"You okay?" she asked, stroking Rae's jaw.

Rae smiled so easy she thought it'd slide right off her face. "Yeah, I'm fine."

Krista grinned down at her. "You look fine."

"Do I?"

"Uh-huh." To Rae's surprise, her eyes welled and a tear slipped down her cheek.

Krista wiped it away, concerned. "What's wrong?"

Rae reached for her hand. "Nothing."

"But you're crying."

Rae kissed her palm and whispered, "I'm living."

CHAPTER TWENTY-FIVE

K rista awoke to the soft sound of a guitar. She opened her eyes against the morning light and squinted, sitting up in the bed.

"Morning," Rae said softly. She was sitting at the foot of the bed, stark naked, guitar in hand.

"Good morning." Krista smiled. "Are you going to serenade me in bed?"

Rae plucked a few strings, her dark hair tousled and hanging down near her eyes. "I thought I might." She grinned and Krista's heart flip-flopped in her chest. "You see, I've been working on this song." She played the familiar tune, then stopped. "But I was having a hard time finishing it." She fell into Krista's eyes. "Until now."

She cleared her throat and scooted closer to Krista. "If you don't mind, I'd like to sing it for you."

Krista felt her body and mind awaken at once, pulsing with nervous energy. "Please," she managed, emotion already working itself up.

Rae nodded and cleared her throat again. Then she lowered her head to look at her guitar as she began to play. The tune was familiar, the rhythm beautiful. Burning hazel eyes found Krista when she started to sing.

I think I know
But I don't
Life and love are pain
And I won't

Then in my life

She walks
Head held high

Her eyes are green
And fierce
Her hair burning fire

She sees right through me
And nails my heart

Her look consumes me
While her words
Her words
Tear me apart

Oh how I thought I knew
What life was
What love meant

But she cuts into me
And life ain't over yet
Life ain't over yet
Life ain't over
Yet

And now I'm seeing
My eyes open wide

Her eyes are green
And fierce
Her touch burning fire

She sees right through me
And ignites my heart

Her look consumes me
While her words
Her words
Bring life

Bring love

They've given me
A whole new start

I think I know
And I do
I think I know
And I do
Yes I do

Life and love…
They're you
Life and love
Yes they're you
They're you

Rae finished playing the tune. When she looked up, her eyes were full of tears. Krista fought to speak, her voice somewhere deep within her chest, burning alongside her heart.

"I don't know what to say," Krista whispered. "I…it was beautiful."

Rae set her guitar to the side and moved closer. She reached out to hold Krista's face.

"It ought to be. It was about you."

Their eyes held as they grew closer and kissed.

"Make love to me?" Krista wanted nothing more than to feel Rae all over her. She'd already covered her body with her words, with her music; now she wanted to feel her mouth.

Rae groaned and lay down atop her. She slipped her thigh between Krista's and rubbed, covering her mouth with a wet, hot kiss.

"Rae," Krista whispered as the dark head moved lower and lower, trailing kisses down her middle.

"Krista," Rae whispered just before kissing her slick flesh just as she'd done her mouth.

Krista lay on her back, her legs spread wide, Rae's mouth working her slow and hard. She thought back to the song and as the words replayed in her mind, the pleasure rising up through her accompanied them.

Rae was right.

This was love.

This was life.

CHAPTER TWENTY-SIX

T hat ought to do it," Dwight said closing the hood to Clinton's old Chevy. He walked to the driver's side door and closed it as well. Krista stood at the hood holding a cover. Dwight took hold of the other side and together they spread it over the vehicle.

"I disconnected the starter," he explained, wiping his hands on his jeans.

Krista smacked her hands together to get rid of the dust from the old cover. "I'll give the keys to Rae."

Sunlight streamed in through the worn wooden slats of the old barn, igniting bits of hay in fiery gold. Jagger, who was now all legs and ears, sniffed around, curious. The walls were lined with old tools, rakes, and worn wooden furniture. Some of it appeared to date back to the 1940s. She couldn't wait to get her hands on one or two to try and restore it.

Excited, she inhaled the barn's musty, earthy scent and walked with Jagger outside the door to watch Dwight close and lock it. He grunted as he worked on securing the latch.

"How are things with Doc?" he asked, trying to sound casual.

Krista smiled. "Fine."

Dwight tugged on the lock and turned, ready to head back to the house. "Just fine?" His eyes twinkled.

"Better than fine."

He grinned. "Glad to hear it."

Krista fell into step next to him, Jagger lingering behind. Repeat ran up from the house, tail wagging, and the two bolted off, chasing one another.

"I wanted to thank you again," Krista said.

"For what?"

"For telling me about Rae."

He spat and squinted up into the sun. "I only did it because I knew Judith would want me to and, well, I love you both like my own daughters." He looked over at her. "Otherwise I would've never told. It wouldn't be my place."

Krista touched his arm. "We're all very lucky to have a loyal friend like you, Dwight."

He stared at the ground, the emotion of the words getting to him.

They walked along in silence for a while until Dwight spoke, changing the subject. "The next group arrives tomorrow?"

Krista studied the house and bunkhouses as they came into view. "Uh-huh." She was pleased with the work that had been done on them. She and Dwight and Cody had done the repairs themselves and they were starting to look as good as new.

After this next run, they were going to finish the bunkhouses and then start on the stables.

"You going to go out on the trail this time?" Dwight asked.

"You bet."

He smiled over at her. "Well, I'll be. That feisty little fifteen-year-old is back."

Krista laughed. "I'll have plenty of help. The two new wranglers arrived this morning. Have you met them?"

Dwight shook his head. "Not yet."

"I think you'll like them. Ben and Everet." She was pleased with the two young cowboys. Their previous employers had nothing but kind words, and neither one had had any run-ins with the law. "Not to mention Cody. He's been a real lifesaver."

"He's a good boy," Dwight said.

"I filed the report on Howie," Krista continued. "The cop told me he had several others. One for indecent exposure and one for voyeurism. One for public drunkenness."

"Son of a bitch."

"Yeah, I should've known. Should've checked."

"What's done is done. You didn't do anything wrong." Dwight moved the ball of tobacco around in his mouth. "'Sides, he won't be back here." His look was serious.

"How can you be so sure?"

"'Cuz Rae and I chased him off with a shotgun last week. I threatened to shoot off his balls."

"What!"

"And that's after I broke his nose."

"Why didn't anyone tell me?"

"We didn't want to upset you." He looked serious. "He won't be back."

"Hopefully, he'll get a little jail time with this last charge," Krista whispered. "But you and Rae have got to quit keeping things from me." She stopped and held his forearm. "Promise me, Dwight."

He bowed his head and sighed. "All right. But you better tell Rae that yourself."

"Oh, I will." She smiled as up ahead Rae's big truck kicked up dirt and crunched gravel along the drive. Krista couldn't help but get excited even though she'd just seen her the night before.

Krista picked up her pace and nearly jumped into her arms as Rae stepped out of the truck.

"Hey!"

Rae grinned, holding her tight. "Hey, yourself."

Krista kissed her short but sweet. Rae blushed, catching sight of Dwight, who merely smiled and tipped his hat as he headed inside.

Rae closed the door to her truck and yanked Krista close for another kiss. This one longer and slower.

"Mmm," Krista managed, her heart fluttering and her knees weakening. She pulled away reluctantly, her desire raging hot and nearing the breaking point. "God, you smell good." She nuzzled Rae's neck, inhaling her cologne.

Rae shuddered when Krista nibbled on her sensitive flesh. "You better stop," she rasped, her fingers digging into Krista's waist.

"I don't want to." Krista bit harder, sucking. She thought of the photos Adam had brought, sitting on the kitchen table. The ones of Rae all hot and glistening, tan and strong in her jeans and cowboy hat. Krista had wanted to eat her alive. She bit again, harder, hungry.

Rae jerked and lifted her off the ground. "Quit it!" she said playfully.

Krista laughed, full of mischief. She wrapped her arms around Rae's neck, her thoughts growing more serious. "I'm going to miss you, you know."

"Me too."

They looked into one another's eyes.

"I wish you didn't have to go."

"I know. But this is my responsibility. I want to go and make sure the new wranglers learn the ropes."

Rae kissed her gently. "I'm proud of you."

Krista smiled. "Thank you."

They kissed again.

"I told Dwight no more secrets," Krista said.

Rae looked confused.

"I know about Howie."

Rae rolled her eyes. "That asshole?"

"Yeah. Sounds like you and Dwight made a lasting impression."

Rae laughed. "We did."

"Next time tell me, okay?"

"I didn't want to alarm you."

"Hey!" Krista said, holding on to Rae's chin.

Again Rae rolled her eyes. "I know, I know. You don't need protecting."

They laughed as they said it in unison.

Krista lightly touched her face. "Can you stay with me tonight?"

Rae looked surprised. "Here at the ranch?" They'd been spending every other night at Rae's, making love well into the morning hours.

Krista nodded. "Sonja asked for the night off. Lindsay's taking her out. I need to stay with Clinton."

Rae chuckled. "Sure."

"Good," Krista said, leaning in to whisper in her ear. Her desire was getting the better of her. Flashing images of her slamming Rae up against the stable wall and tearing down her pants to suck her entered her mind. Then she imagined the two of them in the hay, her straddling Rae, riding her long fingers. She shivered and her skin grew hot.

"Come on." She pulled on Rae's hand.

"Where we going?"

"To the stables."

"Why?"

Krista stopped and nibbled on her ear. "Because I can't wait until tonight."

About the Author

Born in North Carolina, Ronica Black now lives in the desert Southwest where she pursues writing as well as many other forms of creativity. Drawing, photography, and outdoor sports are a few of her other sources of entertainment. She also relishes being an aunt and thoroughly enjoys the time spent with family and friends.

Deeper, her upcoming sequel to the award-winning romantic thriller *In Too Deep*, is due out in 2008. She also has short stories in *Erotic Interludes 2*, *3* and *4* from Bold Strokes Books and *Ultimate Lesbian Erotica 2005* from Alyson Books.

For more info, visit Ronica's Web site at www.ronicablack.com.

Books Available From Bold Strokes Books

Such a Pretty Face by Gabrielle Goldsby. A sexy, sometimes humorous, sometimes biting contemporary romance that gently exposes the damage to heart and soul when we fail to look beneath the surface for what truly matters. (978-1-933110-84-4)

Second Season by Ali Vali. A romance set in New Orleans amidst betrayal, Hurricane Katrina, and the new beginnings hardship and heartbreak sometimes make possible. (978-1-933110-83-7)

Hearts Aflame by Ronica Black. A poignant, erotic romance between a hard-driving businesswoman and a solitary vet. Packed with adventure and set in the harsh beauty of the Arizona countryside. (978-1-933110-82-0)

Red Light by JD Glass. Tori forges her path as an EMT in the New York City 911 system while discovering what matters most to herself and the woman she loves. (978-1-933110-81-3)

Honor Under Siege by Radclyffe. Secret Service agent Cameron Roberts struggles to protect her lover while searching for a traitor who just may be another woman with a claim on her heart. (978-1-933110-80-6)

Dark Valentine by Jennifer Fulton. Danger and desire fuel a high-stakes cat-and-mouse game when an attorney and an endangered witness team up to thwart a killer. (978-1-933110-79-0)

Sequestered Hearts by Erin Dutton. A popular artist suddenly goes into seclusion, a reluctant reporter wants to know why, and a heart locked away yearns to be set free. (978-1-933110-78-3)

Erotic Interludes 5: Road Games, ed. by Radclyffe and Stacia Seaman. Adventure, "sport," and sex on the road—hot stories of travel adventures and games of seduction. (978-1-933110-77-6)

The Spanish Pearl by Catherine Friend. On a trip to Spain, Kate Vincent is accidentally transported back in time—an epic saga spiced with humor, lust, and danger. (978-1-933110-76-9)

Lady Knight by L-J Baker. Loyalty and honor clash with love and ambition in a medieval world of magic when female knight Riannon meets Lady Eleanor. (978-1-933110-75-2)

Dark Dreamer by Jennifer Fulton. Best-selling horror author Rowe Devlin falls under the spell of psychic Phoebe Temple. A Dark Vista romance. (978-1-933110-74-5)

Come and Get Me by Julie Cannon. Elliott Foster isn't used to pursuing women, but alluring attorney Lauren Collier makes her change her mind. (978-1-933110-73-8)

Blind Curves by Diane and Jacob Anderson-Minshall. Private eye Yoshi Yakamota comes to the aid of her ex-lover Velvet Erickson in the first Blind Eye mystery. (978-1-933110-72-1)

Dynasty of Rogues by Jane Fletcher. It's hate at first sight for Ranger Riki Sadiq and her new patrol corporal, Tanya Coppelli—except for their undeniable attraction. (978-1-933110-71-4)

Running With the Wind by Nell Stark. Sailing instructor Corrie Marsten has signed off on love until she meets Quinn Davies—one woman she can't ignore. (978-1-933110-70-7)

More Than Paradise by Jennifer Fulton. Two women battle danger, risk all, and find in each other an unexpected ally and an unforgettable love. (978-1-933110-69-1)

Flight Risk by Kim Baldwin. For Blayne Keller, being in the wrong place at the wrong time just might turn out to be the best thing that ever happened to her. (978-1-933110-68-4)

Rebel's Quest: Supreme Constellations Book Two by Gun Brooke. On a world torn by war, two women discover a love that defies all boundaries. (978-1-933110-67-7)

Punk and Zen by JD Glass. Angst, sex, love, rock. Trace, Candace, Francesca…Samantha. Losing control—and finding the truth within. BSB Victory Editions. (1-933110-66-X)

The Devil Unleashed by Ali Vali. As the heat of violence rises, so does the passion. A Casey Clan crime saga. (1-933110-61-9)

When Dreams Tremble by Radclyffe. Two women whose lives turned out far differently than they'd once imagined discover that sometimes the shape of the future can only be found in the past. (1-933110-64-3)

Stellium in Scorpio by Andrews & Austin. The passionate reunion of two powerful women on the glitzy Las Vegas Strip, where everything is an illusion and love is a gamble. (1-933110-65-1)

Burning Dreams by Susan Smith. The chronicle of the challenges faced by a young drag king and an older woman who share a love "outside the bounds." (1-933110-62-7)

Fresh Tracks by Georgia Beers. Seven women, seven days. A lot can happen when old friends, lovers, and a new girl in town get together in the mountains. (1-933110-63-5)

The Empress and the Acolyte by Jane Fletcher. Jemeryl and Tevi fight to protect the very fabric of their world...time. Lyremouth Chronicles Book Three. (1-933110-60-0)

First Instinct by JLee Meyer. When high-stakes security fraud leads to murder, one woman flees for her life while another risks her heart to protect her. (1-933110-59-7)

Erotic Interludes 4: Extreme Passions, ed. by Radclyffe and Stacia Seaman. Thirty of today's hottest erotica writers set the pages aflame with love, lust, and steamy liaisons. (1-933110-58-9)

Unexpected Ties by Gina L. Dartt. With death before dessert, Kate Shannon and Nikki Harris are swept up in another tale of danger and romance. (1-933110-56-2)

Broken Wings by L-J Baker. When Rye Woods, a fairy, meets the beautiful dryad Flora Withe, her libido, as squashed and hidden as her wings, reawakens along with her heart. (1-933110-55-4)

Combust the Sun by Andrews & Austin. A Richfield and Rivers mystery set in L.A. Murder among the stars. (1-933110-52-X)

Tristaine Rises by Cate Culpepper. Brenna, Jesstin, and the Amazons of Tristaine face their greatest challenge for survival. (1-933110-50-3)

Passion's Bright Fury by Radclyffe. When a trauma surgeon and a filmmaker become reluctant allies on the battleground between life and death, passion strikes without warning. (1-933110-54-6)

Sleep of Reason by Rose Beecham. Nothing is as it seems when Detective Jude Devine finds herself caught up in a small-town soap opera. And her rocky relationship with forensic pathologist Dr. Mercy Westmoreland just got a lot harder. (1-933110-53-8)

Grave Silence by Rose Beecham. Detective Jude Devine's investigation of a series of ritual murders is complicated by her torrid affair with the golden girl of Southwestern forensic pathology, Dr. Mercy Westmoreland. (1-933110-25-2)

Too Close to Touch by Georgia Beers. Kylie O'Brien believes in true love and is willing to wait for it. It doesn't matter one damn bit that Gretchen, her new and off-limits boss, has a voice as rich and smooth as melted chocolate. It absolutely doesn't… (1-933110-47-3)

Carly's Sound by Ali Vali. Poppy Valente and Julia Johnson form a bond of friendship that lays the foundation for something more, until Poppy's past comes back to haunt her—literally. A poignant romance about love and renewal. (1-933110-45-7)

Of Drag Kings and the Wheel of Fate by Susan Smith. A blind date in a drag club leads to an unlikely romance. (1-933110-51-1)

100th Generation by Justine Saracen. Ancient curses, modern-day villains, and a most intriguing woman who keeps appearing when least expected lead archeologist Valerie Foret on the adventure of her life. (1-933110-48-1)

The Traitor and the Chalice by Jane Fletcher. Tevi and Jemeryl risk all in the race to uncover a traitor. The Lyremouth Chronicles Book Two. (1-933110-43-0)

Whitewater Rendezvous by Kim Baldwin. Two women on a wilderness kayak adventure—Chaz Herrick, a laid-back outdoorswoman, and Megan Maxwell, a workaholic news executive—discover that true love may be nothing at all like they imagined. (1-933110-38-4)

Erotic Interludes 3: Lessons in Love, ed. by Radclyffe and Stacia Seaman. Sign on for a class in love…the best lesbian erotica writers take us to "school." (1-9331100-39-2)

Punk Like Me by JD Glass. Twenty-one-year-old Nina writes lyrics and plays guitar in the rock band Adam's Rib, and she doesn't always play by the rules. And oh yeah—she has a way with the girls. (1-933110-40-6)

Forever Found by JLee Meyer. Can time, tragedy, and shattered trust destroy a love that seemed destined? When chance reunites two childhood friends separated by tragedy, the past resurfaces to determine the shape of their future. (1-933110-37-6)

Sword of the Guardian by Merry Shannon. Princess Shasta's bold new bodyguard has a secret that could change both of their lives. *He* is actually a *she*. A passionate romance filled with courtly intrigue, chivalry, and devotion. (1-933110-36-8)

Sweet Creek by Lee Lynch. A celebration of the enduring nature of love, friendship, and community in the quirky, heart-warming lesbian community of Waterfall Falls. (1-933110-29-5)

Wild Abandon by Ronica Black. From their first tumultuous meeting, Dr. Chandler Brogan and Officer Sarah Monroe are drawn together by their common obsessions—sex, speed, and danger. (1-933110-35-X)

The Devil Inside by Ali Vali. Derby Cain Casey, head of a New Orleans crime organization, runs the family business with guts and grit, and no one crosses her. No one, that is, until Emma Verde claims her heart and turns her world upside down. (1-933110-30-9)

Chance by Grace Lennox. At twenty-six, Chance Delaney decides her life isn't working, so she swaps it for a different one. What follows is the sexy, funny, touching story of two women who, in finding themselves, also find one another. (1-933110-31-7)

Erotic Interludes 2: Stolen Moments, ed. by Stacia Seaman and Radclyffe. Love on the run, in the office, in the shadows…Fast, furious, and almost too hot to handle. (1-933110-16-3)

Turn Back Time by Radclyffe. Pearce Rifkin and Wynter Thompson have nothing in common but a shared passion for surgery. They clash at every opportunity, especially when matters of the heart are suddenly at stake. (1-933110-34-1)

Promising Hearts by Radclyffe. Dr. Vance Phelps lost everything in the War Between the States and arrives in New Hope, Montana, with no hope of happiness and no desire for anything except forgetting—until she meets Mae, a frontier madam. (1-933110-44-9)

Innocent Hearts by Radclyffe. In a wild and unforgiving land, two women learn about love, passion, and the wonders of the heart. (1-933110-21-X)

Protector of the Realm: Supreme Constellations Book One by Gun Brooke. A space adventure filled with suspense and a daring intergalactic romance featuring Commodore Rae Jacelon and a stunning, but decidedly lethal Kellen O'Dal. (1-933110-26-0)

Course of Action by Gun Brooke. Actress Carolyn Black desperately wants the starring role in an upcoming film produced by Annelie Peterson. Just how far will she go for the dream part of a lifetime? (1-933110-22-8)

Coffee Sonata by Gun Brooke. Four women whose lives unexpectedly intersect in a small town by the sea have one thing in common—they all have secrets. (1-933110-41-4)

The Temple at Landfall by Jane Fletcher. An imprinter, one of Celaeno's most revered servants of the Goddess, is also a prisoner to the faith—until a Ranger frees her by claiming her heart. (1-933110-27-9)

Rangers at Roadsend by Jane Fletcher. Sergeant Chip Coppelli has learned to spot trouble coming, and that is exactly what she sees in her new recruit, Katryn Nagata. The Celaeno series. (1-933110-28-7)

The Walls of Westernfort by Jane Fletcher. All Temple Guard Natasha Ionadis wants is to serve the Goddess—until she falls in love with one of the rebels she is sworn to destroy. The Celaeno series. (1-933110-24-4)

The Exile and the Sorcerer by Jane Fletcher. First in the Lyremouth Chronicles. Tevi and a shy young sorcerer face monsters, magic, and the challenge of loving. (1-933110-32-5)

Force of Nature by Kim Baldwin. From tornados to forest fires, the forces of nature conspire to bring Gable McCoy and Erin Richards close to danger, and closer to each other. (1-933110-23-6)

In Too Deep by Ronica Black. Undercover homicide cop Erin McKenzie tracks a femme fatale who just might be a real killer...with love and danger hot on her heels. (1-933110-17-1)

Hunter's Pursuit by Kim Baldwin. A raging blizzard, a mountain hideaway, and a killer-for-hire set a scene for disaster—or desire—when Katarzyna Demetrious rescues a beautiful stranger. (1-933110-09-0)

Erotic Interludes: Change of Pace by Radclyffe. Twenty-five hot-wired encounters guaranteed to spark more than just your imagination. Erotica as you've always dreamed of it. (1-933110-07-4)

Justice Served by Radclyffe. Lieutenant Rebecca Frye and her lover, Dr. Catherine Rawlings, embark on a deadly game of hide-and-seek with an underworld kingpin who traffics in human souls. (1-933110-15-5)

Justice in the Shadows by Radclyffe. In a shadow world of secrets and lies, Detective Sergeant Rebecca Frye and her lover, Dr. Catherine Rawlings, join forces in the elusive search for justice. (1-933110-03-1)

A Matter of Trust by Radclyffe. JT Sloan is a cybersleuth who doesn't like attachments. Michael Lassiter is leaving her husband, and she needs Sloan's expertise to safeguard her company. It should just be business—but it turns into much more. (1-933110-33-3)

Fated Love by Radclyffe. Amidst the chaos and drama of a busy emergency room, two women must contend not only with the fragile nature of life, but also with the irresistible forces of fate. (1-933110-05-8)

Storms of Change by Radclyffe. In the continuing saga of the Provincetown Tales, duty and love are at odds as Reese and Tory face their greatest challenge. (1-933110-57-0)

Distant Shores, Silent Thunder by Radclyffe. Dr. Tory King—along with the women who love her—is forced to examine the boundaries of love, friendship, and the ties that transcend time. (1-933110-08-2)

Beyond the Breakwater by Radclyffe. One Provincetown summer, three women learn the true meaning of love, friendship, and family. (1-933110-06-6)

Safe Harbor by Radclyffe. A mysterious newcomer, a reclusive doctor, and a troubled gay teenager learn about love, friendship, and trust during one tumultuous summer in Provincetown. (1-933110-13-9)

shadowland by Radclyffe. In a world on the far edge of desire, two women are drawn together by power, passion, and dark pleasures. An erotic romance. (1-933110-11-2)

Love's Masquerade by Radclyffe. Plunged into the indistinguishable realms of fiction, fantasy, and hidden desires, Auden Frost is forced to question all she believes about the nature of love. (1-933110-14-7)

Honor Reclaimed by Radclyffe. In the aftermath of 9/11, Secret Service Agent Cameron Roberts and Blair Powell close ranks with a trusted few to find the would-be assassins who nearly claimed Blair's life. (1-933110-18-X)

Honor Guards by Radclyffe. In a wild flight for their lives, the president's daughter and those who are sworn to protect her wage a desperate struggle for survival. (1-933110-01-5)

Love & Honor by Radclyffe. The president's daughter and her lover are faced with difficult choices as they battle a tangled web of Washington intrigue for…love and honor. (1-933110-10-4)

Honor Bound by Radclyffe. Secret Service Agent Cameron Roberts and Blair Powell face political intrigue, a clandestine threat to Blair's safety, and the seemingly irreconcilable personal differences that force them ever farther apart. (1-933110-20-1)

Above All, Honor by Radclyffe. Secret Service Agent Cameron Roberts fights her desire for the one woman she can't have—Blair Powell, the daughter of the president of the United States. (1-933110-04-X)